LOST IN LOVE

A **CITY LOVE** NOVEL

SUSANE COLASANTI

KT KATHERINE TEGEN BOOKS
An Imprint of HarperCollins Publishers

Katherine Tegen Books is an imprint of HarperCollins Publishers.

Library of Congress Control Number: 2015952417
ISBN 978-0-06-230774-3

Typography by Erin Fitzsimmons
17 18 19 20 21   PC/LSCH   10 9 8 7 6 5 4 3 2 1
❖
First paperback edition, 2017

THREE **GIRLS,**

THREE DIFFERENT STORIES . . .

AND THE **SUMMER** THAT

WILL CHANGE THEIR LIVES

FOREVER.

To Emily van Beek

*for dreaming big with me
and turning those dreams into reality*

ONE
SADIE

MONDAYS ARE HARSH. YOU DON'T want to go to school. You don't want to go to work. And what's with getting up so freaking early? Mondays bust in after Sunday nights, those murky nights that are always infused with dread. Mondays are a nagging reminder that your real life isn't as exhilarating as the movie version of your life. Not even close. Especially when compared to the adventures you're pretty sure everyone else is having.

But I'm one of those annoying people who actually like Mondays. Mondays have always symbolized starting over to me. What better chance for a fresh start than the beginning of a shiny new week?

Except for this Monday. Today is the worst Monday in the history of calendars. I can't believe Saturday was only two days ago. A boy slept over in my room—in my bed—for the first time. Austin was spending the whole weekend at my place. It felt like one of those really good dreams you never want to end. We were having a blissful New York City weekend where we could do whatever we wanted. The city belonged to us and we belonged to each other.

Until Saturday night. When I found out Austin is married.

Tears seep onto the bright stripes of my pillowcase. I brought my pillow out to the couch yesterday morning. I've been sacked out here binge-watching movies and shows ever since. My brain can't handle anything else. I cannot function like a normal person. Even lying on my bed is too painful. I already called out sick from my internship today. Even if there wasn't a chance of running into Austin in our building, there's no way I'm showing up at the office with my eyes all red and puffy from the kind of relentless crying that might never end. I just want to lie on this couch forever.

How pathetic am I? All miserable and heartbroken over some boy. Only . . . Austin wasn't some boy. With him, I felt the way I'd always wanted to feel. We were perfect for each other. Or so it seemed. Now I'm a binge-watching hot mess on the couch. All I need is a pint of Ben & Jerry's to complete this cliché. Or chocolates to throw at the screen whenever the leading man finally kisses the girl.

Darcy and Rosanna are sneaking looks at me from the

open kitchen. They're pretending to eat breakfast, but they're really watching and whispering about me. The same way my parents did before I moved out. I didn't want to deal with what happened to my sister then and I don't want to deal with Austin now. All I want to do is block out the world. My roommates can whisper all they want. I'm not going anywhere. I didn't even get up to go to bed last night. I just slept right here on the couch, much to Darcy's dismay. Darcy and the couch have developed an intimate relationship. She's not home that much between her summer session classes during the day and staying out all night, but when she is here, she enjoys her lounging time. Sorry, Darcy. The couch is taken indefinitely.

The thought of going back to my internship twists my stomach into knots. At least no one there knew our secret. Imagine if I had to explain why we broke up on top of worrying that I'm going to run into Austin any second. If he didn't work on a different floor, I would seriously have to consider quitting.

"Hey, Sadie," Rosanna says. Her face is covered with concern. Somehow her camp counselor tee and gray cotton shorts are making her look more tentative than usual. She's careful not to stand in front of the TV as she takes in the full view of my sorry state. She's also careful not to stand too close to me. The last time I took a shower was two days ago. "We have to leave. Can I get you anything?"

"I'm good," I say, my voice cracking.

"You sure?"

The energy it takes to nod exhausts me. Every part of me is weighed down with cinder blocks.

"Okay, well . . . call Darcy if you need anything. Or you can call camp if you need to get in touch with me."

Darcy breezes into the living room on a cloud of her signature Vera Wang Princess fragrance. She has her hair pinned up in a high bun and is rocking a mod red knee-length dress with black polka dots and a wide black belt. The dress looks extra glam with her new black wedges and matching red tote. I'd tell her how cute she looks if I hadn't just used up all of my energy nodding to Rosanna.

"You called out sick?" Darcy asks me.

"Yeah." It wasn't even a lie. My eyelids are so heavy I can hardly keep my eyes open. As soon as Darcy and Rosanna leave, I'll be drifting toward sleep again. Heartbreak is a serious illness.

"I say we track Austin down and hurt him," she proclaims. "Didn't you tell me he likes *Breaking Bad*? How about we get the hookup on some of that ricin?"

"Let me think on it." Darcy might be only half joking about the powdered poison that dissolves in someone's drink and leaves no trace.

"You get a little more time to mope. Then we are physically removing you from this couch and reuniting you with the outdoors. Right, Rosanna?"

"Right." Rosanna is trying to be supportive, but I can

tell she's nervous that I might actually take Darcy up on that ricin.

"Comfort food tonight," Darcy says. "We're ordering in. My treat."

"Sure you don't need anything?" Rosanna asks me again.

Two weeks ago, I didn't even know these girls. The University of New York's housing department placed us together in this apartment for the summer. I could have ended up with anyone. Instead I was placed with two incredible roommates who couldn't be more different, but are equally concerned about me. Almost as if karma started restoring balance before the Austin travesty even happened.

"Don't worry about me," I tell them. "I'll be okay."

After they leave, I sink back into my pillow, plunging into memories I would rather forget. The smaller things bother me the most. I held Austin's hand, the same hand where his wedding ring should have been, walking along Hudson River Park as I let the excitement of our epic love story wash over me. Then he said the view of the Manhattan skyline was better from Hoboken than Jersey City. Now it's clear he wanted to keep me away from Jersey City, where he lives, to avoid running into people he knew.

Like his wife.

I remember this couple I saw at Coffee Shop. They were

obviously so in love. The way she gazed into his eyes. The way he stroked her arm so tenderly. You could tell they were soul mates just by looking at them. They were meant to be together. It felt like I had the same connection with Austin.

But I was wrong. I never knew who Austin really was. And now I never will.

TWO
DARCY

"HAS SHE BEEN THERE ALL night?" I whisper to Rosanna.

"I think so," she whispers back.

Our vantage point behind the breakfast bar provides us with a stark view of a disheveled Sadie on an even more disheveled couch. Half of the matching mugs she bought for the apartment are scattered around the floor and coffee table. The mugs' cheerful stripes are a sharp contrast to the Girl Formerly Known as Sadie. Balled-up tissues are strewn everywhere. Even on top of her. She's sprawled on the couch in a crooked diagonal, with her feet dangling off the edge, watching *Crazy, Stupid, Love.* The tank and shorts of her Forever 21 pajama set (a super cute set that has "Love is all around you" printed all over the shorts) are beyond rumpled. Poor thing. She doesn't even have the motivation to change. All signs point to lack of showering. Sadie is the last person I'd have expected to see shattered by boy drama. Or any drama, really. She's the most positive person I know.

"How can we help her?" Rosanna whispers.

"Well, eventually we have to throw her in the shower," I say. No question there.

"I'm really worried. It's like her whole life was destroyed overnight."

I hate to admit it, but I kind of knew Sadie was going to crash and burn. There was no way I knew Austin was lying about his life or anything. I just knew her relationship would come to an end. When relationships are crashing and burning all around you, you tend to not be that optimistic about love.

"The best way to help her is to be there for her," I whisper to Rosanna.

Her bagel pops out of the toaster. She goes to put it on a plate, then comes back over to the breakfast bar where we've been huddled together. Rosanna takes the lid off her tub of Breakstone's whipped butter. She slowly scrapes a knife along the top of the butter and spreads it thinly on the bagel. She's so precise you'd think she was conducting brain surgery. How can she not be sick of bagels? She eats them like every day. Maybe she couldn't get good bagels back in Chicago, where she's from.

"What are you doing tonight?" I ask.

"Nothing."

"So D isn't whisking you off anywhere before South Beach?" That boy is totally spoiling her. D is taking Rosanna to Miami for Fourth of July weekend. I'm sure they'll be staying at the most exclusive hotel and eating at the best restaurants. That's how D rolls. D and all the other trust-fund kids aspiring to investment banker status. I was surprised Rosanna agreed to go. When it comes to boy adventures, she and I are on opposite ends of the pleasure spectrum. She's only going because D reserved separate rooms for them.

We sit on our stools at the bar, Rosanna crunching on her toasted bagel, me spooning my boysenberry yogurt, looking everywhere but at what could be mistaken for a dead body on the couch. My heart aches for Sadie. It sucks that boys have the power to break even the strongest girls. I wish I didn't know how she feels. I wish no one had to know how she feels.

"There's not much we can do for her," I say. "She just has to feel it." Time is the only thing that can heal the devastation of boy betrayal. Not that I had enough time to get over mine. . . .

As much as I wanted to be over Logan before he showed up at my door Saturday night, I wasn't. There was a little less aching in my chest when I thought about him, but the pain was still there.

The first time Logan kissed me was near the end of our

first date. We were hanging out on Ocean Front Walk after dinner and Logan was talking about how college is not his thing. He didn't know what his thing was, but he was only twenty-one so there was plenty of time to figure it out. Maybe he would join a circus. Or a band, even though he didn't play an instrument. Or maybe he would be a nomad, picking up odd jobs in odder towns until he was ready to move on to his next unknown destination. I loved the way he had no problem going with the flow. How he refused to let anyone force him into being someone he's not. We were connecting on a hundred different levels, all firing synapses and racing heartbeats.

And then there was a moment. The electric crackle of our charged conversation defused to a hypnotic hum. Logan leaned back against a palm tree, pulling me toward him. He put his arms around me. And then he kissed me. He tasted like honey.

Maybe I would have been over Logan if he had waited a year to fly across the country and announce what an idiot he was for dumping me right before I moved here. But he didn't. And I wasn't. He came all the way from California to tell me he wanted me back after only a couple weeks. I swear I felt like one of those flustered-but-adorable girls from a Nora Ephron movie. When does the boy ever come after the girl he dumped in real life?

Not that this changes my opinion of relationships in any way. Relationships are destined for failure. Everything has to end eventually. But it validates what I already knew. Logan is here in New York because what we had meant something. Before he threw it all away.

I don't know if I can trust him again. I don't know if I can give up Summer Fun Darcy to be exclusive with the boy who broke my heart. All I know is that giving Logan a second chance is the right thing to do. However long it takes, he deserves the chance to show how he really feels.

Logan was my heart. Could he be again?

I wish I could swoop in on Sadie the way Logan swooped in on me and take away her pain. We were talking with Rosanna about going to the beach this weekend. But that was before the scandalous exposure of Austin's double life. Sadie doesn't want to go to the beach now. She doesn't even want to get off the couch. And Rosanna will be away with D.

After we say goodbye to Sadie, we head down the long flights of our fourth-floor walk-up: me clomping along in my three-inch wedges and Rosanna bouncing in her comfy sneakers. Comfort does not interest me. The price of fashion includes deft maneuvering on everything from steep stairs to cobblestone streets. I wouldn't have it any other way. When it comes to couture, the more alarming the better.

Rosanna's subway stop is in the same direction as UNY, so we walk together for a few blocks. I quickly call Logan to cancel our plans for tonight. We were going to hit up some static dancing at this Polish rec center. You know, typical Monday night stuff. When my call goes to voice mail, I explain that Sadie needs some emergency girl time, but I'd love to see him tomorrow night if he's free. Logan got the hookup on a friend of a friend's apartment in Chelsea. The apartment belongs to an older guy, like twenty-five, who travels a lot for work. All Logan has to do is take care of the plants, bring in the mail, and pay part of the rent. I guess Logan had a decent amount saved before he came here, because he's still looking for a job.

The boy drama gloom inside our apartment distracted us from realizing what a gorgeous day it is. I smile in the morning sunshine as I saunter down 5th Avenue. But then a boy who looks like Jude passes us. The shock of that first millisecond wipes the smile right off my face. My heart is slamming out an entire repertoire on the steel drum. It takes a few seconds for my body to register that I did not just encounter Jude. I don't have to figure out what to say to him. I don't have to watch him walk away dejected again. My adrenaline level returns to normal. I'm off the hook for now.

Jude has been ignoring my messages. Which might be a good thing, considering I have no idea what's going to come out of my mouth when I talk to him. I know I owe him an explanation. The question is how much to explain.

THREE
ROSANNA

WHEN WE GET TO MY subway stop and Darcy branches off toward class, I start obsessing over the call I'm going to make at work. All weekend I've been dying to call the Upper East Side camp to get Addison's number. I cannot wait to find out what her damage is. She has to tell me why she wants to hurt me. Why would a person I don't even know hate me? This whole Nasty Girl thing is stressing me out so much I can't even enjoy the anticipation of going away with D. My mind still can't wrap itself around the fact that we are going to South Beach together.

D could not be a sweeter, more generous person. The first thing I did when he called Sunday night and invited me to South Beach was refuse. There was no way I could let him pay for such an elaborate trip. I told him that I would love to go away with him one day, but I couldn't afford to yet.

"We're going," D said. "I want to treat you the way you deserve to be treated."

"But it's not right that you would have to pay for everything."

"Oh, it's right. I want to take you away for a trip you will never forget."

"Could we wait until I can save up enough to pay my way? Or at least pay for most of it?"

"Aren't you putting yourself through college? Haven't you taken out student loans?"

He was right. I was delusional to think I could afford to go anywhere before I'm thirty.

"Let me do this for you," D said. "You'd be doing *me* the favor. I want to go away, but I don't want to go alone. I really want you to come with me. Please let me take you?"

We went back and forth for a long time. But I finally accepted that D really did want to treat me. And it's not like he couldn't afford to. Donovan Clark is from a rich family. He can afford to do anything.

All I want to do is get on the subway and lose myself in a few minutes of swooning over D. But I can't. Because Addison is so nasty she's even invading my fantasy life.

The Lower East Side day camp where I'm a counselor is affiliated with a camp on the Upper East Side where Addison works. There was a party for the counselors and staff of both camps. Addison threw me a nasty glare as soon as I got there. Like she hated me even though I'd never seen her before. Then she intentionally spilled red punch all over my best going-out top (which was white, of course) and went over to a group of girls and started laughing.

And then she ran into Mica, the only counselor at camp I've clicked with, and told her all these nasty lies about me. Lies about things I've said and done that came out of nowhere. Mica believed everything Addison said. Now she won't talk to me.

I was really hoping that Mica and I would become good friends. Our connection was so much more than the superficial friendships I had in high school. We have tons in common, like our strong opinions, high expectations, and affection for quirky cool activities. We both come from poor families. People who grew up poor understand other people who grew up poor in a way no one else can. We've experienced the same hard times. I don't have to explain myself like I do with everyone else. She doesn't make me feel like I have to defend why I don't have a cell phone the way every other person I've ever met has. Mica isn't confused about why I've been eating bagels for dinner most nights since I moved to New York City. Or why I wear old shirts that have holes in them instead of buying new ones. Mica knows that when money is extremely tight, luxuries like cell phones and square meals and new clothes aren't always an option.

I hope Darcy appreciates how lucky she is with her parents paying her bills. She won't have a pile of student loan debt towering over her for the next ten years. I'll be in debt long after I've graduated and am finally a social worker. Not that I'll be making good money. I don't care about being rich. I care about helping other people and making their lives better.

The subway comes just as I'm passing through the turnstile. I get to camp—which is in part of an elementary school we're allowed to use for the summer—ten minutes early and rush over to the main office before first period starts. The camp's administrative assistant, Cecelia, is always so nice to everyone. The world would be a better place with more kind people like Cecelia in it. She gives me the number to the Upper East Side camp and lets me use the office phone. My palms sweat as I dial.

"Hi," I say when a woman answers the phone. "This is Rosanna Tranelli. I'm a counselor at the Lower East Side camp? I was wondering if it would be possible to get the phone number of one of your counselors."

"Which counselor?" she asks.

"Addison. I don't know her last name." I take out the red pen and small notebook I always carry in my bag. Addison is probably at camp already, but maybe she'll answer her cell before first period. Waiting until tonight to talk would be excruciating.

One of the older girls streaks into the main office. She

runs over to Cecelia and starts squealing about some doctor's note. I press a finger against my free ear.

"There's no Addison here," the assistant says. "I didn't think we had a counselor by that name, but I just checked the system to make sure. Could she work at our affiliated location?"

"I'm calling from that location right now."

"You're sure she doesn't work there?"

"Yes. I'm a counselor here. I know all of the other counselors."

"Well, I'm sorry," she says, her tone taking on a sharp edge. "I don't know what to tell you."

"That's okay," I reply. "Thanks for checking. Bye." I hang up and stare at the phone. How can Addison not work there? The camp party was only for counselors and staff from both camps. She told Mica she works at the Upper East camp. Why would she lie about where she works?

"Is everything okay?" Cecelia asks me.

"Yeah." I put my pen and notebook away. "Thanks for all your help."

"Anytime." Cecelia gives me a warm smile before answering a call.

I head over to the cafeteria to pick up my group of campers. I'm assigned to six eight-year-old girls. We go to activities together in the morning, sit together at lunch, and then have more activities and free play in the afternoon. At the end of the day, I take the girls to the pickup area in front of the school and wait with them until they're all picked up by guardians or put on the buses that take them home. I love kids in general, but girls this age are the best.

Momo and Jenny, two girls from my group, are at their table in the cafeteria. The camp provides free breakfast to kids who qualify.

"Ready for nature?" I ask them. Learning about nature at an indoor camp isn't the most ideal situation. But we're making the best of having camp at a school. We've renamed and repurposed some of the rooms to sound more like a real campground. The cafeteria is the dining hall. The tables with benches in the courtyard are the arts and crafts area. The set of lockers we're allowed to use are cubbies. The yoga studio is really just a classroom. Street games take place in the gym. Once a week all the groups leave for a special activity off campus. We've been to the Central Park Harlem Meer for fishing and gone swimming at a nearby public pool. Coming up we have kayaking in the Hudson River, roller-skating in Brooklyn, and an afternoon at the Museum of Natural History.

"Boo." Momo frowns into her chocolate milk. "Why do we have to do nature?"

"How else are you going to learn about the environment?" I say, even though the "nature" they're learning about is hardly enough.

"Do we have arts and crafts today?" Momo asks.

"You know we do."

Momo brightens. Arts and crafts is her favorite activity. She also likes street games and yoga.

"I heard we're making jewelry in arts and crafts this week," Jenny says. "Monday is earrings—that's today—Tuesday is bracelets, Wednesday and Thursday are necklaces, and Friday is tiaras."

"That sounds awesome," I say. "I can't wait to see what you girls make."

"I'm using pink and purple beads on my bracelet," Momo informs us.

"I'm making a rainbow one," Jenny says. Jenny loves everything rainbow. Even her sneaker shoelaces are tie-dyed rainbow.

The bell rings over the loudspeaker. Time for first period.

"Let's go," I say. The girls take their trays up to the counter. The smell of hash browns is making my mouth water even though I just had a bagel. If counselors qualified for free breakfast, I'd be all over that.

Nature takes place in a classroom with southern exposure. All sorts of plants are growing in ceramic pots along the counter that runs under the windows. Today we're learning how to repot plants. Then everyone will decorate a pot. At the end of the summer, the kids will get to take their plants home.

"It's very important that you water your plant right after

you repot it," the nature instructor explains to the group. He's repotting a plant on a table in the front of the room for everyone to watch before they repot theirs. "Plants are in trauma when their pot is changed. Make sure you give them plenty of water right away."

After the demo, the girls begin prepping their areas to repot their plants. They spread newspaper on the floor. They bring watering cans over to their stations. Momo digs her trowel into a bucket of soil, then pulls too hard when she scoops the soil out. Soil goes flying all over her shirt. She tries to rub it off, but then she has streaks of soil down her white shirt.

This is why every camper is required to keep a change of clothes in the main office.

"Come on," I tell her. "Let's go change."

"My shirt is ruined."

"No it's not. That soil will come out in the wash."

"Are you sure?" Momo sounds more worried than she should be about getting her shirt dirty.

"Absolutely."

"Good. My mom would be mad if I ruined another shirt."

We go to the main office. Cecelia makes pouty lips at Momo's shirt.

"Your nice white shirt," she sympathizes. "I'm always spilling things on my white shirts."

"Tell me about it," I mumble. The white top that

Addison spilled punch on was permanently stained. And that was my only presentable top until Darcy gave me all those fancy clothes. "Can we grab Momo's backup shirt?"

"You bet." Cecelia unlocks the door to a storage room and returns with Momo's extra shirt. "Just have your mom send another clean shirt with you to camp tomorrow, okay?" Cecelia instructs Momo.

"Okay," Momo says.

"Or I can call her for you."

"No!" Momo yells. "It's okay. I won't forget to tell her."

"All righty then." Cecelia throws me a look. I press my lips together to prevent myself from saying something I shouldn't. At least in front of Momo.

We find an empty classroom where Momo can change. The girls usually have no problem changing in front of one another. On days when we go to the public pool, they all take their clothes off to change into bathing suits in the same room. But Momo darts to the corner to change into her clean shirt. She faces away from me, hunkered down.

"Can you not look?" she says.

I turn away from her. "I'm not looking."

She changes quickly. On the way back to nature, we stop at her locker to put her dirty shirt in her backpack.

"Are you sure this dirt will come out?" she asks me again.

"Yes. Just tell your mom to wash the shirt in hot water."

"Maybe she didn't do that last time."

"What happened last time?"

Momo pauses for a second. Then she runs back into nature without answering me.

I follow her in, lingering near the door. The last thing I want to do is crowd Momo and scare her off from telling me something I should know. I'm getting worried about her. Most of the time she seems fine. She gets along with everyone. She acts like a normal girl. But sometimes she'll say or do something that seems a little off. Something that strikes a familiar chord.

She jumped a mile when a metal tub fell in arts and crafts. Then she ran over to the water fountain, sweaty and shaken. Her reaction reminded me of how panicked I was when that guy grabbed me at Come Out and Play. When he grabbed me from behind, all I could feel was being grabbed by the man who molested me.

Momo said she told something she was supposed to keep secret. Her jewelry box was taken away as punishment. Permanently. And now she's stressing over a dirty shirt. What eight-year-old gets that concerned about dirty clothes? I wonder what happened the last time she got a shirt dirty.

I wonder what her mom did to her.

After the kids go home, I stay late to talk to the camp director. Frank is not someone you'd guess works with kids. He's a gruff guy in his fifties with leathery skin and a bald spot, and doesn't appear to enjoy his job. The kind of guy who starts watching the clock when it's almost time to go. He's not mean to the kids and he's not rude to the counselors. He's just not the easygoing, energetic, enthusiastic camp director I was hoping for.

Frank is using one of the classrooms as his office. Papers are scattered over his desk. A few file folder boxes are stacked on the floor nearby. The room smells musty. I knock on the open door.

"Come on in," Frank says from behind his desk. He looks back down at his paperwork.

I stand there awkwardly, waiting for him to look at me.

Eventually he does. "Pull up a chair," he says, gesturing to a stack of orange plastic chairs against the wall.

I pull the top chair off the stack and place it in front of his desk. I sit down without knowing exactly what I'm going to say. The blinds on the windows behind Frank are all the way down with their slits half-open. An office building is next door. People are working at their desks, but none of them are looking over here. Do they ever watch the kids in class during the school year? Or is this school just part of the background scenery?

"So," Frank says. He folds his hands together and rests them on the desk. "What's up?"

"There's a camper who . . . I mean, I'm not completely sure, but . . . I think she's being abused."

"Do you have hard evidence of abuse?"

"No."

"Then what makes you suspect this is an issue?"

I tell Frank about the way Momo's been acting. The things she's said that sound like red flags. The way she jumped a mile and ran away from the table when that metal tub fell. How she was so worried about showing her dirty shirt to her mom. It's difficult to look him in the eye as I'm talking. A torrent of embarrassment from my own past makes it hard to articulate what I want to say. I can't help but recognize a part of myself in Momo. I know I shouldn't be embarrassed about what happened to me. It wasn't my fault. But talking about Momo is bringing up all of those ashamed feelings I buried at the bottom of my emotional suitcase a long time ago.

Memories of the neighbor who molested me when I was eleven come rushing back. I kept it secret for a long time. He threatened to do the same thing to my little sister if I told anyone. But I finally told my friend and then my dad found out. My dad ran that monster right out of town. I made a deal with myself to forget what happened and move on. By the time I started high school in a different town, no one around me knew about it except my family. I wanted to rewrite my life. I wanted to be a better version of myself, the one I always knew I could be. It turns out that reinventing yourself is hard when you want to lock up painful emotions and throw away the key.

"Have you spoken to her mother?" Frank asks.

"No."

"Good. Let's keep it that way. Parents prefer to deal with these situations directly with me."

"But if a camper is being abused by their parents, wouldn't they just deny it?"

"You'd be surprised. I've heard it all. Some parents have no problem describing the methods they choose to discipline their kids, even when they sound inappropriate."

I wait to hear some examples. Frank doesn't offer any.

"So, um . . . what are you going to do?" I ask.

"I'll call Momo's mother. Get to the bottom of this."

"How will you do that exactly?"

"We won't know specifics until I make contact."

I wait for more information. Frank doesn't offer any.

Is it just me, or is this guy brushing me off? Why can't Frank be a stereotypical hippie camp director who's all about singing around the campfire and making s'mores? That guy would be racing to call Momo's mom.

"Anything else?" he asks. He actually has the nerve to look at the clock over the door behind me.

"No." Isn't suspected abuse enough?

"Thanks for bringing this to my attention. I'll let you know when I hear back." Frank stands, shuffling papers together to make a messy pile. Several other messy piles sigh in exasperation. "Are you walking out?"

"Um . . . I have to go by my locker."

"See you tomorrow, then."

"Have a good night."

"Oh, I will." He scurries off like he can't wait to get home, change into sweats, and hit the La-Z-Boy.

People like Frank don't seem to be motivated by anything. They go to work only because they have to and count down the days to the weekend. How is that enough for them? Aren't they constantly feeling the lack of deeper meaning in their lives?

My goal in life is to help make the world a better place in any small ways I can. That's why I can't wait to be a social worker. I want to work with underprivileged kids in the toughest areas of New York City. Kids like Momo need people in their lives who truly care about them. But being in New York isn't all about my career. I've always known that this city is my true home. This is where I was meant to be. Moving here was the ultimate way to reinvent myself. I can be the best version of myself in the best city. No one ever has to know about the damaged parts of me.

When I moved to New York City, I wasn't only running from my past. I was running toward my future.

FOUR

SADIE

I WAS LANGUISHING ON THE couch for the fourth consecutive day when Darcy declared an end to my pity party. She said it was time to pick myself up and dust myself off. I had called out sick again yesterday, and the office was closed today for Fourth of July. The couch was all mine and there was no way I was moving. Until Darcy made me move.

Darcy and Rosanna had been leaving me alone. They knew I needed space and that binge-watching was the only activity I could tolerate. But when Darcy threatened to physically remove me from the couch, she wasn't playing. She came home this afternoon, turned off the TV, and demanded that I march myself into the shower. She was probably just jealous that her couch was having an affair. Darcy led me toward the bathroom when it became clear that marching was not about to happen. I caught Rosanna in my peripheral vision peeling the sheets, pillows, and fuzzy throw off the couch.

Standing in the shower under the hot water might be making me feel better. It's hard to tell. Everything unrelated to Austin feels blurry. And even the unrelated stuff ends up being related by the time I get finished thinking about it. Like the soap I'm using. One minute I'm lathering up, inhaling the calming scent of lavender, washing away the past four days of the worst emotional trauma I have ever known. The next minute I'm remembering how Austin used this same bar of soap just four days ago, came back into my room, and joked that he smelled girly.

I want to throw out this bar of soap and the other bars of lavender soap in the bathroom cabinet. I want to destroy every bar of lavender soap in the world. But that would be a slippery slope. It's not like I can get rid of every single thing that reminds me of him. There wouldn't be anything left.

My arms get tired when I'm rinsing out my hair. I have to rest them, waiting for the ache to subside, before I finish rinsing the shampoo out. Forget conditioner. What would be the point? It's not like I'm going anywhere. I stand still and let the water wash the suds away. I try visualizing Austin's lies rinsing away with the soap and shampoo, a foamy froth of deception swirling down the drain. But a fresh wave of nausea washes over me with the water as I remember each betrayal, my tears mixing in. How he said he loved me more than he's ever loved anyone. How he said he was the happiest he's ever been when we were together. How being with me made him want to be a better man.

Except he wasn't a better man. He was a man who was married the whole time.

Freshly showered and dressed in a clean cami and leggings, I go back out to the living room. Darcy and Rosanna have taken over the couch. Probably to prevent me from wasting any more of my life on it.

"Feeling better?" Rosanna asks me.

I sit on the puffy armchair. It feels weird to sit upright after reclining for so long.

"A little," I say.

"Do you want to watch the fireworks in Tribeca tonight?" Darcy says.

"Who's going?"

Rosanna and Darcy exchange a look.

"Logan and Donovan are meeting up with us," Rosanna admits. "But then D and I are leaving for Miami before the fireworks. He's letting Darcy and Logan up to his roof so they can stay and watch them. He says the view is incredible."

"Enjoy."

"You don't want to come?"

Every year I look forward to the Fourth of July. Where else do you get a front-row seat to the best fireworks in the country? Everyone else watches the fireworks on TV while New Yorkers get to see them live. But there is no way I'm watching the fireworks this year. Not after that ginormous non-coincidence with Austin. We were talking about the Fourth of July a week ago and how much we love the fireworks. Then he drove me to New Jersey so I could see the Manhattan skyline from his side of the water. That's when we saw a short practice run for tonight's fireworks over the Hudson River. Right after we were talking about them. At the time I thought the non-coincidence was a sign that we were meant to be together. But I guess that non-coincidence happened for a reason I don't understand.

"I can't watch the fireworks," I say.

"Why not?" Darcy asks.

"Remember that ginormous fireworks non-coincidence with Austin?"

"Oh yeah."

"So I'm not really feeling up to it." I'm also not really feeling up to being around two happy couples. "I'm staying in."

"Um . . . that's not happening."

"Why not?"

"I called—"

The door buzzes, cutting Darcy off. My heart jumps into my throat. "Who's here?" I ask Darcy.

"It's for you," she says.

"It's not Austin," Rosanna quickly adds.

My heart recedes back to where it belongs. I go over to the intercom and press the talk button. "Hello?"

"Hey, Sadie," says a familiar girl's voice. "It's me."

I buzz her up.

"Hope you don't mind that I asked her to come over," Darcy says.

"No, it's cool. How did you get her number?"

"Your phone. Excuse the invasion of privacy. Desperate times call for desperate measures."

When I open the door, I'm happy to see Brooke. Just seeing that she looks the same after so much has changed—wavy brown hair, brown eyes, skinny, tough, two inches taller than me—is oddly comforting. Brooke is my best friend from high school. She understands about soul mates better than anyone else I know. But I didn't tell her about breaking up with Austin. Even the thought of talking about it made me want to throw up.

"Hey," I say, relieved that I was forced to take a shower and change.

Brooke folds me into a tight hug. "Why didn't you tell me?" she says against my wet hair.

"I didn't tell anyone except Rosanna and Darcy. But only because they live here."

"The comatose body on the couch was pretty hard to miss," Darcy quips.

"Thanks again for calling me," Brooke tells her. "I wish you would have called me sooner."

"We wouldn't have been able to get her out of the apartment before. She's ready now."

"Ready for what?" I wonder.

"We're going out, just the two of us," Brooke says. "To Kitchenette. For cupcakes."

This makes sense. Brooke is a fellow cupcake addict. She is a big believer in the power of a cupcake to mitigate boy drama.

Brooke talks to Darcy and Rosanna while I go to my room to get ready. Leaving the apartment feels like something I used to do a million years ago. I stand in front of my dresser, figuring out what to wear. The girl looking back at me in the mirror is a girl I don't entirely recognize. She looks shell-shocked, a survivor of serious destruction. Sparkly eye shadow and mascara aren't helping. I run a comb through my wet hair. That's one thing I love about summer. You can go out with wet hair and it doesn't matter. People think you just came from the pool.

Brooke and I take the subway to Kitchenette. She sits next to me in silence the whole ride down. We've never been quiet together for this long before. She can tell that I don't feel like talking yet. But when I do, I know Brooke will listen without judgment. That's the kind of true friend she is.

The first thing I realize at Kitchenette is that they're out of my favorite cupcake. The vanilla rainbow sprinkles ones are always in the same place in the dessert case. There's a big gap where rainbow sprinkles should be.

"Of course," I grumble at the gap.

"But they have peanut butter chocolate," Brooke points out. She knows why I'm grumbly.

We settle in at a table with our cupcakes and coffee. I still don't feel like talking even though we're totally at home here. There's a little girl with her mom at the next table. The girl is about three years old. She's eating a cupcake while her mom yaps away on her phone. Doesn't her mom realize this time is fleeting? That her little girl will be grown up before she knows it? If I were that girl's mom, I would be fully focused on her. Or if I were that girl's big sister.

I had a chance to be a big sister. That chance was taken away from me. Those two guys arguing on the subway . . . one of them pushing the other, who shoved my pregnant mom so hard she fell. . . . The scene replays against my resistance for the billionth time.

My stomach twists in knots. Any hint of an appetite is gone.

Brooke is concerned. Typically I would be on my second cupcake by now.

"I made you something," Brooke says. She reaches into her bag on the chair next to her and pulls out a bright yellow origami flower. Flowing script in orange glitter pen spirals on each flower petal.

"A warm fuzzy?" I ask. My throat gets tight. Brooke

was so cynical when I met her. She scoffed at the first warm fuzzy I gave her, assuming I had some ulterior motive. Now she not only gets warm fuzzies, she made one for me.

"I learned from the best," Brooke says.

My eyes well up with tears. It takes every bit of energy I have not to start bawling in the middle of Kitchenette.

"Thank you," I manage to say. "And thanks for getting me out of the apartment. Sorry to be such a drag."

"No apologies allowed. Austin is the one who should be apologizing."

"He did. I didn't want to hear it."

"I'm so sorry things turned out this way."

"He was cheating with me the whole time," I say miserably. "I was the other woman. But I swear it felt like we were meant to be together." How can I explain the epic love I thought we had? How can I make her understand how it felt to be with him? To touch him? To kiss him? "What if I never find that kind of love again?"

"You will," Brooke insists. "You're the most positive person I know. You'll get back to your optimistic place. And it will be even better next time because the person you're meant to be with won't be married."

I really want to believe Brooke. I want to believe that time will heal. That one day I'll be over this. But there are some things you just never get over. Brooke doesn't know about my sister. Maybe she wouldn't think I'm so positive if she knew about the loss and fear under my optimism.

I feel like a fraud. Brooke thinks she knows me. But she only knows the shiny happy parts of me. The bright parts I show the world while I hide the darkness.

"I just feel so unhinged," I say. "It's hard to explain. It's like . . . I can't trust anyone the way I thought I could. Like I can't even trust reality as I know it. Because what do I really know? Nothing is guaranteed. Bad things happen to good people. Anything can fall apart when you least expect it."

"But there's the Knowing. Sometimes deep down you do know."

The Knowing is what Brooke calls this feeling of absolute certainty she sometimes has. The Knowing is rare, but when it happens, Brooke never questions it. It's a gut instinct guiding her with unshakable clarity. Even when the Knowing sounds crazy, about something that seems totally illogical or impossible, it is always right.

I had the Knowing about Austin. I knew he was my soul mate. And the scary truth? Even after everything that happened . . . I still do. If we had met another time when we were both available, we would be together. The timing wasn't right for us. And the lying wasn't right for me.

But it doesn't matter. There's no way I can forgive him.

My eternal optimist side still knows that following my heart is the right thing to do. That's how I will eventually end up where I belong with the person I'm meant to be with. Brooke wouldn't even be here if she hadn't followed her heart. She moved here senior year even though that meant she'd have to live with her dad. She had a Knowing it was the right thing for her. Coming to New York has shown her so many possibilities. Possibilities she never even imagined before she moved here.

Brooke's story gives me hope. Just being with her is helping me start to heal. It will be a long time until I feel like myself again. But right now, my best friend is helping me find my way home.

FIVE
DARCY

THERE'S THE POSSIBILITY THAT I might have figured out what to say to Jude. There's also the possibility that he will hate me forever once I say it.

Things could go either way.

I swing by Jude's spot in Washington Square Park after my last class. He's performing a magic trick with big bubbles. Could the boy be any cuter?

The last time I saw Jude was Saturday night. I couldn't wait for him to come over. Words I needed to say to him were boiling inside of me. My lid was about to pop any second. When the door buzzed, I ran down the stairs instead of buzzing him in. That's how excited I was to see him. I couldn't even wait for him to climb the freaking stairs. But it wasn't Jude at the door. It was Logan, saying all the things I'd been wanting to hear since I left home.

Logan was telling me that he wanted me back when Jude came around the corner. Logan was totally focused on me. He didn't see Jude until Jude was climbing the steps with a big smile. His smile faltered when Logan turned to look at him.

I did not know how to introduce Logan to Jude. My brain blew a fuse from stimuli overload.

Mental note: Boys from different parts of my life should never meet.

Jude stuck his hand out to Logan.

"Hey, man," he said. "I'm Jude."

They shook hands. I had never seen Logan shake anyone's hand in any circumstance ever. Logan is not the hand-shaking type.

"I'm Logan. Darcy's boyfriend."

"Ex-boyfriend," I quickly clarified. "'Ex' as in 'not anymore.'"

Jude looked confused. "Ex-boyfriend . . . from Santa Monica?"

"Yeah. I'm living in New York for a while."

"I didn't know he was coming," I told Jude. "He surprised me."

"That makes two of us."

Logan raised his eyebrows at Jude. "Is there something I should know?"

See, that's when I should have spoken up. I should have

just come out and told Logan that Jude and I were sort of together. Or hanging out or whatever. But I just couldn't. I couldn't do that to the boy I loved ferociously not too long ago, my first love, who came all the way here to win me back. Even after what he did to me.

So I didn't say anything. Neither did Jude. He mumbled something about needing to go. I tried to get him to stay, but he wasn't hearing it. It was awful.

I was awful.

This is my chance to apologize for my awfulness. Hopefully he will forgive me and understand that I need to give Logan a second chance. I want to be with Logan, at least to see where it goes . . . but what I had with Jude felt so right. Trying to do the right thing is not going to be easy. Jude hasn't tried to get in touch with me. He hasn't responded to any of my messages. The only way to beg his forgiveness is in person.

The crowd watching Jude in an enthusiastic semicircle breaks into applause. Jude thanks everyone for coming. He'll go on break now before starting another show.

I take a deep breath and approach him. He's taking a picture with a little girl, hamming it up for her mom. Early evening sunlight is making his blue eyes glow like neon. He sees me when the last of the crowd leaves.

I approach him. "How's it going?"

"Decent crowds so far." Jude takes a sip from his water

bottle. I love that I know his water bottle always sits by his yellow collection bucket with the smiley face. I love that I know he changes into his hipster magician costume (violet-and-black striped cigarette pants, fitted violet T-shirt, turquoise high-tops) in café bathrooms. I love that I know things all the people who've stopped to watch him never will.

"That little girl was so excited to take a picture with you. You're like a rock star with the ten-and-under crowd."

Normally Jude would laugh at that. He'd crack an aw-shucks grin, then try to hide it by looking down. But none of that is happening. He's staring at me with the blankest expression I've ever seen on him.

"You know that's how I roll," he says absently.

The real Jude isn't showing. He isn't being his usual warm and wonderful self with me. This is some other version of him I've never seen before. The cold and wary version I created. I want the real Jude back.

"So . . . I just . . . I wanted to come by and say I'm sorry. About Saturday night."

"I got your messages."

"But you didn't respond."

"No. I didn't."

"I'm really sorry Logan showed up like that. Seriously, I thought it was you at the door. That's why we were on my stoop. I ran down when he buzzed because I couldn't wait to see you."

"Too bad it wasn't me."

What if it had been Jude? Where would we be right now?

"Logan totally surprised me," I say. "He didn't tell me he was coming to New York."

"You had no idea he was coming."

"None! He showed up out of nowhere. The last time I saw him before Saturday was when he dumped me. Oh wait, it was when I threw that drink in his face. But yeah, so—"

"You threw a drink in his face?"

"You didn't know I was a badass?"

"No, I knew."

"Anyway." I give Jude a shy smile to test the waters. He smiles back. Not the dazzling Jude smile I know and love. But at least he's giving me something. "I'm sorry it was weird. It won't happen again."

Jude's tight expression softens. Then he reaches out and hugs me. He lingers against me, sliding his hands down my arms.

"Thanks for coming to find me," he says. "Not seeing you for so long was a bummer."

"We can't let that happen."

"What are you doing tonight?" Jude has defrosted. I

hate that I have to tell him this next part. But now that he's warmed back up to me, maybe it won't be so bad.

"Actually, I have plans tonight. With . . . um. With Logan."

Jude drops his hands from my arms. "Why?"

I fidget uncomfortably on my peacock espadrilles. "It's . . . kind of complicated." I want to be completely honest with Jude. He deserves to know what's going on. I desperately want to rip off the Band-Aid. Just tell him, get it over with, and move on. But the words are playing a killer game of hide-and-seek and they are crazy determined not to be found. Leave it to words to find the best hiding places.

"He's your ex, right?" Jude says. "So he shouldn't get in the way of us. Right?"

"He wants me back. That's why he came here."

"What do you want?"

I face him like a wide-open sky. Nothing to hide.

"I don't know," I admit. "I'm figuring that out."

Jude would look less hurt if I had just smacked him across the face. I watch helplessly as the scalding shock turns to icy indifference. Any defrosting that might have occurred is over. The boy is back in the freezer. Way back with some old meat that expired a year ago.

"Good luck with that," he says. He bends down to his collection bucket. He takes out a few bills, lining them up neatly before putting them in his wallet.

"Can we . . . do you still want to hang out?" I ask.

"We're done."

Tears spring to my eyes. "Why does it have to be like that? We have so much fun together."

"I don't want to share you."

"But you were okay with not being exclusive."

"No, *you* were okay with not being exclusive. That's never what I wanted. From the first time I saw you, I knew I wanted more."

"Then why didn't you tell me?"

"I thought it was better to have part of you than not have you at all."

"But we can still—"

"No." Jude glares at me, blue eyes ice cold instead of glowing like neon. "There's no 'we' anymore. There was a chance at a 'we.' But you blew it."

Part of me wants to tell Jude what I was dying to tell him before Logan showed up. That I want us to be exclusive casual. That I don't want to put Summer Fun Darcy on a shelf, but I don't need boy adventures with other guys to have a good time. Jude is the only boy adventure I need. Except he didn't want to be part of an adventure. He wanted the kind of commitment that's all official where people start throwing down rules and making demands and the magic dies after six months.

And now Logan is here. For real. He's back in my life the way I wished he would be. Even while I was looking forward to a summer of fun with New York City as my playground, a secret place in my heart hoped we would get back together. I can't shut him down. But Logan can't erase all the trauma he caused just by showing up like some leading man in a rom-com. This isn't a movie. Real life doesn't work that way, all happy resolutions and polished Hollywood endings. Real life doesn't come with a big red bow at the end of a conflict. It comes with two miserable people who now have even more crushing disappointment to add to their emotional baggage. Two people who end up alone.

"You made your choice," Jude says. "You just didn't choose me." He turns away from me and starts getting ready for his next show. Like I'm already gone.

Real life endings suck.

SIX
ROSANNA

"WOULD YOU CARE FOR ANOTHER fresh water-melon juice, miss?"

I look up from my book at the pool waiter. Are they even called pool waiters? This hotel is so fancy I don't even have the right vocabulary.

When I came out to the rooftop pool earlier, I practically had the whole place to myself. A couple in lounge chairs were the only other hotel guests out here. I worried that they weren't wearing enough sunblock. They were an astonishing shade of pale. I looked around for towels to put on my lounge chair and the lounge chair next to me so it would be all ready for Donovan. But The Hotel of South Beach doesn't work that way.

The Hotel ensures that your stay is so relaxing you don't

even have to lift a pool towel. They have staff to make up your chair for you.

"Um . . . excuse me?" I asked a guy in a white polo shirt, white pants, and black sneakers. "Where are the towels?"

"Would you like a chair set up, miss?"

"Oh. Yes, that . . . thank you. May I have two towels? My boyfriend's coming out soon." There was a moment of internal freakout after calling D my boyfriend. That was the first time I called him my boyfriend out loud.

"Of course," the pool attendant said. He quickly gathered the four fluffiest, largest, whitest towels I'd ever seen. "Right this way." I followed him over to a row of lounge chairs facing the ocean. As we walked by the shimmering pool, I was mesmerized by the ribbons of sunlight dancing in the water. The water looked so clear I wanted to jump right in. But first I wanted to be decadent with my fluffy towels.

The pool attendant placed the stack of towels on one of the oversize lounge chairs. Then he spread out two towels on two of the chairs, covering each chair completely and tucking in the top and bottom of the towels. Every move he made was crisp efficiency and expert precision. The two other towels were rolled and placed near the top of each chair. Because of course neck pillows were included.

As if the lounge chair preparation wasn't impressive enough, now the pool waiter is asking me if I want another fresh watermelon juice. Um, that would be a yes *please*.

My first sip was so delicious I almost cried. Is it possible to become addicted to watermelon juice after your first sip? How could I have lived eighteen years without tasting watermelon juice?

When the waiter brings my second glass, I take a minute to admire it. Slices of pineapple and kiwi are wedged on the rim of the glass. A paper cocktail umbrella sticks out of a chunk of watermelon in the juice. The color palette of the pink juice, yellow and green fruit, and orange umbrella is so pretty and summery. Even the glass is festive. It's one of those grown-up cocktail glasses with a stem. My instinct is to take a picture before I start drinking. I really need to get a cell phone. I had a camera, but it broke last year and I couldn't afford to buy a new one. Taking a mental snapshot will have to be good enough. Once I read that experiences we have alone end up being the ones we remember most clearly. I will remember this watermelon juice in vivid detail. I lift the glass and sniff the juice. It smells like sunshine and summer.

Even though D told me to order whatever I wanted, I was planning to just have water. I already feel bad enough that D is paying for the entire trip. But he keeps saying that it's his pleasure. He wants to make me happy. He said I deserve a fun vacation. He said I deserve to be treated right.

I cannot believe this is my life right now.

Here I am, chilling on the softest lounge chair in the

world with a perfect view of the ocean sparkling in the sunshine. Watching palm trees sway in the warm Florida breeze. No longer regretting taking two days off from camp. Reading a good book and sipping fresh watermelon juice. Time slips away as I savor every second of it.

"Look at you, lounging it up by the pool," D says from behind me. He slides onto the lounge chair I was saving for him. Good thing I did. I've been out here for a few hours (slathered in SPF 80, of course) and there are only a few free lounge chairs left.

"How was parasailing?" I ask.

"Unreal. I wish you'd tried it with me."

"Maybe tomorrow."

"Really?"

"Maybe."

"You'd love it."

Floating 600 feet above the ocean while a motorboat pulls me along is not something I think I'd love. That's 38 stories above the ground. Thirty-eight stories that I do not want to fall to my tragic, premature death. But D could not wait to go. He's gone parasailing twice before. The first time was on a family vacation to Maui when he was fourteen. The second was a few years ago at the New Jersey shore. He told me all about what a rush it was to fly through the air, nothing but blue sky around him, with the sickest view.

I'm all set on my fluffy towel, thanks.

D takes his shirt off. I try not to stare. He is one boy who is almost impossible not to stare at. Everywhere you look are features that add up to gorgeous: hazel almond-shaped eyes, sandy blond hair with a bit of a wave, cleft chin, sun-kissed skin. He's even tall, which is perfect for a tall girl like me. D has the kind of confidence that makes people notice. He has this calm stillness while he waits for someone at a café or on the corner, something I will strive to master my whole life and never achieve. I am always uncomfortable waiting for someone. I feel like I have to be checking a screen (that I don't have) or rummaging through my bag (for something I don't need) or adjusting my sandals/dress straps/hair (which are fine except for the hair). But D has a peaceful tranquility wherever he is, whatever he's doing. I really admire that about him.

"Can you do my back?" he asks. He holds up a tube of sunblock, turning his back to me.

I flip the top open and squeeze out some lotion. Then I panic that I squeezed out too much. Putting the extra lotion back in the tube would be impossible. I'll just have to go with it and hope I don't soak his back. That would not be sexy. Some lotion drips on the towel as I begin to spread it on his tan skin. He's been laying out on his roof all summer and it shows. It also shows that I have no idea what I'm doing. This is my first time rubbing sunblock on a boy. Should I be spreading the lotion in circles? Or up and down? Or in various directions to make sure I'm covering his entire back? Does skin safety come first, or is the sensation of how the lotion is rubbed in more important?

Sunblock application shouldn't make me this nervous.

Last night made me way more nervous. After our flight got in and we checked into our hotel, D took me out for an amazing dinner at Joe's Stone Crab. Then we walked along Ocean Drive. D told me people stay out there partying all night. Was he hoping I'd want to stay out all night, too? Is that what he'd do if he were here alone? Partying all night is not my thing. I hope D doesn't think that's lame.

When we got back to our hotel, we took the elevator up to our floor and paused where the hallway split in two directions. Our rooms were at different ends of the hall. I was nervous all over again. How much would D expect from me? Was he going to come to my room? Would he ask me to go to his? What guy takes a girl on an elaborate vacation and doesn't expect to sleep with her?

"This is where I leave you," D said. He knows Jonathan Tropper is one of my favorite authors.

"Thanks for dinner. And for everything else. Tonight was amazing."

"Like I said. You deserve the best." D put his arms around me, holding me close. The elevator dinged. A glamorous older couple got off the elevator. They smiled at us as they passed by. You could tell they thought we were cute.

D pulled back just enough to look at me. His hazel eyes were golden in the warm light of the hallway.

"See you tomorrow for breakfast?" he asked.

I nodded.

"News Café at eight?"

I nodded some more.

And then he kissed me. A perfect good-night kiss at a fabulous hotel in beautiful Miami.

"Sweet dreams," he said.

I had been nervous for nothing.

Last night was something out of a dream. It was a night other people get to experience. And now I get to be other people. D and I have three more nights here. I will never want to leave.

We lay out together in the soothing sunshine. I savor the rest of my watermelon juice. D says I should order another one, but I've already decided that two is my limit. What they're charging for one watermelon juice is my grocery budget for the week.

The sun is much lower in the sky when we start getting restless.

"Ready to head in?" D asks. "We have that surprise I told you about."

I nod with excitement. D wouldn't tell me what we're doing. Just that I'm going to love it.

Getting into the shower back in my room and working the knobs smoothly, I already feel like a fancy hotel pro.

It took me a while to figure out how to work the posh shower fixtures when I took my first shower here. The hot and cold water knobs I was used to seeing were nowhere to be found. Instead there were two polished chrome knobs and a major lack of information about what each knob did. I was scared that I would have to call the front desk to ask how to use the shower and that D would somehow find out. Eventually I determined that the top knob switched the water from overhead rain shower flow to hand faucet flow. The bottom knob controlled the water temperature.

D is waiting for me in the lobby when I come downstairs. He told me to dress casual for the surprise activity. I hope cutoffs, a flowy floral-print tank, and my destroyed old pair of Converse is okay.

"You look pretty," D says when he sees me.

"Thanks." You look gorgeous. As always. Why are you even with me?

"Ready to go?"

"I can't wait."

The surprise turns out to be bike riding along this little boardwalk that runs between a strip of hotels and the beach. I'm surprised D picked such a low-key, old-school activity. He picked it because he knew I'd love it. I can't believe he already knows me so well.

We ride single file with me in front of D. I go slowly, taking in the ocean views and letting the heat soak into my skin like a salve. I ding my bell when people up ahead are in the way. Or not even in the way. Ringing the bell is fun.

The seat of my bike is a little too high. When we have to stop at a crossing, I wobble and almost fall over.

"Do you want me to lower your seat?" D asks, straddling his bike next to mine.

"You don't have to."

"I want to." D gets off his bike. He leans it against the boardwalk railing. Then he adjusts my seat. The muscles in his arms flex as he works. Everything about him is golden. Not only does he have a heart of gold, but amber sun rays are making him glow all over. The blond highlights in his hair look like they're sparking. His eyes are all glittery. His skin is more sun-kissed than ever. I resist the urge to reach out and run my hand up his arm, his chest, his shoulder. For a second I almost topple over again, I'm swooning so hard.

"You're all set." D holds my bike while I swing my leg over. He glides his hand slowly down my hair. "Your hair is glowing."

"So is yours."

"Really?"

"More like sparking."

"My hair's on fire?"

"That's how it looks."

"Cool. I can't tell you how long I've been going for the hair-on-fire look."

We smile at each other in the shimmering sunshine. I'm trying to come up with a witty response when D moves closer to me. He holds my bike handle with one hand and puts his other hand on my waist. I forget what I was trying to say.

When he kisses me, I glow even brighter than the sun.

SEVEN

SADIE

PARKER ASKED HOW I WAS feeling when I came back to my internship yesterday. A zap of fear stung me. Did Parker know about Austin? If my supervisor found out that Austin and I were together, we would both get suspended. Office romances are strictly prohibited. But then I remembered that I called out sick Monday and Tuesday. Parker wasn't suspecting the truth. He just thought I really was sick.

I hate lying. Some people think that a small lie doesn't count. Of course it counts. Even a small lie is a lie. When I told Parker I was feeling better, I was lying some more. I'm on a lying roll. Just like Austin was.

Before I found out Austin was married, there was always this current of excitement running underneath whatever work I was doing at the office. There was always the possibility of bumping into him. Maybe he'd make up some excuse to come see me. Maybe I would sneak up to his floor just to say hi. Snippets of daydreams infiltrated everything I was supposed to be concentrating on.

And then there was the time we hooked up in the copy room. . . .

We stayed late after everyone else left. We were naughty interns making out in the copy room and it was scary hot. Until someone came back into the office and started talking on the phone. They could have come into the copy room anytime. The possibility of getting caught switched our hookup to less hot and more scary.

Blueprints are spread out on the long glass conference room table. I stare at them blankly without processing any information. My mind is only half on this project. The other half is terrified that Austin might come down to my floor for some reason. Maybe even try to talk to me. I do not want to talk to him ever again. And definitely not here.

Why do we have to have internships at the same office? Why couldn't we have met in a café or a bookstore or the park or any one of a zillion other places? I used to go to those places with the hope that I would meet my soul mate there. The hope that he might walk through the door any second was fluttering in my heart the whole time. I didn't know what he would look like, but I would know him when I saw him. Talking with a friend at my regular coffeehouse, I looked up expectantly whenever someone came in. Reading at a bookstore, I glanced down the aisles in anticipation. Going for a walk in the park, I scanned the benches overlooking the river to see if he was sitting there. He could have been anywhere. So of course I found a soul mate in the one place I wasn't looking. A guy I never want to see again.

Enough.

I snap myself out of my Austin haze. I won't let him ruin the rest of my internship experience. I hardly ever saw him here anyway, unless we planned to meet up or he came down to flirt. Good thing he works up on the fifth floor and I'm on the third. Plus he has a job placement coming up in August. He won't even be in the building next month.

My internship is at the Department of City Planning. Right now I'm working on a project for a new green space in Midtown. A vacant lot is being converted into a public area. The concept of starting with a blank slate and having the power to convert that space into anything we want is remarkable. Working on this project makes me want to be an urban designer even more. I can't wait until college starts. I'm going to major in urban planning and design with a focus on environmental conservation and wellness. My professional life is going to rule. But my love life? Remains unclear.

"Hey, Sadie," Parker says, coming into the conference

room. My heart leaps into my throat before I realize he's not Austin.

"Hey."

"What do you think of these?" he asks about the blueprints.

"They're incredible. I love the use of trees in this section." I point at a circular area in the center of the space. Trees will be planted in bunches along the border of the circle. Pathways extending out from the center will originate between each bunch of trees. When Parker first explained this project to me and the rest of the group assigned to revise and refine the layout, he talked about the importance of making urban areas functional, attractive, and sustainable. He said that form and function should be the cornerstone of design. This section with the trees is a good example of what he was talking about, both aesthetically pleasing and user-friendly.

Parker leans a hand on the table, bending down closer to the blueprints. "Do you think there's enough lawn space?"

"Totally. I love the idea of creating a peaceful enclave right in the middle of a busy neighborhood. And the benches are placed far enough away from the main lawn so people can choose to have quiet time. The main lawn might attract rowdy groups."

"We hope not. But yes, that's the philosophy behind the bench placement. We might even do a wading pond along this edge of the lawn." Parker slowly traces his finger along a line of the blueprint. He was one of the original architects of this plan.

The green space project is still on my mind when I fall asleep that night. As I drift off, I visualize my future life as one of the most innovative urban designers in New York City. I'm trying to focus on happy thoughts. I heard that if you concentrate on something happy when you're falling asleep, you will have happy dreams. So it doesn't make sense that I have another nightmare. I was hoping the nightmares would stop when I moved out. Sometimes the nightmares were so terrifying back home that I woke up yelling. Those dreams were so realistic, like I was right back there on the subway when my mom fell. Two guys were fighting. I knew that one of them was going to shove the other. I reached out to stop him, but I couldn't. I couldn't stop him from slamming into my pregnant mom.

I couldn't stop him from killing my little sister.

Different versions of this nightmare played out almost every night for a few weeks before graduation. I was help-less to change the outcome every time. One time I stood up and got between the men. Even though I was seven when the assault happened, I was eighteen in my nightmare. I was brave enough to wedge myself between the men, but I wasn't strong enough to stop their fury. Another time I tried to seduce the man who shoved my mom. I wanted to distract him long enough for my mom and me to get to our stop. Then we would run off the train. He seemed interested at first. Then his face contorted in rage when he realized I was tricking him, and he pushed me aside. He shoved me right into my mom. That was the worst version of the nightmare. In that version, I was the one who killed my little sister.

I woke up screaming that time.

My mom came rushing in. She had been asking what was wrong for a while. She heard me yelling the other times I woke up from nightmares, but my words were incomprehensible. I told her I didn't remember what I was dreaming about. I was exhausted all the time because it was impossible to go back to sleep after one of those nightmares. I would stay awake the rest of the night, staring at the darkness, playing scenarios over and over in my mind that would result in my sister being alive today. When my mom rushed in that time I screamed, I was so frustrated and sleep deprived that I finally told her what was going on.

But I never should have told her. She would not drop it. She kept having these whispered conversations with my dad. They kept throwing me worried looks all the time. I'm like the last person you need to walk on eggshells around. People like being with me. They like my positive energy. They like that I have an optimistic attitude no matter how bad things get. My bright outlook inspires them to be positive, too. Brooke even said that being around me was like a shot of sunshine. So it was infuriating to have the people who were supposed to love me more than anyone suddenly treat me like a different person. I couldn't stand to be around them for another minute. I had to get out of there.

Moving into a new place was supposed to give me a fresh start that would make the nightmares go away. I kept telling my mom that I didn't need counseling. Or a support group. Or medication. I kept telling her that the annual Remembrance Walk was enough.

But maybe I was wrong.

There were times when I thought my brother, Marnix, should have gotten help. He basically locked himself in his room for all of high school. When my parents tried to talk to him, he'd yell at them and slam his door. Marnix slammed his door in my face lots of times, too. I know my parents are relieved that he's away at college now. It's hard to live with someone who shuts you out. Especially if they're family.

I'm not slamming doors in people's faces. But am I shutting my mom out when I should be letting her in?

EIGHT
DARCY

LOGAN WANTED TO TAKE ME out tonight. But there was no way I would desert Sadie in her moment of need. So I threw down some girl-time plans. I told Logan we could go out tomorrow night instead. Then I told Sadie to get ready to love the nightlife. Hoes over bros.

This girl in my art history class is friends with a bouncer who works at the hottest new club. A bouncer who happens to be on tonight. She totally hooked me up. After dropping her name and working my charms, the bouncer let us in but made us swear not to drink or his ass would be grass. We'd never be let in here again if we crossed the adult beverage line. And I intend to crash this place more than once. So we scored a table and I ordered us virgin mojitos to enjoy while we watch everyone else making fools of their drunk selves.

The DJ is on fire. He's been laying down some sweet tracks that are making everyone rock to the beat. The dance floor is packed. Summer Fun Darcy would love this place if she were still on the prowl for boy adventures.

"What's in this?" Sadie asks after she takes the first sip of her drink.

"Ginger ale. Mint. Lime juice. Um . . . and sugar?"

"This is delicious."

"Yay. So you're happy to be out?"

Sadie smiles. "Well, we haven't seen anyone freak out yet. You promised a freakout."

"Oh, there'll be freaking out. Just you wait."

"Maybe some girl will even throw a drink in her boyfriend's face."

"Nice one." I told Sadie all about how I threw that drink in Logan's face after he dumped me. The day after he dumped me, to be exact. At Urth Caffe, which was our place. He was laughing with his friends like nothing catastrophic went down the day before. Like he wasn't even a little bit sorry for ripping us apart. So yeah. I picked up his drink and threw it in his face. It was a badass move I've never regretted for a second.

"Do you think it would make me feel better if I threw a drink in Austin's face?" Sadie ponders.

"I know I'd feel better. And you'd get to diss him publicly. We could track him down in Jersey City. Oooh, maybe his wife would even be there!"

"Like I would want to see her. Think I'll pass on finding out how gorgeous she is."

"How do you know she's gorgeous?"

"Because Austin is gorgeous. Why wouldn't his wife be?" Sadie washes down the word *wife* with a few gulps of her drink.

Sadie doesn't have to tell me how gorgeous that boy was. I remember running into Sadie and Austin on the stoop one time when I was leaving for a date. They had a vibe like they'd been together for a while. Like they were already boyfriend and girlfriend. But then I found out they had just met.

I scope out the scene. Two guys at the bar have been looking at us since we got here. They're cute in a frat boy way.

"See those guys at the bar?" I tilt my head slightly in their direction. "They've been staring at you this whole time."

"Which guys?" Sadie turns to look. The guys notice her looking. One of them raises his glass.

"The ones who just saw you gawking at them."

"Who cares if they saw?"

"It's better to play it cool. They might lose interest if you seem desperate."

"Are you seriously trying to hook me up with some random bar dudes?"

"Too soon?"

Sadie takes another look at the glass raiser, surreptitiously this time. "He's not even half as cute as Austin."

"Okay, rule number one for moving on? You need to get over how cute Austin was. His cuteness factor is entirely irrelevant. The boy broke your heart. He's an asshole."

"But that's the thing. He's not an asshole. He's actually a good person."

"Name one good thing he's doing."

"He's dedicating his life to green design for urban environments."

"I'm sorry, but just because a guy is environmentally aware doesn't exempt him from being an asshole. A person can be a prick and still advocate wind turbines."

"You know that's not the only good thing about him. He's caring. And protective. And a dreamer like me. Being with him felt the way I'd always wanted to feel with a boyfriend. Being with him was . . . everything."

We sit in silence with dancehall pounding and club lights pulsing and hundreds of trendy twentysomethings getting hammered. Normally I'd love a place like this. Here you can escape for the night. You can be anyone. You can turn a stranger into your next boy adventure. You can be completely anonymous or spill your life story. Whatever you want to be, whomever you want to be, however you want to be are all within your reach.

But Sadie is not having a good time. I need to step up my support system game. Time for a subject change.

"Can you believe Rosanna is in South Beach?" I say. "With a *man*?"

"I know!"

"How have we not talked about this?"

"I'm really happy for her."

"Rosanna is radical on the DL. That's hot. I was hoping she had a wild side that was going to emerge. There's nothing like dating a trust-fund kid with the world at his disposal to yank you out of your shell."

"This is her first vacation anywhere."

"Seriously?"

"That's what she said."

My mouth drops open. "She never went on any family vacays?"

"Her family isn't . . . they don't have a lot of money. You know Rosanna is one of five kids, right?"

That I knew. But I didn't know money was so tight in her family. I just thought she needed a style hack. That's why I treated her to some new clothes and accessories. She didn't want to accept them, but I insisted. I even ripped the tags off and destroyed the receipts so she couldn't return anything. I wanted her to feel good about herself. Now that she's with D, I bet she appreciates not having to come incorrect for dinner at Babbo in some busted threads. Just because Mario Batali can pop out from the kitchen in orange Crocs to add the finishing touches to a crackling duck wing or whatever doesn't mean you get to slum it in daytime attire when you're eating there.

My dad gave me a credit card that I'm allowed to use for almost anything. The deal is he pays the bill every month as long as I stay serious about college. He's not loving that I don't know what I want to do with my life. But the way he sees it, at least I'm in school. He digs that I'm taking summer session to make up some of the credits I missed last year while I was backpacking through Europe. Daddy doesn't want my gap year turning into a gap decade.

"I hope she's okay," Sadie says.

"She's more than okay. They're staying at like the swankiest hotel there."

"Do you think she'd call us if she wasn't okay? We're pretty much her only friends in New York so far. I want her to know she can count on us if she's in trouble."

This is why Sadie is so endearing. She even worries about other people when she's the one people should be worrying about.

"I wonder how the separate rooms thing is going," I say.

"That makes me like Donovan even more. He knows Rosanna wants to take things slow and he totally respects that. She's smart. I'd only known Austin for ten days when he stayed over at our place. Look where it got me."

"You're different. Rosanna is way more cautious. More reserved. You know how to take a chance. There's no way you could have known what Austin was hiding. You fell in love. That's a beautiful thing. No regrets."

"Excuse me, but what have you done with my friend Darcy?"

"She's right here. Did you not recognize me in these wild shoes?" I reach down to adjust the straps of my new Dolce platform sandals. These are proving to be among the most challenging shoes I've ever worn. Challenge accepted.

"Since when do you think falling in love is a beautiful thing?"

I remember how Logan and I used to be. He was my first love, and falling in love with him was like diving into a clear blue sea. I thought I could see everything we were, everything we were meant to be. I was wrong. But the falling part . . . The falling part was pure ecstasy.

"Falling in love is beautiful," I say. "It's the being in love part that sucks."

"Maybe you haven't been in love with the right person yet. True love makes people happy more than anything."

"How can you be so positive about love after what just happened to you?"

Sadie gives me a reflective smile. "That's just how I am. I'm an eternal optimist."

"Well, I hope the eternal optimist will stop worrying about Rosanna. She's having the time of her life."

"Bonus—she's getting a break from your snoring."

"For the zillionth time. I do not snore."

Sadie presses her lips together but can't hide her smile. "You snore."

I put my hand up, palm facing Sadie. Then I turn my hand around and give it a confused look. "The hand's not even listening. I was going to be like, 'Talk to the hand.' But then it wasn't listening to you, either."

"You should apologize to your hand for keeping it up at night with your snoring."

"You have me confused with someone who snores."

"I don't think so." Sadie takes her phone out of her bag. She searches for something. Then she holds it out triumphantly for me to see. "We recorded you. Snoring."

"What? When?"

"Right after you insisted you don't snore. Rosanna and I snuck into your room and recorded you. I wish she was here to see this."

"How did you . . . ?" I examine her screen. A graph is being displayed with sound waves. I can't hear the sound over the loud music, but I get the gist. Whoever thought it was cute to think up this snore app has another thing coming. "You seriously recorded me snoring?"

"We did."

"Seriously?"

Sadie leans over to see the screen. "Oh, here's the best part. This is where you do a snorting thing that almost wakes you up. Check out how the waves peak."

Other people might be mad at being recorded without their consent. Or think that their roommates sneaking into their room to record them was creepy. But I'm not other people. I think it's freaking hilarious.

I start laughing so hard I have to put the phone down on the table before I smash it in a convulsive fit. My spazzing makes Sadie bust out laughing. The more I laugh, the harder she cracks up. Tears are running down our faces. Sadie is bent over like her stomach hurts from laughing so hard.

A group of girls on the couch across from us are throwing us contorted looks like we're the crazy ones. But they're the ones all posing on the couch in their micro dresses and overglossed lips, zinging judgment our way for having a genuinely good time.

They make us crack up even harder.

NINE
ROSANNA

WE COULDN'T BREAK OUT OF South Beach mode after we flew home this morning. And we didn't want to go our separate ways after having such a perfect time together. So we took a car service from the airport to D's place, dropped our bags off, got our beach stuff together, and came over to Soho House. D explained that Soho House has a ridiculous rooftop pool. He also explained that Soho House has an extremely exclusive membership policy. I wasn't surprised to find out that D's parents are also members. D can use the pool anytime he wants. Fortunately for me, he's allowed to bring a guest.

The backdrop of this rooftop pool in the Meatpacking District is strikingly different from our view in South Beach. Instead of gazing out over the ocean with palm trees swaying in the breeze, we are surrounded by buildings.

Not right on top of us. They're a bit in the distance, but close enough for you to know where you are. It's pretty cool to be up in this special place most people down on the street don't even know exists. It's like we have our own secret hiding place with some other exclusive members. D orders me a watermelon juice, and we sit in a prime spot on the lounge couch.

I cannot get over how drastically my life has changed since I moved here last month. How bizarre is it that D is treating me to the best restaurants and venues on the nights I see him, but I'm eating bagels for dinner and collecting coupons on the nights I don't?

D smiles at me. "It's like you were meant for this," he says.

"You could say I'm having a decent time. I mean"—I fake-scoff at the rooftop with its insane pool and lush land-scaping and beautiful people—"if you're into perfection or whatever."

"What I love about you is that you appreciate it. All of it. Every last detail. Most people up here don't give their lifestyle a second thought. This is what they've known their whole life. But you . . . you're different."

Um. Did D just say he loves something about me? As in a part of me he loves? As in he also loves other parts of me?

"Remember three days ago?" he asks.

We've been doing this thing where we reminisce about our trip like it happened a long time ago. On the plane we were like, "Remember last night? Remember Friday morning? Remember Wednesday?" Our vacation was even more perfect than I imagined the perfect vacation would be.

"Let's see," I say, pretending to have a hard time remembering. "That was . . . Thursday. Rooftop pool, bike riding, and another best dinner ever."

"Remember two days ago?"

"Sunset beach walk." D took me for the most romantic walk on the beach. I'd always thought the idea of a romantic sunset beach walk was too cliché to not be corny. But the beach at sunset in real life was breathtaking. It was my first time seeing an ocean for real. My first time walking on beach sand. My first time hearing the crashing waves, feeling the foaming water lapping at my legs, smelling the salt and tang of the ocean. Beaches in photos or movies could never have prepared me for the vast beauty of being there in person. It felt like a place inside of me that had been sealed tightly closed flew wide open. The ocean went on forever. We walked along the water's edge as the sky fused pink into purple. D held my hand the whole time. Even when he reached down to pick up a shell he knew I'd love, he didn't let go of me. The shell is small, white, and smooth, with light pink stripes. I'm going to put it on the windowsill in my room when I get home.

D shifts closer to me on the lounge couch, pressing his leg against mine. "Remember last night?" he says.

My face gets hot. I slept in D's room last night. I didn't mean to. We got back to the hotel late and D walked me to my room. He kissed me good-night outside my room, just like he did the night before. Only this time we couldn't stop kissing.

"Let's go to your room," I said. The words came out of my mouth before I could think about them. Like I was someone who wasn't me. Like I was a girl who went to boys' rooms late at night.

We made out on D's bed for hours.

Making out with him wasn't scary the way I thought it would be. The only scary part was wondering how far we would go next time. And the time after that.

At some point I must have crashed. I'd been so tired when we'd gotten back to the hotel, I'd been running on a supercharged combo of lust and adrenaline. When I woke up, the first thing I saw were bright lines of sunlight around the edges of the curtains. For a second I thought I was in my own room. Except I didn't remember closing the curtains. I liked sleeping with the curtains and window open so I could hear the ocean waves as I fell asleep. Then it hit me that I was still in D's room. On D's bed. I was on top of the covers in my underwear. Nervous excitement zipped through me.

D woke up and turned toward me. He didn't say anything. He didn't even open his eyes. He just spooned me. I could feel his bare chest pressed against my back, his arm slung over my waist, his legs bending against the backs of mine. I was afraid to move. I didn't want to wake him up in case he was falling back to sleep. After a while, D hugged me close. Then he turned me gently to face him.

"I'm the luckiest guy in the world for getting to wake up next to you," he said.

I didn't want to leave. Ever.

You'd think after that stretch of intense time together I'd be okay with a break when we got back to New York. Going back to my apartment, unpacking, doing laundry. Finding out how Sadie was doing. Getting ready for the week. But I just wanted us to stay together for as long as we could. Going back to the real world will be weird after this extension of paradise.

"Do you want another drink?" D asks.

"No, thanks." One drink at Soho House is my limit. Drinks are more expensive here than they were at The Hotel "But I never want to leave this rooftop."

"Don't worry. We still have mine. Minus the pool."

D is opening my eyes to a whole new way of life. Not worrying about money for a few days has been amazing. Letting D treat me the way he wants to, the way he says I deserve, makes me feel like I can relax for the first time ever. I don't even think I need a Plan D the same way I used to. Having a Plan D means always having a backup plan for when catastrophe strikes. Scraping by in an expensive city and putting myself through college is not going to be easy. My mental backup planning allows me to defuse the tornado of anxieties that is constantly whirring in my mind. Once I can visualize the worst-case scenario, I realize that my situation isn't as bad as I thought.

My new Plan D is all about D. Donovan D. He is integral to the shiny new version of myself I established when I moved to New York. Part of redefining myself means accepting the kind of love I want. And believing D when he says I deserve to be treated to all the good things he wants to give me.

I reach out to hold D's hand. He looks at me with his intense laser focus that makes my heart pound. What we have is more than physical attraction. It's more than an emotional connection. The way he's looking at me, it's like I can see him seeing the potential in me. Seeing my future. And being impressed with what he sees.

TEN

SADIE

THE FIRST THING I NOTICE when I emerge from my nap is a weird crack in the ceiling. Did that crack just get here? I never noticed it before. The crack is near the center of the ceiling with thinner cracks extending from it like tree branches. What caused the tree crack? Did someone in the apartment above ours drop something crazy heavy in the middle of their room? Is the crazy-heavy thing still sitting there? Will their floor keep supporting the weight of it? Or will I be sleeping one night when my ceiling splits open and the crazy-heavy thing falls on top of me and crushes me to death?

No. None of that is happening. It's a harmless weird crack.

I spring off the bed, yanking my sheet with me that somehow had gotten twisted around my leg. The sheet pulls my leg back and almost makes me fall on my face. I recover my balance, throw the sheet back on the bed, and glance around as if someone who films these kinds of klutzy moments might arrive. Or there could be a hidden camera. How do I know the person who lived here before me didn't install a hidden camera in the crown molding? They could have been watching me ever since I moved in. They could be watching me right now.

No. None of that is happening. There are no hidden cameras.

Exaggerated negative thoughts like these have been harassing me for the past week. Normally I'm able to keep myself in eternal optimist mode. But Austin changed me. He was the harshest reminder that the world can be a cold, nasty place. That people you love can turn out to be poseurs. That life can be taken away in a random instant. That the one thing you believed in the most could be nothing more than a lie.

A girl is entitled to throw herself a pity party when she discovers that the boy she thought was her destiny turns out to be a lying scumbag. Austin had taken over every part of me: my mind, my body, my soul. For the rest of my life, I will never forget how consuming that heartbreak was. Not only did he steal a part of my life from me, but for a time he shattered my optimism.

Enough. I cannot waste any more time being angry. It's time to pick myself up and dust myself off.

My pity party is over.

The first thing is to put away all reminders of Austin. I'm not ready to throw out our mementos. Maybe I never will be. But leaving them out where I can see them is not an option. I scrounge around in my closet for an old photo box that's mostly empty. The box has some notes and ticket stubs and fortune cookie fortunes in it. I grab the box when I find it stashed behind a blanket on the top shelf. Then I go around my room filling it with Austin stuff. Our scorecard from mini golf. The tiny pencil I stole from mini golf. The photo strip we took in Bubby's photo booth. A game piece one of the guys in Austin's board-gaming group gave me that time I went with him. A dried flower Austin picked for me that night in New Jersey. Everything goes in the box. The box goes back behind the blanket in my closet. I close the closet door with a satisfying thud.

Cleaning is up next. My room is disgusting. I open both of my windows all the way to let fresh air in. The hardwood floor peeks out here and there from under the mess. I pick up everything that's on the floor, sorting into four piles: dirty clothes, garbage, recycling, and other. I drag the old vacuum cleaner my mom gave us from the front closet into my room. Running it a few times over my floor helps tremendously. Then I mop my floor until it shines. I push the mop forward and pull it back in slow, deliberate strokes, visualizing my problems being washed away with every swipe. By the time my mind is clear, the floor looks better than it did when we moved in.

My dirty clothes get added to the hamper. I lug the heavy hamper down to the laundry room and start two loads. Back upstairs, I sit at the breakfast bar to make a grocery list. In my catatonic stupor I can't guarantee that I didn't eat some things that did not belong to me. I want to replenish everything that's missing or we're almost out of.

As I'm adding maple syrup to the list, Rosanna comes home from South Beach. She wheels her luggage into the living room.

"Hey!" she says when she sees that I am showered, sitting upright, and fully functional. "How are you feeling?"

"Better. But enough about me. You're so tan! How was it?"

"Amazing. We had the best time. I could have stayed there forever."

"Tell me everything."

Rosanna tells me all about relaxing by the pool, romantic bike rides and sunset beach walks, her new addiction to watermelon juice, and the incredible dinners they had. The more I hear about Donovan, the more I love him. I tear up when she tells me about seeing the ocean for the first time. D made that monumental experience possible.

"He sounds like the sweetest guy," I say. "Super generous."

Rosanna nods, her eyes sparkling. "He said that I

deserve good things and he wants to be the one to give them to me."

"Aww!"

"We didn't want to leave each other when we got back. So you know where he took me?"

"Where?"

"Soho House."

"What."

"I know."

"He's a member?"

"Yeah, and so are his parents."

That is amazing. I've lived here my whole life and have never even seen the pool. "Dude. It's like impossible to get a membership there. Everyone wants to get in."

"I know!"

"You're so lucky."

"I would feel just as lucky without anything fancy, though. D makes me feel lucky just to be with him."

That's exactly how I felt about Austin. It didn't matter what we did or where we went. Being with him was the best feeling in the world.

I hope Rosanna and D don't disintegrate like we did.

"I'm really happy for you," I say, and I mean it.

"Thanks. I kept wondering how you were doing."

"Today woke me up. Have you ever gotten to a point in your life where you've had enough?"

"You mean like when I moved to New York to start over?"

"Exactly. I kind of had a mental move from the corner of Miserable and Pathetic to Done and Moving On."

"Awesome. Can I help with anything?"

"Nope. Enjoy being home. I have to put clothes in the dryer. Can I throw anything in the wash for you?"

Rosanna smiles at me.

"What?" I ask.

"It's good to have you back."

"It's good to be back."

By the time I've put my clothes in the dryer, added a Spring Fresh fabric softener sheet, and started the machine, I've made a resolution. Most people wait until the new year to make resolutions. Not me. I like to make resolutions throughout the year. I resolve to keep myself in the light. This past week was the worst. Trying to focus on anything beyond my heartbreak was like trying to see the world from underwater, gazing up at images wobbling above the surface, but being too weak to break through to them. Drowning was so much easier. But now there's no turning back to that dark underwater world. I will ignore boys for the foreseeable future. I will focus on taking care of myself and helping others. I will put more effort into planning for my future. I will make healthy lifestyle choices so I can feel good every day. These are the priorities that matter.

Coming up for air is a powerful thing. Like pressing an

internal reset button. Or replacing all of your groggy old cells with glittery new ones. I feel better right down to the core of me. I can already feel my internal light shining brighter than ever.

Sometimes to start feeling like yourself again, you just have to remember who you are.

ELEVEN
DARCY

LOGAN TOLD ME TO MEET him at Pier 40. He wouldn't tell me what for. As if showing up in New York to win me back wasn't enough of a surprise, the boy wants to surprise me even more.

I say bring it.

Pier 40 turns out to be a big building in Hudson River Park. I thought it was going to be an actual pier with like seagulls and attractions and stuff. Not that I was expecting anything as dope as the Santa Monica Pier. There is only one Pacific Wheel. But I wasn't expecting Pier 40 to be a . . . recreation center? No wonder Logan told me to dress down.

Logan is doing his sexy sloucher thing near the entrance. He's leaning against the wall, all tall and lanky with his dark hair falling across his face. I always loved that he was tall. I could wear my highest stilettos without towering over him. And those smoldering dark eyes. I used to get lost in those eyes for days.

"Hey, Gorgeous," Logan drawls. He's got the same megachill vibe as always. Same half smirk like you just did something risqué and he knows every last detail about it. Same magnetic aura that draws you in and won't let go.

Mental note: This boy tore your heart into a million bloody shreds. Proceed with caution.

"So what are we doing here?" I ask. "Playing baseball?"

"Think bigger."

"Basketball?"

"Think higher."

"Volleyball on trampolines?"

Logan pushes off the wall. He takes my hand and walks me away from the building.

"Check it." He points to the roof.

Part of the roof is covered with clear netting. I can see dangling ropes through the nets. Like swings . . .

A big smile breaks out on my face. "Trapeze?" I ask.

"Time to catch some air, shorty."

"This is just like—"

"Our first date? Yeah. I remember."

Logan took me to a class at the Trapeze School on the Santa Monica Pier for our first date. We had dinner at a hella good taco truck after. This girl couldn't have asked for a better first date. I was beyond impressed how Logan knew what I wanted even before he knew me. Almost like we were meant to be together. If you believe in that sort of thing.

Our trapeze class is an open class with three other students. We'll all take turns on the trapeze while everyone else watches from the AstroTurf green below. When it's my turn to go, I climb the ladder up to the board we jump off. The instructor is a cute blond girl who tells me how to get into position for my first attempt. She stands behind me on the board after I'm strapped into my safety belt. I remember some things from the class we took before, like how I have to tilt my hips forward and bring the bar up to eye level. This bar is surprisingly heavy, just like the one in Santa Monica.

"When I say *ready*, give me a little bend in the knees," the instructor says from behind me. "When I say *go*, bunny-hop off the board and hang straight."

I have my faults. Being afraid to let go is not one of them. I'm swinging through the air, gripping the bar, when I hear the instructor yell, "Let go!" I release my grasp and fly at the other bar that's swinging toward me. My hands find the new bar and I grip it tight. Logan hoots from where he's watching with the rest of our group.

This is the way I hoped living in New York City would be. Exhilarating, tantalizing, and just the right amount of dangerous. Being in the Now is not hard when you're flying through the air far above the ground. I can see for miles up here. Night is my favorite time of day, but I've always loved this summer evening pre-sunset time when the anticipation of night makes your pulse race and your imagination run wild. You never know what the night can do. One night can change your life forever.

Logan's tall lankiness does not interfere with his agility. I watch as he takes his turn. He puts power behind his swing, flipping up to bend his knees over the bar. I hoot for him even louder than he hooted for me.

"You were awesome," Logan tells me as we're leaving Pier 40. "You always were."

"Awesome at the flying trapeze?"

"Awesome at everything."

We stop on the sidewalk, staring at each other. The people weaving around us are barely detectable beyond my trance. This is how it was with us back home. This is how we were.

I want to kiss him. I want to kiss him until we become the way we were again. But I remind myself what he did. The bitter memory is enough to hold me back.

Logan doesn't kiss me when he puts his arm around my waist. He just walks me over to one of the cute West Village streets. Did he want to kiss me, too? Could he tell I wasn't ready? He stops next to a shiny black motorcycle parked between two cars.

"This is us." He unlocks a compartment at the back and takes out two helmets.

"How is this us? This isn't your motorcycle."

"It's my friend's."

"The guy who's letting you stay at his place?"

"Another guy."

"How do you know so many people in New York?"

"I know like three or four guys. That's not so many people." Logan puts his helmet on. It's black with red flames. "Put your helmet on."

My helmet is red with black flames in a reverse pattern of Logan's. I'm bummed that it will flatten the beachy tousled look my hair cooperated in achieving this morning but delighted that it matches my candy-colored oversize tank, black leggings, and cherry-red BOBS. I grin at the irony of wearing sneakers tonight compared to the stilettos I was wearing the first time Logan took me motorcycle riding. We rode down the California coast on our second date.

"Wait," I say before Logan gets on. "Why are we doing the same things we did on our first and second dates?"

"Are we?" Logan asks in an overly inquisitive tone.

I wait for him to spill.

"Tonight is all about going back to the good times," he reveals. "So, I don't know . . . I thought re-creating highlights from our first three dates might be romantic."

My heart swells. It's amazing that this boy can still surprise me in the most unexpected ways.

"Look . . . I can tell you're reluctant to trust me again,"

he says. "I get it. I messed up big-time. I'd probably feel the same way if I were in your position. That's why I want to show you that you can trust me. I want to remind you of what we had."

This is an absurd conversation to be having in motorcycle helmets. Will helmets protect us in case of an emotional crash? Nervous laughter bubbles up in my throat. I tamp it down.

"Do you remember how good it was?" he asks.

Of course I do. But I also remember him dumping me. Why did he break us apart?

Logan gets on the motorcycle and starts the engine. I get on behind him, put my arms around his waist, and hang on tight.

We ride way up the West Side Highway. I watch the skyscrapers of Midtown fade to the shorter buildings of uptown. The terrain changes into a picturesque countryside filled with trees. Are we even in New York City anymore? Is this what New Jersey looks like? I wrap my arms tighter around Logan, excited to see where he's taking me.

Logan stops the motorcycle in a grassy area with more trees and flowers. A blue butterfly lands on a purple flower. I absorb the Now like a sponge, taking a mental photo of everything all at once. Sadie told me about how she sometimes has epic feelings. She'll be walking down the street and she'll see something that will trigger an overwhelming emotion. Is this what she was talking about?

We get off the motorcycle. Logan stashes our helmets. I attempt to salvage my hair by stabbing at it with my fingers like a pick. Good thing my look today was beachy bedhead.

"Where are we?" I ask.

"Fort Tryon Park."

"In New Jersey?"

Logan laughs. "We're still in Manhattan, babe."

"What street is this?"

"We're above One-Ninetieth."

"The streets go up that far?"

"They go to like Two-Eighteenth."

I have a flashback of watching the sunrise with one of my boy adventures on the East Side Promenade. I had no idea what we were looking at across the river. I told myself that I should look closer at a map of New York City so I could actually understand the geography of where I live. Really need to get on that.

We walk around the park for a while. The summer air feels so green and fresh that it permeates my skin. The slight humidity seals in the sensation, pressing summer into my bones. I can even feel summer in my teeth. Logan tells me about the Cloisters, this old monastery up here that displays medieval art.

"Righteous," I say. "Should we go check it out?"

"We would if we weren't already doing a related activity after this."

"Related to . . . a monastery?"

"Do you really want to know?"

"You're right. Surprises are way better."

"Like when the guy who loves you shows up at your door, begging you to take him back?" Logan leans on a tree, pulling me up against him. He puts his arms around me. He looks at me more intensely than I've ever seen. "I'm sorry. I'm sorry I messed up. I'm sorry I got scared. You're the first girl I've ever loved. The first and only. When you said you were moving . . . I couldn't stand the thought of us being so far apart. I didn't think I could swing the long-distance thing. But I think you were right. We can make it work."

I'm speechless. The boy has taken all my words.

Logan slides his hand through my hair. I try to concentrate on him instead of worrying about how tangled my hair is.

"Whatever it takes," he says. "That's what I'm going to do to win you back."

I press up against Logan with my cheek on his chest. Listening to his heartbeat. Feeling his heat. We stay like that for a long time. Night birds chirp around us and a summer breeze rustles some tall grass, and it could not be more romantic. The strong connection we had back in California comes rushing at me. This must be one of those epic feelings Sadie has. It's like the entire history of our relationship flashes by in an instant, transmitting its intensity in a sonic boom. I remember everything we had, everything we were. I can feel it in the air.

Almost as if none of the badness ever happened.

Before I realize what's happening, Logan kisses me. Our first kiss was just like this. Pressed up against a palm tree near the Santa Monica Pier. I remember how sweet that kiss was. How he tasted like honey.

"Wow," I say after. "You even re-created our first kiss."

"That part wasn't planned."

"Yeah, no, you're clearly a horrible planner."

"Maybe I'd be better if I had some inspiration. I wonder what would inspire me to plan a whole special night?"

"Hmmm. Maybe a special girl?"

"She would have to be really special. The most special."

"So." I pull away from Logan a little. "That was our first two dates. What about the third?"

"What do you remember?"

Logan took me to the Santa Monica Museum of Art on our third date. There was an amazing exhibit with light and color I had been dying to see. I was stoked when he told me he got us tickets.

"Everything," I say.

"Next stop, east side. With a ride through Central Park on the way."

We ride back down the West Side Highway. I feel like I'm flying in the glimmery sunset. I press the side of my helmet against Logan's strong back and close my eyes, wrapping my arms around him even tighter. I remember this. This feeling of being with Logan like we were the only ones in the world who could ever feel this much. This much passion. This much contentment.

When Logan turns off the highway, I lean into the steep turn. I love the way we lean into turns together. You have to completely trust the person you're riding a motorcycle with. If you don't lean into the turn with him, the imbalance will throw you both off.

To re-create our third date at the museum, Logan brings me to the Metropolitan Museum of Art. They're having a Sunday night special exhibit.

"I'm not dressed for this," I say outside the museum.

"That's okay. We're not going in."

"We're not?"

"Trust me. What we're doing is much better. Come on."

Logan brings me around to the side of the museum. In the soft glow of the lamplights, I can see a perfectly manicured lawn extending from the museum wall. He takes us onto the lawn close to the wall and stops under a tall, skinny open window. The soothing musical sound of a string quartet glides out to us.

"You're right," I say as he takes me in his arms. "Being outside the reception is way better than being inside the reception."

"I told you, you could trust me."

We dance. We dance in the lamplight, under the music, pressed together on a hot summer night.

"Do you remember dancing on that roof we snuck up to?" Logan asks. "After that party we crashed when the roofdeck door was open? I put one earbud in your ear and the other in mine. We played our favorite songs. God, that was amazing. I could have danced with you all night."

Yes. I remember.

I remember us.

TWELVE
ROSANNA

FRANK STILL HASN'T DONE ANYTHING about Momo. A camp director not even bothering to follow up on a camper who might be in danger. Nice. I thought by now Frank would have gotten in touch with Momo's mom. I assumed everything would get taken care of. But I just stopped by his office and I can't believe what I am hearing.

"What happened when you called?" I ask.

Behind his desk, Frank huffs. He's sitting in front of several piles of paper, looking frazzled like he is every Monday morning. A sharp, acrid smell is coming from somewhere. Frank picks one sheet of paper off the top of a pile, glances at it, and puts it on top of another pile. "I left a message. She hasn't called me back yet."

I cannot believe that's all he's done. He basically hasn't

done anything. Why isn't he treating this as a potential emergency? It's like he's not even taking his job seriously. Or taking *me* seriously. He should be worried about Momo as much as I am.

"Is there anything I can do to help?" I ask.

"Better to stay out of it." He shuffles another paper between piles. "Like I said, parents prefer to deal with the camp director personally."

But he's not dealing with the parent. Why is he being so lazy? He's acting like a typical administrative tool, with all of the power and none of the heart.

"When did you leave that message?" I ask.

"I don't remember," he says, all defensive. "A few days ago." He looks up from his paper shuffle. "Don't worry. I'll handle it."

All day I fume about Frank's lack of action. Camp directors should want to help every single kid at their camp. When a counselor reports suspected abuse, the director should be relentless in investigating instead of waiting for a call that may never come. It makes me sick that Frank isn't burning to discover the truth like I am.

When my sexual abuse was reported to the police, nothing was done about it. The police didn't have sufficient evidence to convict the guy who was molesting me. Reporting suspected abuse to authorities without sufficient evidence is a big waste of time. They don't do anything and you deal with a lot of extra stress for nothing.

Date rapists are exonerated all the time. Husbands who beat their wives walk free. The system is a joke. Thinking about every raped woman who never saw justice, every abused wife who was tortured into silence, every molested girl without an advocate, makes me infuriated to the brink of insanity. I would do anything to help them. Anything.

I wish I had enough evidence to file a police report about Momo. Or at least to try to find someone who could help me. All I have is a gut feeling that something is not right. Police can't take action if all you can tell them is that a kid is jumpy and worried that she got her shirt dirty. If I want to file a report with sufficient evidence to the police, I'm the one who has to find that evidence.

I want answers. And it's becoming clear that I'll have to get them myself.

There's no way I could talk to Momo's mom on the phone. I highly doubt her mom would call back a counselor if she's not calling back the director. Even if she did call me back, she could easily lie about the situation. I really don't expect her to admit anything over the phone. The only way to get a real sense of what's going on is to confront Momo's mom face-to-face. That means going to her apartment.

I really want to talk to D about this. He might come up with a better strategy.

After camp I go home to take a shower and change. Then I head over to D's place. The burst of cold air that hits me when his doorman opens the door is such a relief from the suffocating humidity that I actually feel faint for a minute. The doorman tells me that D isn't home, but I can wait for him in the lobby. I cross the polished marble floor to the nearest seating area. I glide onto a satin upholstered wing chair and rummage through my bag for one of the small tubes of lotion I snuck home from The Hotel. This lotion smells so good I should have collected an entire bag of it. I kept calling housekeeping for more lotion until I had stockpiled ten tubes. Now I can smell lemon-minty-cucumber fresh all summer. Probably all year. I am officially addicted to this lotion along with watermelon juice, which I unfortunately could not sneak back to New York in my bag. Who knew going to South Beach would be stimulating on so many levels?

I watch the front door as I rub lotion on my arms and legs. Then I take out the book I'm reading. Even though it's a Rainbow Rowell novel, I can't concentrate on anything besides watching the front door. You know you're stressing hardcore if you can't even concentrate on Rainbow. And you know you're a stalker when you show up at your boyfriend's place uninvited. But I can't help myself. My nerves are jangling, my mind is spinning, and I need someone to help me figure out what to do.

At first I don't even realize it's D when he finally comes home. I gave up on watching the door an hour ago. Immersed in my book, I catch D coming in out of the corner of my eye. But I assume it's someone else because he's not alone. Then I look up and realize it is D.

With a girl.

A girl who is hanging on his arm, laughing hysterically at something he just said.

She's one of those annoying size-zero girls who irrationally irritate me. Girls like her can get away with wearing whatever they want. They can wear three-inch heels and still look cute. I tried wearing three-inch heels once. As if I'm not already tall enough. What an embarrassing catastrophe. It was my cousin's wedding. I had just turned sixteen and wanted to look as sophisticated as possible, so I borrowed three-inch heels from my friend. I spent the whole time lurching around, towering over everyone else and hunching down to hear what people were saying. It was not pretty. But this girl with D is pretty. Really pretty. She has long, pin-straight blond hair. Big blue eyes. The kind of girl who would set the fashion trends in high school. The girl who ruled the cool table at lunch. She was the most popular girl who dated the most popular boy. They were expected to have popular babies.

Girls like her can have any boy they want. Including mine.

D looks over and sees me in the wing chair. He reclaims his arm from the girl's grasp.

"Hey," he says, coming over. "What are you doing here?"

"It's good to see you, too," I mutter.

"Of course it's good to see you. I'm just surprised."

I don't mean to glare at the girl. But I'm pretty sure I'm glaring anyway. She was touching my boyfriend. More than touching. She was *clinging* to him.

"Rosanna, this is Shayla." D turns to the girl. "Shayla, Rosanna."

"Hi!" Shayla bubbles.

I do not bubble back.

They look at me expectantly. What, am I supposed to make small talk? Who is she? And why was she hanging on to D's arm, laughing like that?

"Um." Shayla gives D a heavy look. A look like she knows I'm bothered. "I'm taking off. See you tomorrow?"

D nods.

Shayla gives us a tinkly wave and saunters out, perfectly poised. Could her dress be any shorter?

"So what's up?" D says. Acting like he doesn't owe me an explanation. Acting like nothing's wrong.

"Who was that?"

"Shayla? She's my friend."

She didn't look like a friend.

The doorman is throwing us glances like he's keeping tabs on a potentially explosive situation. I take D over to the couch farthest from the door so the doorman can't spy on us. We don't sit down.

"How do you know her?" I ask.

"Shayla is a good friend of mine. From high school."

"You've never mentioned her before."

D smiles, shaking his head like he thinks I'm joking. "Have you told me about all of your friends from high school?"

"No, but my high school friends aren't here." Hanging all over me. Flaunting their size-zero perfection.

"That's because you're from Chicago. I grew up on the Upper West Side, remember? Lots of my high school friends still live here. Or their families are here and I see them when they come home on breaks."

"Does she know I'm your girlfriend?"

"Not yet."

"Not yet? If she's such a good friend, why didn't you tell her?"

"It didn't come up. We were mostly talking about her."

"Then why didn't you say I'm your girlfriend when you introduced me?"

D sighs. "I'm sorry I didn't tell you who she was. I'm sorry I didn't introduce you as my girlfriend. I'll tell her all about you when I see her tomorrow. Okay?"

"Why are you seeing her tomorrow?" I hate how I sound. I wish I weren't so paranoid. But that's the thing with trust issues. They take control of every part of your life and make you say nasty things. Especially to the one person you're supposed to trust the most.

"She's been going through a hard time," D says. "Family

drama. That's why she got back in touch with me. She needed a good friend she could trust."

"Wait. You haven't been in touch with her since high school?"

"Not until recently."

"Why would she contact you after three years?"

"Her parents are high-profile. No one can know what's happening. She can't talk to anyone else about it."

There has to be someone else she can talk to. There has to be more to this story. I hate that she's making me feel this way.

No. That I'm letting myself feel this way. I need to get a grip.

"Can we go up to my place now?" D says. "Or did you want to chill in the lobby all night?"

"What's the family drama?" I ask. Maybe if I felt bad for her, I wouldn't be as jealous.

"I can't tell you."

"Why not?"

"I promised Shayla I wouldn't tell anybody."

"Not even me?"

"How would you feel if I promised to keep a secret you told me and then I went and told someone else?"

"You don't trust me?"

"It's not a matter of trust. I gave her my word. I can't break my promise."

Okay, that's . . . wow. That's like saying Shayla and I

are on the same level to him. That we are both equally important.

D is one of the most important people in my life. I was hoping he felt the same way.

My eyes fill with tears. I blink them back.

"Hey." D hugs me. He holds me close, rubbing my back. "You have nothing to worry about. Shayla and I are just friends. That's all."

It doesn't feel like that's all. It feels like she was there first and she wanted me to know it. Like there's something more between them. She managed to make me feel totally insecure in less than a minute. And now I have to accept that my boyfriend is hanging out with her.

Feeling powerless really bothers me. I get that this is one of those things I can't control. When I feel this way, like there's something out of my control I want to change so desperately but can't, it makes me want to take control of the things I *can* change even more.

Like what I suspect is happening to Momo.

I will help her. No matter what it takes.

THIRTEEN
SADIE

I'VE BEEN MAKING WARM FUZZIES for my friends and people going through hard times for years. I used to give warm fuzzies to kids at school who seemed like they had it rough, just to let them know someone cared. Everyone in my Random Acts of Kindness Meetup group started making their own warm fuzzies after I told them about mine. Of course they loved the idea. The Random Acts of Kindness Foundation is all about spreading the love. Their philosophy is that anyone can help others simply by practicing kindness. My group wanted to extend the warm fuzzy circle to people we don't know. How cool would it be to make a bunch of warm fuzzies and leave them around for strangers to find?

Our plan to paper lower Manhattan with warm fuzzies is a go.

Tonight we are papering our neighborhoods with the warm fuzzies we've been making for a few weeks. Like a warm fuzzy bomb is about to explode. Warm fuzzies cannot be rushed. You have to use special paper and quality pens. Your handwriting has to be impeccable. Script is preferred but is optional. Nice printing works just fine. I usually bedazzle my notes with stickers, rhinestones, sequins, or glitter.

Each of us made twenty-five warm fuzzies. Tonight we split up into our respective neighborhoods. I'm covering the West Village with another girl from my group. She's doing the Far West Village. Bleecker Street to 5th Avenue is my territory.

The first stop I make is at a diner on Greenwich Avenue. But I don't go inside. I take out a warm fuzzy cut into a star shape on watercolored paper. *What we think, we become.* —*Buddha* is written in black Sharpie against the watercolor background. I stick the star in the takeout menu box hanging outside the door of the diner. Next I hit the library. I go up to the children's section and find *The Grouchy Ladybug.* This book is getting a warm fuzzy with sequins and feathers that says: *Have a happy day!* All of our warm fuzzies are stickered with the Random Acts of Kindness seal on the back so people will understand our initiative.

Back on the street, I check my list of papering locations. The ginormous bag I usually lug around is at home. Tonight I just have my mom's High Line member tote I accidentally on purpose packed when I moved out. I feel so free without a big, heavy bag weighing me down. My plan is to start carrying smaller bags. Not just because it's too hot for big bags in the summer. Escaping the confines of my ginormous bag is part of the whole Enough Mode. Feeling lighter and freer physically will help me feel that way emotionally. Everything is connected. Ditching my actual baggage will help me let go of the secret baggage I've been carrying in my heart like dead weight. And it's definitely part of getting over Austin.

The next stop on my list is Joe, a cute coffeehouse on Waverly. Good karma is totally in the air tonight. My corner window table with the vintage filament bulb hanging over it is free. I rush in and claim the table before anyone else can. New York City cafés can be cutthroat when it comes to seating. If you want a seat that's free, you better go for it without hesitation.

I was so excited to see my table free that I sat down without thinking about it. Now I have to stay for a coffee out of habit. One of my favorite things to do is kick back at a window table and people-watch. This area of the West Village is filled with locals who have been here for decades. And a lot of celebs. One time I was leaving and Keri Russell was right outside. My love for *Felicity* is profound and unwavering. I wanted to take a picture with Keri Russell so bad. But she was with a friend who was introducing her to someone. I didn't want to bother her when she was trying to have a normal day. "Hi, I'm Keri," she said to the person she was being introduced to. As if anyone would be dense enough not to know who she was. Keri's sweetness put her right at the top of my celebrity crush list.

After I get my coffee and add cream and sugar, I come back to my table to decide which warm fuzzy I'll leave here. I remember how I used to make warm fuzzies for Marnix and slip them under his door. Sometimes he'd say thanks. Sometimes he wouldn't say anything. But at least he knew I was there for him. That's why I'm knitting Marnix something for Christmas. I want him to know I'm thinking of him every time he sees it. I'm just not sure what to make him. Arizona is warm in the winter, but it gets cold at night. A fun scarf? A hat? Or maybe something cute. A quirky stuffed animal for his desk?

Selecting which warm fuzzy to leave at Joe is not easy. Ultimately I decide to go with a rainbow that disappears into a cloud at one end. In green glitter Gelly Roll pen, I had written inside the cloud: *Anything you visualize, you can create. Dream big.* A croton plant is sitting on the window ledge next to me. I tuck the warm fuzzy under its pot with most of it sticking out. Then I change my mind and stand it up against the pot.

"Scavenger hunt?" someone asks me.

I look up. A boy in his early twenties is standing by my table. A really cute boy with blue eyes and wavy brown hair. He looks familiar, like we've met before, but I can't remember where.

"What?" I ask, borderline rudely. His blue eyes caught me off guard. They're almost the same shade of blue as Austin's.

"Are you doing one of those city scavenger hunts where you take something from a designated place and leave something else behind in exchange? I forget what they're called, but I've always wanted to do one."

"No. I'm just doing the leaving-behind part."

"What are you leaving behind?"

"This." I hold the rainbow out for him. He takes it, his smile brightening.

"That is so sweet. Did you make this?"

I nod.

"And you're just leaving it here for someone to find? How awesome are you?"

"My Random Acts of Kindness group is papering Manhattan with these warm fuzzies tonight. I'm covering the West Village."

"No. Way." The boy points at me. "How do I know you?" he asks.

And then it hits me. He's Danny. We met right before last summer at Strawberry Fields, this place in Central Park where Beatles fans get together. There's usually at least one guy playing guitar and singing Beatles songs. Danny was playing guitar with some other guys there when we met. I went up to him after. We only talked for a few minutes, but I remember that he was just learning to play the guitar back then.

"I think we met at Strawberry Fields like a year ago," I say. "You were playing guitar and we talked after."

"That's it." He cracks a bright smile, his eyes glittering. "I knew I knew you from somewhere. I wanted to come over and ask you, but *Where do I know you from?* is such a line."

"You're Danny, right?"

"Good memory." He extends his hand over the table for me to shake. "Danny Trager."

"Sadie Hall." Normally I wouldn't give my last name out to random boys for safety reasons. But I can tell Danny is a genuinely nice guy.

Danny gives the rainbow back to me. "May I join you?" he asks. "I have to hear more about these warm fuzzies."

There's a second of hesitation where I remind myself that I am not interested in boys right now. Especially boys with glittering blue eyes. Those are the most dangerous ones. But then I get over myself. He's interested in warm fuzzies. Not me.

"Okay," I tell him.

He pulls out the chair across from mine and settles in. I can't help noticing how gracefully he moves for a boy. Most boys slam themselves down into chairs.

"I've heard about your group," he says. "You're doing magnificent things."

"Um . . . I'm just, you know. Leaving some warm fuzzies around."

"But that's impressive. What inspired you to join Random Acts?"

"I like trying to help make the world a better place. Even a little note can make a big difference."

"That is so true." Danny glances over his shoulder, then quickly turns back. "Wanted to make sure my laptop was still there."

Danny was sitting across from me the whole time and I didn't even notice him. My lack of cute boy radar shows how tuned out I am right now. I used to come into this place dreaming of my soul mate walking in the door. Or my soul mate sitting at my corner window table and offering to let me sit with him. My cute boy radar was permanently set to red alert. But I didn't even see Danny when I came in, and he's a cute boy I sort of already know.

"So how's the papering going?" he asks. His blue eyes scorch mine. I actually have to look away to cool my eyes off.

"This counts as an early break. I couldn't resist staying when I saw that my table was free."

"I love this table, too! I always try to get it. Someone was sitting here when I came in. I was getting ready to move over after they left. But you got here first."

"Oh, I'm sorry! I didn't know."

"How dare you not know I was here. And that I wanted this table." Danny's eyes glitter some more as he teases me. Where was he all those times I hoped to meet a boy like him?

"Anyway . . ." I put the other warm fuzzies I was considering back into my bag. "I better get back to leaving these around. Three down, twenty-two to go."

"Have fun. Hey, and if you're ever in Strawberry Fields again, come on by. I play there most Wednesday nights." More glittering eyes. More bright smile.

"Thanks. I might do that."

Danny goes back to his table. On the way out, I slip a warm fuzzy behind his laptop.

FOURTEEN
DARCY

YOU KNOW HOW SOME PEOPLE drone on in a monotone that's so flat their voice is more effective than a sleeping pill?

Yeah. That's my art history professor.

This art history class might be more interesting if the professor wasn't the most boring man alive. Apparently his idea of fun is being able to recite all the artists and titles and dates in the entire history of artistic creation. Why would you still have all that stuff memorized years after the test if you weren't obsessed? He told us he studied at the Sorbonne in Paris. And that he's been to every major museum in Europe. So the dude has passion. It's just hidden under a wrinkled polo and extremely unfortunate khakis. What is it with middle-aged guys and khakis? Are khakis part of a uniform for guys over thirty? Do they think khakis are flattering? Khakis are flattering to no one.

My professor could definitely use a fashion hack. A fresh wardrobe might even motivate him to bring some pep and zing to his classes. He might actually be handsome with the right clothes. I can totally see him looking sharp in a tailored suit. Or even just a fitted button-down. He doesn't wear a wedding ring. The poor guy is probably living a lonely bachelor life, coming home every night to frozen dinners and dreary TV. He is clearly in desperate need of a woman's touch.

Restraining myself from daydreaming is a test of strength. I can't stand being cooped up in a lobotomizing class when it's so gorgeous outside. This girl likes to run with the wind. But I'm also a girl who wants to graduate on time. Taking summer session to make up some general credits I missed while I was in Europe sounded like a better option than graduating a year late. Until summer session actually started. I can't believe I'm cramming classes that normally take an entire semester into one summer.

Class mercifully ends with a slide of Magritte's *The Son of Man*. You have to respect an artist who paints apples over people's faces as a metaphor for the conflict between the visible and the hidden in everything we observe. Magritte was the bomb.

On the way out of class, a shy girl with thick black hair piled on top of her head trips over a chair. She crashes into the girl in front of her, who was talking to another girl—both of those girls get shoved in the kerfuffle. The first girl who got crashed into drops her large coffee cup. Coffee splashes on the shy girl who tripped.

"I'm so sorry!" she says. She looks mortified.

"That's okay," the girl she crashed into says. "It happens. The coffee was cold, so."

"Can I buy you another one?"

"Oh, no. I was just going to throw it out."

Shy Girl still looks mortified. The shoved girls are staring at her as she blushes harder. I'm compelled to do something to smooth out the tension.

"You meant to do that, right?" I ask. "As a performance art piece exposing the hidden from the visible? Anything could have been in that cup. We assume it was coffee because she was holding a coffee cup. But it could have been anything. Even a Magritte apple."

All three girls laugh. Shy Girl gives me a grateful smile.

"You're dropping some serious spin," a boy who sits in the back says on his way out. "You should be in PR."

And just like that, it clicks.

It clicks so hard I'm pretty sure I hear a clicking sound.

The boy is right. I should be in public relations. My social butterfly tendencies and solid extrovert skills are perfect for public relations. What better way to promote people I believe in while constantly making new connections? I can definitely see myself loving the PR world. The image is fuzzy, but for the first time I can make out some rough edges of my future.

How wild is it that I might have figured out what I want to do with my life on the way out of class, standing around with a bunch of people I don't really know? You never know when an epiphany will strike.

Sadie and Rosanna are loving the epiphany story when I tell them about it in my room later. There's something about having them hang in my room that's more fun than chilling in the living room. I filled my room with as many floor pillows, beanbag chairs, and poufs as it could hold exactly for this purpose. The splashes of bright colors everywhere make my room inviting. You want to come in and you don't want to leave.

"That boy has no idea how much of an impact he had," Rosanna says from her turquoise beanbag. Sadie has the violet pouf. I'm sprawled out on my bed. "Do you even know his name?"

"Not yet. But I feel like I should get him a thank-you gift. Is that weird? It has to be something generic while coming across as personal. What do all guys like? Gadgets? Hardware? Steakhouses?"

"Sex," Sadie says. She lifts another slice of pizza from the box on my Jonathan Adler area rug.

"Nothing says 'Thanks for figuring out my life' like the gift of sex," I confirm.

"What's your budget?" Rosanna asks.

"Sky's the limit on this one. Without, you know,

coming off as a creeper."

"Do you know anything about him?" Sadie says.

"Nothing. Today was the first time we ever talked. And I didn't even get a chance to talk back. I was still in delirium mode when he was out the door."

"How about a pogo stick?" Rosanna offers.

"Why a pogo stick?"

"It's pretty much guaranteed he doesn't have one."

"Maybe I should just ask him what he wants?"

Rosanna snorts. "Then he'll be like, 'A new phone is good. Or whatever. A new laptop works.'"

"You really don't have to get him anything," Sadie says. "You can just tell him what happened and say thanks."

"But money's not an issue. Daddy will be stoked to hear that I finally figured out my life. Well, my career, which is the same to him. He'll probably give me a new credit card to celebrate."

Sadie laughs. Rosanna scowls at her pizza.

"Was it something I said?" I ask her.

"No, you're right. He probably will. He gives you everything else."

I exchange a glance with Sadie. Sometimes it's hard to tell what's going on with Rosanna.

"Are you mad at me?" I ask.

"Not mad. Just annoyed." Rosanna rips the ponytail holder out of her hair. "Everything comes so easily to you. You don't know what it's like to not get whatever you want. It's hard." She scrapes her hair back up into a tighter ponytail, looking at me. "Sorry. I'm in a repulsive mood. I shouldn't be taking it out on you."

"No worries." What Rosanna said stings a little. But I brush it off. She's obviously under a lot of stress. I want to help her as much as I can, regardless of her repulsive mood. We've all been there.

"What's wrong?" Sadie asks Rosanna.

"D is out with some girl he knows from high school. This girl Shayla."

"Shayla?" I ask, incredulous. "Her name is *Shayla*?"

"Allegedly."

"I hate her already." Being vehemently on Rosanna's side should help make her feel better.

"He says they're just friends. But it felt like there was something more between them when I met her. I was waiting for D in his lobby last night and he came home with her. She was hanging on his arm, laughing way too hard. He didn't even say I was his girlfriend when he introduced me."

"Wait. He didn't tell her you're his girlfriend? That's messed up."

"She doesn't even know he has a girlfriend. She just got back in touch with him recently. They stopped talking after graduation."

"Oh!" Sadie says. "Then they're still catching up on old times. It's not like they've been talking all these years and he didn't tell her about you."

"Why did she contact him?" I ask.

"Some family crisis she's going through. Apparently D is the only good friend she can trust not to tell anyone. Her parents are public figures or something."

"What's her last name?"

"I don't know."

"I don't like that he didn't tell her about you right away. Isn't that what you do when you get back in touch with someone after a long time? At least mention the person you're in a relationship with?"

"Thank you."

"Where are they right now?" The rage I had back when Logan broke up with me is poking at my ribs like a red-hot skewer. I better check myself at the door before I go and throw a drink in D's face. And Austin's face. Morons.

"I don't know."

"Could you find out?"

"You guys." Sadie holds her hands up in a stop-everything motion. "Donovan and Shayla are just friends. There's nothing to get worked up about."

"Right, because boys and girls can just be friends," I huff.

"They totally can. How is Donovan having a friend who's a girl any different than Rosanna having a friend who's a boy?"

Sadie might have a point.

"It didn't feel like they were just friends," Rosanna says. "There was this . . . vibe coming from them. You could feel their history."

"That's what it's like with old friends," Sadie justifies. "They have history. But if D says they're just friends, I trust him."

"Do you trust him?" I ask Rosanna.

"I want to . . ."

"What if the bad feeling you had was just . . . like, jealousy?" Sadie asks carefully. "Could that have been possible?"

"Of course she was jealous!" I boom. "Any girl would be jealous of her boyfriend coming home with some girl clawing at him." I throw Rosanna a cautious look. "Was she hot?"

"Really?" Sadie says. "How are you going to ask her that?"

"It matters." I bite my lip. "Was she?"

"Super hot," Rosanna grumbles.

"Damn," I say.

"Um, okay." Sadie gets up from the pouf. Even though I only met her a month ago, I know Rosanna and I are about to get schooled. Or attempted schooled. Sadie's positive energy can have a hard time penetrating our cynicism. This girl would defend Walter White *and* Dexter Morgan. "First off, can we remember that Donovan just took Rosanna down to South Beach for four nights? There's no way he would have done that if he wasn't serious about her."

"That doesn't change how Rosanna felt when she saw him with Shayla," I interject.

"Exactly. How she *felt*." Sadie turns to Rosanna. "Did you see Donovan acting like she was more than a friend?"

"No."

"And he told you that they're just friends, right?"

"Yes."

"So why don't you believe him?"

Rosanna shakes her head. "I just don't."

"Why don't you tell him how you're feeling? It's better to be honest and put everything out there."

I almost choke on my pizza. "Again with this? Didn't we agree that it's not always better to share every little thing you're feeling?"

"When was that?" Sadie asks.

"After we watched *Unfaithful*."

"No, *you* said it was better to hide stuff. I think it's better to be honest. Austin lied to me and look how that turned out."

"Being married is not a little thing. It is monumental. There's a huge difference between having an affair and not bothering the person you're with about crap that could be your own issue." I look at Rosanna. "Not that this is crap. I would have been furious if Logan walked in with some clingy hottie."

"This could be my own issue," Rosanna says slowly. "You know how we were talking about how we all have baggage? I wouldn't be surprised if trust issues were buried in mine."

"Why?" I ask. But Rosanna doesn't answer.

Sadie purses her lips like I shouldn't be so nosy. Again, the girl has a point. A good publicist knows when to shut up.

Sadie sits back down on the pouf. She looks around my room. "We could do some fun feng shui in here," she says.

"'Fun' and 'feng shui' should not be used in the same sentence," I protest.

"Have you ever tried it?"

"What do you think?"

"I'm guessing not so much. But it really is fun. We could move those two glass bottles on your dresser to your nightstand. That way they'll be against the southern wall. Objects in pairs against the southern wall are good for relationship prosperity."

My gaze flicks over to the shopping bag hanging on my closet door. The *Princess Bride* shirt I bought for Jude is inside. I can't believe I haven't given it to him yet. But what did I expect after the Logan debacle? Jude looked so disappointed at the park last week. I hate to disappoint anyone. But disappointing Jude? That's really, really bad.

I wish this summer hadn't turned into such a complicated mess of boy drama. Everything was so simple when

Summer Fun Darcy ruled Manhattan. Now my head is spinning. Jude wants to be exclusive, but Logan is the one I have to be exclusive with. Logan was my first love. As much as I want to be with both boys, that wouldn't be fair to either one of them. Logan deserves my full attention.

But I can't help thinking about Jude.

There was a light that used to be in Jude's eyes when he looked at me. I wish I knew how to find it again.

FIFTEEN
ROSANNA

I KEEP STARING AT THE phone.

The phone remains quiet.

I refuse to back down.

The phone refuses to ring.

This is how my night has been going since our pizza party in Darcy's room wrapped up and I came back to my room. All I can think about is D out with Shayla. I can't stop wondering where they are and what they're doing and if D has told Shayla about me like he said he would.

Waiting for D to call is excruciating. Sadie was probably right that there's no reason not to trust him. But I'm not sure he's acting like someone who can be trusted.

I stare at the phone.

The phone stares back in defiant silence.

I need a distraction. Getting more research done on Do

Something might work. I sit on my bed and wrangle with my old laptop until the Do Something site appears with its extensive lists of volunteer opportunities. Volunteer work is important to me. Everyone should give back to their community in some way. That's why Sadie is my new role model. Sadie rocks at random acts of kindness. She's completely confident about taking action. Like when she ran up ahead on the sidewalk to open that door for an old lady trying to maneuver her walker into a deli. Sadie didn't hesitate. I don't want to be shy about approaching strangers on the street. I want to be as confident as she is. No hesitation.

Studies have shown that people in a group watching someone who needs help, even if that person is in danger, will often keep watching without taking action. No one wants to be the next potential target by drawing attention to themselves. People usually rely on someone else to be the first person to do something because it's easier to be a follower than a leader. It takes a person on a mission to zing into action like Sadie does. She doesn't care what everyone else is doing. She's a natural leader people want to follow. I want to zing into action the way she does.

I want to be more like Darcy, too. A little. I want to have the courage to put myself out there more and meet new people. That's not easy to do when you're an extreme introvert. Darcy is an extreme extrovert. Our social skills couldn't be more diametrically opposed. She's a natural people person. She told me that engaging people and figuring out what makes them tick has always come easily to her. She thinks everyone is interesting in their own way. Darcy is charming and witty and draws out the uninhibited side of people. Her enthusiasm loosens me up when we go out. Maybe she even affected my decision to go to South Beach with D. Old Rosanna never would have gone away with a boy she'd just met. But Shiny New Rosanna totally went. And had the best time ever.

When the UNY housing department placed the three of us together for the summer, they had no idea they were matching me up with two girls who would push me out of my comfort zone and inspire me to grow.

I open my notebook to a running list of volunteer opportunities. Working with my kids at camp has been lots of fun, so maybe I should work with kids as a Big Sister or a Girl Scout leader. There are a bunch of other programs for children and teens all over the city. Looking over my list, I wonder how much free time I'll have when the semester starts. I'll have to work at least twenty hours a week on top of my financial aid package. Maybe it would be better to wait until classes and my work-study job start to decide on volunteering. The last thing I would want to do is begin building connections with kids and then have to scale back. I know what it's like to have someone you trust shatter a relationship you were counting on to never change. The kind of relationship a person should always be able to count on. I don't want anyone to get attached to me if I can't guarantee a commitment. My biological mother left when I was one. I was too young to remember her, but her abandonment still hurts.

The phone finally rings a million years later, making my heart hammer. The screen says it's D. I let it ring two more times while I steady my breathing.

"Hello?" I say all casual.

"Hey."

"Hi."

"How's it going?"

"Okay. Just having pizza with Darcy and Sadie."

"Sorry to call so late."

"That's okay. Did you just get back?"

"Yeah."

Then . . . silence. D offers no elaboration on the *yeah*. Like why they were out so late. Or what happened. Or even where they went.

"How was your day?" D asks.

"Good." Horrible. My stomach has been twisted in knots since last night. All day at camp I kept seeing flashbacks of Shayla clinging to D's arm. Laughing too hard at whatever he said. Clacking away in her absurdly high heels. I could barely keep my lunch down. And we had fried chicken.

"Anything exciting happen at camp?" D tries again.

"No." Enough. I'm not going to slide past D going out with Shayla without finding out the most basic information. "So how was it?"

"How was what?"

"Getting together with . . . Shayla?"

"Okay. I mean, she's not okay. She's a mess. It's so frustrating when you want to help a friend but there's not really anything you can do, you know?"

If it's anywhere near as frustrating as your boyfriend going out with a hot girl he has a secret shared history with even though it makes you uncomfortable, then yeah. I know.

"What did you guys talk about?" I ask.

"You know I can't tell you."

"She talked about her family drama the whole time? You didn't talk about anything else?"

"Some other stuff came up."

"Like what?"

D sighs. He is clearly annoyed with me. I know I should simmer down and let D be friends with whomever he wants and not fixate on Shayla. But I can't help it. I can't pretend she doesn't bother me.

"Can we not do this?" D says.

"I'm not allowed to know what you and your friend talked about?"

"You never ask what Jesse and I talk about." Jesse is D's friend from high school. He goes to UNY. They played basketball together in high school and still get together to play on one of the public courts.

"Jesse's different."

"Why? Because he's not a girl?"

"Shayla's not some girl. She's a girl you have a past with. She's a girl who trusts you more than any of her other friends."

"I don't know about that."

"That's what you said."

"Rosanna. I'm with you. I want to be with you. You are my girlfriend."

My jealous frost melts a bit.

"Didn't we just have an amazing time in South Beach?" D says.

"We had the best time."

"This is only the beginning. We'll have lots more best times. Because we're good together. I love being with you. You love being with me, right?"

"You know I do."

"So why can't we focus on that?"

"Okay," I relent. He's right. I'm being a crazy jealous girlfriend. I need to dial back the crazy and amplify the girlfriend. Or I might ruin everything.

"I have something for you," D says. "Guess what it is."

"A pogo stick?"

"What?"

"Never mind. Long story. Um . . . fresh watermelon juice from South Beach?"

"So close."

"Really?"

"No."

"Give me a hint."

"You asked me for it when we were having dinner at that Italian place on the beach."

That dinner was ridiculous. I'd never tasted pasta so fresh. I didn't even know pasta could be that fresh. But I don't remember—"Oh! You got her number!"

"Nailed it."

D's sister runs a campus activity group that's sponsoring my camp and the affiliated camp on the Upper East Side. Her group threw the party for both camps where I met D. I was stuffing bags of chips and pretzels into my cross-body like the scavenger I am. He saw the whole thing. I was mortified. But not as mortified as I was when he saw Addison spill punch on me. D offered to ask his sister for Addison's number so I could find out what her damage is. At first I said no. I wanted to ignore the situation, hoping it would go away. Then Addison went and turned Mica against me. And now she doesn't even work at the Upper East camp?

What happened with Mica was something I was hiding from D. I didn't want to bother him with my immature girl problems. But it really hurts that Mica won't talk to me or even look at me at camp. Right before I left for South Beach, Mica actually spoke to me for a minute. Just long enough to tell me that she's hanging out with Addison now. Mica is making friends with Addison instead of becoming better friends with me. The injustice kept bothering me in South Beach. So when D and I were talking about our friends at that restaurant, the unabridged Addison drama came out. D said he'd ask his sister for Addison's number. This time I didn't protest.

"What did your sister say?" I ask.

"She thought Addison worked at the Upper East camp. She couldn't believe it when I told her you called there and they had no record of her. But she's texted Addison before. So we know this is her real number." D gives me the number. I write it down in the margin of my notebook.

"I wish I didn't have to confront her. Even over the phone, it's going to be nasty."

"Do you want me to call her?"

"No, thanks. I can do it." This will be a test. A test of building confidence. A test of confronting my problems instead of running away from them.

The second I get off the phone with D, I take a deep breath and dial Addison's number. She doesn't pick up. I leave a message for her to call me back right away.

I call Addison a few more times that night. And the next day. Every time she doesn't pick up, every time I leave another message she'll probably never respond to, I get angrier.

Addison is definitely ignoring me. What a disgusting way to treat someone. The ignoring is a form of bullying. When and where will Addison strike again? What if she decides to hurt more of my friends? Or D?

Who will she hurt next to get to me?

SIXTEEN

SADIE

IT HAPPENS LIKE A HURRICANE. Actually, more like a flash flood or an avalanche. They give you warning if a hurricane is coming.

I do not see him coming. I am not prepared for the onslaught. I cannot even take a breath before he crashes into me.

Austin. Is confronting me. At internship.

We didn't run into each other randomly. Austin came down to my floor to find me. He expected to find me in my cubicle. He did not expect to slam right into me as I was rounding the corner on the way back from the bathroom.

I freeze in front of the windows, paralyzed.

"Sorry!" Austin says. "Are you okay?"

Suddenly seeing him without warning is even more

horrible than I've imagined. All I can hear is a whoosh of blood rushing to my head. All I can feel is my heart pounding in my ears.

"We need to talk," he says.

This is the first time I've seen Austin since the night I found out he's married. The first time his eyes have sparkled silver in the sunlight since I discovered how he lied. The first time he's wearing his blue polo shirt with the frayed string on the second button from the bottom while I understand that his wife has never cared enough to snip it off. The first time I've seen him without a wedding ring, knowing he takes it off when he leaves home every day.

We don't need to talk. We need to stay far away from each other.

"There's nothing left to say," I whisper.

"That's not true. There's so much I have to say to you. So much I owe you."

I walked out on him the night I found out he's married. But I can't walk out on him now. Not unless I want to give up my internship. There's no way that's happening. Austin destroyed my love life. I will not let him destroy my professional life.

"Just leave me alone," I say. "Walk away."

"I can't walk away from you. We're soul mates."

"A soul mate wouldn't—" I shut up while two interns discussing solar arrays walk by. When they are out of hearing range, I say, "Soul mates don't treat each other the way you treated me."

"I know, and I can't tell you how sorry I am. Please let me explain."

"What could you possibly say that would change anything?"

"I left her, Sadie. I moved out."

Oh. My. God.

He did it.

Darcy was ranting that when a guy is cheating on his wife, he promises to leave her but never does. The other woman always ends up devastated and alone.

But Austin did it. He left her.

There's a chance he's lying again. But something about the intense look in his eyes, something about the way he's opening up to me, tells me he's not.

My heart leaps like it wants to pull me back to Austin. I can't let that happen. He completely shattered my world. Even if he did leave his wife, he's still married. This is one mess I do not want to get tangled up in. There is no way I'm letting him take me back to that dark and twisty place. I picked myself up. I dusted myself off. Austin is not going to drag me down again.

He's still talking, but I'm not listening. I don't trust myself to hear any more.

"Um," I interrupt. "I need to get back to work."

"Can we—"

"We're done here." I dart back to my cubicle. Continue working where I left off. Pretend like he did not just crash into me. If you act like nothing's wrong at work or school or really anywhere, that's how people will perceive you. Like a fully functional person going about her daily routine. Not like a girl whose heart was ripped to shreds.

I leave the office at 5:00. Austin starts calling me at 5:01.

His first call goes to voice mail while I'm in the elevator. I haven't even had a chance to turn my phone on yet.

He calls again three minutes later.

By the time I get home, take a shower, and start making dinner, Austin has left me nine messages.

My phone rings again as I empty a box of pasta into a pot of boiling water. I refuse to pick up. There's a moment of panic that Austin will come over if I keep avoiding his calls. But I get over it. I will not be intimidated into picking up.

"Who keeps calling you?" Darcy asks, coming into the kitchen. Darcy does not cook. We've gotten into a groove where she treats for dinner sometimes and I cook for the three of us sometimes. Most nights she's out.

"Austin." I throw some garlic bread into the oven.

"Wait. What?" Darcy's mouth hangs open.

"Oh yeah. He came down to my floor today. He said we needed to talk."

"Did you talk to him?"

"Only long enough to hear that he left his wife."

"WHAT."

"He moved out."

"When?"

"Don't know."

"Where is he staying?"

"Don't know."

"Does she know about you?"

"Don't know."

"Why am I the only one interested in these answers?"

"Because I've moved on. Or I'm trying to move on. Moving on isn't exactly the easiest thing if you get bogged down in the situation all over again."

"But the situation has changed. He's free. Isn't that what you wanted?"

"No. I wanted to not fall in love with a married man. That's what I wanted."

Keys jangle on the other side of the front door. Rosanna bangs in, her face twisted in irritation. She drops her keys, bends down to pick them up, and chucks them into her bag.

"What's wrong?" I ask her.

"Nothing."

"I'm making pasta. Do you want some?"

"That would be awesome. Thank you."

"No problem. It'll be ready in ten."

My phone rings again.

"Why don't you turn it off?" Darcy asks. She sits at the

breakfast bar, peering down at the phone on the counter. "Or we could record a fun outgoing message just for Austin. Please don't call again, eff you very much."

"Then he'll know I care."

"Do you?"

"Why is Austin calling you?" Rosanna asks. She was on her way to her room, but her head snapped around when she heard Darcy.

"He left his wife," Darcy tells Rosanna. Darcy gives her big drama eyes, one elbow propped up on the counter, chin in hand.

"What?"

"I know, right? When does that ever happen?"

"When someone's really in love."

Rosanna looks at me. Darcy flicks her big drama eyes my way.

"Can we all kindly remember that this is the same man who lied to me? Over and over? How am I supposed to trust anything he says?"

"Why would he lie about leaving his wife?" Rosanna asks.

"For the same reason he lied about having a wife in the first place. He's a lying liar."

"Boys lie," Darcy confirms.

Sing it, sister.

After dinner, I hang out by myself in my room. Rosanna insisted on doing the dishes. Darcy did not protest. I'd turned off my phone when dinner was ready. Now I turn it back on.

Twenty-three messages. All from Austin.

So he's frantic to get in touch with me because he finally left his wife. I get it. But that doesn't mean I'm required to let him manipulate me. Whether or not Austin takes over my entire life again is up to me. And I say I've had enough.

There's no way I'm listening to these. I am not remotely interested in what he has to say.

But that's a crazy lot of messages. I wonder if he said the same thing in all of them. Maybe I should listen to the first one? Or two? Just to see what they sound like?

Stay strong, Sadie. Do not get pulled back in.

I come detached from time for a while. Lying on my bed, listening to Adele, my earbuds drowning out voices in the living room, floating in a bubble of nostalgia. Will I ever forget how good it felt to be with Austin? Will I ever find that intense connection and chemistry with someone else?

My phone rings. I glance at the screen.

It's Trey. Austin's friend.

Austin and I went to a party on Trey's rooftop in Brooklyn. Trey's parents' rooftop, actually. Austin and Trey have been good friends since high school.

I shouldn't pick up. But if I talk to Trey, I can tell him to tell Austin to stop calling me. I don't want to communicate directly with Austin. I can't trust him, but I'm not completely sure I can trust myself, either.

"Hello?" I answer.

"Sadie? It's Trey. Austin's friend?"

"Hi, Trey."

"We met at my rooftop party?"

"Yeah, I remember you."

"Oh, cool. Well . . . um. Austin wanted me to call you. He's not doing too well. There's—is this a good time for you to talk? Are you busy?"

"I can talk for a minute."

"Austin is destroyed, Sadie. He can't believe he messed things up with you. The way he talks about you, the things he told me when you guys met . . . he loves you."

"He's married."

"He's separated. He moved out."

"Where is he staying?"

"With me. Until he finds a place. The dude's a wreck. He couldn't get out of bed for like a week."

Austin was miserable like I was? Did he call out sick, too?

"He needs to talk to you," Trey says.

"I don't want to talk to him."

"Five minutes. That's all he's asking for."

"That's five more minutes than I want to give him."

"Look. I know you're pissed. I get it. But Austin wants to make things right with you. Can you please just let him apologize? He owes you at least that much."

Trey is right about that. Austin owes me a huge apology. Not that it would change anything. What's done is done.

"Sorry, Trey," I tell him. "I have to go." I hang up before Trey can say anything else.

I am completely drained. I want to go to bed early. Lose the rest of this day to sleep. Wake up tomorrow on a fresh new day with no Austin in it. I decide to brush my teeth, wash my face, and drift away under the covers. When I open my door to go to the bathroom, Rosanna is still doing the dishes while Darcy is picking up mugs she left around the living room. She never cleans up. She usually leaves her dirty mugs around until we run out of mugs. Then Rosanna or I end up washing them. She must really feel bad for me.

I'm almost asleep when the doorbell buzzes. A minute later, someone knocks lightly on my door.

"Yeah?" I say.

Rosanna opens my door slowly. "Sadie? Are you awake?"

"Sort of."

"I hate to tell you this, but Austin's downstairs."

I sit up in bed. "Seriously?"

"He wants to talk to you."

This is ridiculous. This will never end unless I make it end. To his face.

"I'll be right out," I tell Rosanna.

"Are you sure? I can tell him to go away."

"No. It's okay."

I put on my glasses, slip into some flip-flops, and throw my robe over my tank-and-shorts pajama set. They're the ones that say YOU'RE MY TYPE all over them. How ironic that I'm wearing these. But good. Let Austin feel my pain.

He's waiting outside on the stoop.

I stand in the open doorway, one hand on the door handle, the other on my hip.

"What do you want?" I ask.

"To be with you," Austin says quickly. "That's all I want. If I could have only one thing in the whole world, being with you would be it. You're all I need."

"You had me."

"I know—"

"And then you destroyed us."

"I know I messed up. More than messed up. I made the biggest mistake of my life. I am so sorry I hurt you. I'll do anything to get you back."

"You had plenty of chances to tell me the truth. You chose not to. You made the wrong choice."

"But now I'm trying to make the right ones. That's why I moved out. We're separated, Sadie. It's over."

"Does she know about me?"

"Yes. I told her everything."

"Everything? Like how . . . we were soul mates?"

"She knows."

"What did she say?"

"Why does it matter?"

"Because I was responsible for ruining her life! I feel horrible!"

"You didn't ruin her life."

"I broke up her marriage."

"That's not true. We would have gotten separated anyway. I can't tell you how sorry I am that I didn't tell you I was married. But everything else I said to you was true. I never thought about things like soul mates or the total package before I met you." A pack of twentysomething girls strides by on the sidewalk. One of them is laughing so hard she's screaming. Austin waits for them to pass by. "Before we met, I had been regretting that I got married so young," he continues. "I thought that's why I was feeling a void with her. But you showed me what it's like to be in love for real. I thought I was in love before. Until I found you, I had no idea what real love felt like. Now I'm in love for the first time in my life, and I can't believe how amazing it is."

Maybe it's a trick of the streetlights. But it looks like Austin has tears in his eyes.

"Now I understand why I felt that void," he says. "The kind of love you and I have is what was missing. There's no way I can go back from that. How can anyone feel the way we did about each other and settle for less with someone else? What we have happens once in a lifetime.

If that. Do you really want to throw us away just because I was stupid?"

My throat constricts. A car passes by slowly, its headlights making minerals in the sidewalk sparkle. I keep my eyes down.

"You're the love of my life, Sadie," Austin says. "You don't give up on the love of your life."

I look at Austin closely for the first time since I opened the door. He's all sweaty. His white T-shirt and navy basketball shorts are rumpled, like he pulled them out of the hamper and yanked them on. The shoelace on his right sneaker is untied. His face is scruffy. It looks like he hasn't shaved in a few days. Why didn't I notice that this morning?

"There is one thing I want to know," I say.

"Anything."

"How did you pull off spending the whole weekend with me?"

"My wife was away for the weekend. I might have talked her into visiting her mom. She'd been talking about visiting her for a while. She knew things between us weren't good. They hadn't been good for a long time. She didn't need much convincing to leave."

My wife.

Not me. Someone else.

I remember the huge fireworks non-coincidence. I

thought it was a sign that the Universe had brought us together at the exact right time.

Then I remember that I asked Darcy and Rosanna if Austin could stay at our place for the weekend the same night we watched *Unfaithful*. There was no way for me to know that was a huge non-coincidence at the time. Huge. A glaring sign right in front of my face and I didn't even see it.

"There's one more thing I want to know," I say.

"You can ask me anything. No more secrets, I swear. I'm going to be one hundred percent honest with you from now on."

"Honesty doesn't have percentages."

Austin runs his hand through his hair, smiling ruefully. "I realize that now. I thought I was saving you at the time. Protecting you. I thought as long as we didn't have sex, it wasn't really an affair. But an emotional affair can be much more serious than a physical one. What we have . . . this is the kind of love people hope to find. Some people search their whole lives for what we have and never find it."

"Did you tell your wife that? Did you tell her I'm the love of your life?"

"Not yet."

"Why not?"

"I've already hurt her enough. But I will tell her. I just want to give it some time."

"I thought you wanted to be one hundred percent honest?"

"Do you want me to tell her now? Or can it wait until she's not going to be glued to the floor crying, like she was when I first told her about you?"

I need her to know that I'm not some random person who destroyed her marriage. I need her to know I didn't know.

"She knows I didn't know you were married, right?"

Austin nods. "I told her."

"And that if I knew you were married, there's no way I would have been with you, right?"

"I don't remember if I used those exact words, but I'm sure she knows."

Not good enough. His wife deserves to know the truth.

Wait. What am I even talking about? I can't be with him anyway. But she still needs to know the truth. Without percentages.

"Let me know when you've told her everything," I say.

"And then you'll come back to me?"

I don't bother to answer him. I just close the door.

SEVENTEEN
DARCY

THERE'S THIS APARTMENT AROUND THE corner from our place that is so freaking beautiful I can't even. It always gives me a rush when I look in the window. Every time I pass by, I have to stop and stare in the enormous picture window as if the glass has hypnotic powers. My attraction is not just about the high-end pieces like the cow-print Eames sofa or the Bang & Olufsen floor speakers. There's something about the apartment that just gets me. I could totally picture myself living there. I'd have to replace the cow-print sofa with a zebra-print, but still. Everything down to the last detail—the big arc lamp swooping over the sofa, the color-block area rug, the Paul Klee print—are things I would have selected for my own place. The living room looks so cozy at night with the warm glow of the lamplight and candles lit on the coffee table and fresh flowers in a blown-glass vase. Darcy Stewart is not a homebody, but that home could be mine.

Standing at the gate in front of the picture window in the bright morning sunlight, separated from the building by an enclosed area with perfectly landscaped plants and potted flowers, I envision myself on the other side of the glass. How cool would it be to live there? You can tell the apartment goes all the way back. It probably opens into a back garden.

What about the man on the other side of the glass? I wonder what he's like. I've never seen anyone inside, but a man obviously lives here. The only thing that saved his apartment from looking like a bachelor pad was the expensive interior designer he clearly hired. How old is he? Where does he work? Is he in a relationship? He could be like me. A free agent who got sucked back into the past.

I've walked around with Sadie a few times at night. She's always looking in people's windows and pointing out beautiful things in their apartments. I get why she's always so mesmerized. Stopping to look into this apartment the way Sadie does has become a thing. The hypnotic powers of this place force me to be still and enjoy the Now. I only stop for a minute or two. But with the frenetic activity of New York City incessantly vibrating around me, it feels like much longer. I love being able to control time this way. To have the power to stretch one minute into five, five into ten. The power to choose how I want to spend each of those minutes, adding up to days and weeks and months, small units of time building up to become my entire life. That's how powerful the Now is. It defines you every second, whether you are aware of it or not.

You know those days when everything clicks perfectly into place? Today has been one of those days. Like ribbons from every thread of my life swirling together in a Technicolor starburst of happiness. After my voyeuristic apartment therapy, I have a really good Social Foundations class where the professor is firing on all cylinders, sparking our interest in that way you always hope a class will. Revved up on intellectual stimulation, I treat myself to some shopping before my next class. There's a cute retro fit-and-flare dress at a boutique near campus that I must possess. I go in to try it on. The dress clings to my curves in all the right places. We were made for each other. And we all know you can't fight destiny.

I stroll back to campus with my glossy boutique bag. There's something about carrying an upscale store bag around downtown Manhattan that makes me happy. I smile at everyone I pass. Some people smile back.

My next class is Communications. It only meets once a week for three hours. We get a twenty-minute break in the middle. People usually grab a snack or coffee or just sit outside during the break. I usually sit outside with a cluster of people from class. But today I break away to meet up with Logan. He's waiting for me at Washington Square

Park, sitting on the edge of the fountain. My nerves tingle as I glance around for Jude's crowd, but I don't see him performing anywhere. I wonder if he was out here earlier this morning or if he'll be starting soon. Or maybe he's working on his start-up company. It feels weird not knowing even the simplest things about his life anymore.

I sneak up behind Logan and put my hands over his eyes.

"Guess who?" I ask.

"The sexiest girl in New York?"

"Good guess." I sit down next to Logan. I remember sitting in almost this same place at the fountain a few weeks ago, hostile over the boy drama I left behind. Now I'm right here next to the boy who caused that drama. The boy I never thought I'd see again for the rest of my life.

"How's your day going?" he asks.

"Perfectly. What about yours?"

"Just got better." Logan kisses me. He puts his arms around me and kisses me harder. That's another thing I love about New York. You can totally make out in the street or wherever and no one cares.

"I wish I didn't have to go back to class," I say when we stop kissing. "We could go to your place."

"Tempting. But I have a job interview in half an hour."

"Where?"

"This bike shop on Charles Street."

Logan has been looking for a job, but he's only had two

other interviews. One place didn't work out. The other place did, but Logan said he wasn't feeling it. This bike shop sounds more like his speed. He was working at an electrical repair shop back in Santa Monica and living in a beat-up condo near the beach. He didn't love the work. It was one of those jobs you do to get by. But that's how Logan rolls.

Logan splays his hands behind him, leaning back in the afternoon sun. His hair falls over his face as he turns to me with those big dark smoldering eyes. "You don't have to go back to class if you don't want to," he says.

I want to tell him about my decision to go into public relations. How I was checking out the course schedule for fall and found some cool classes I could take. I found out that my major would be Media, Culture, and Communication, which even sounds cool. Except that's not who we are. Logan has no interest in college and he probably never will. We just don't talk about things like career goals and future plans that would limit us to a singular path. We live in the Now. Later will work itself out.

But maybe the Now is more complex. Choosing how to spend the minutes that add up to the hours and days and weeks of my life might be more powerful than I realize.

"Yeah, well, I want my diploma, so . . ." I stand and stretch. "I kind of do have to take this class."

Logan gets up and wraps his arms around me. "When did you get so responsible?" he asks.

"When did you get so romantic?"

"I've always been romantic."

"Not like this. Not like crossing the country to win me back or re-creating our first three dates. You've taken things to a whole new level."

"There's more tricks up my sleeve where those came from."

"Oh? Like what?"

"Come over tonight and I'll show you."

"I'm already there. What time?"

"Around ten?"

"What are you doing before?"

"Happy hour with the boys."

"You better be ready for me."

"Bring it, sexy."

We kiss for a long time in the summer heat. Then I break away and rush back to class.

That night at my place, I can still feel Logan's lips on mine. Sprawled on the couch after the pasta dinner Sadie made, watching Rosanna do the dishes, I'm anticipating what we'll do tonight. I wasn't exaggerating when I said Logan better be ready for me.

A crash of glass breaking against the kitchen floor startles me out of my lust haze.

"Dammit," Rosanna says. She bends down behind the breakfast bar.

I go over to help her. Pieces of broken glass are everywhere.

"Be careful," I say. I rummage under the sink for a

dustpan. There's no dustpan here. Where else would people keep a dustpan? Do we even have a dustpan?

"Could you give me a hand?" Rosanna huffs. There's been this cloud of stank attitude over her since she got home. I don't know what her deal is, but throwing a tizzy fit in my direction is not the best way to go.

"I'm trying," I say. "Do we have a dustpan?"

Rosanna springs up off the floor, exasperated. "How can you not know if we have a dustpan?"

"Um, because if we do, I haven't used it yet?"

Rosanna pounds over to the little utility closet outside the bathroom. She whips out a dustpan and slams the door.

"Yeah," she says, bending down to sweep up the glass. "We have a dustpan." The way she says it sounds like an accusation. Like I'm supposed to know everything everyone has and where it is.

"What's with you? You've been hissy ever since you got home."

"I'm not having the best day."

"So you're taking it out on me? I'm trying to help you."

"By lying on the couch while I do the dishes? How is that helping?"

"You offered to do them."

"And you couldn't offer to help?"

"You didn't say you needed help."

"I don't!"

"Then why are you mad at me?"

Rosanna sweeps up the last shards of glass. Then she brushes the glass into the garbage can and puts the dustpan away. She comes back to the kitchen, turning the water on to wash the rest of the dishes. I'm still waiting for her to answer me.

"Forget it," she says. Rosanna stares down at the colander she's washing. She shakes her head.

"Is this about D?" I ask. "Did something happen?"

"Other than Shayla?"

"Forget her. D is obviously crazy about you. She's not worth thinking about."

"How can I not think about her? She's a problem."

"Situations only become problems if we let them."

"Says the girl with no problems," Rosanna mutters, turning the water off.

"Oh, so that's why you're mad at me. What you said last night about how I get whatever I want. That everything comes so easily to me. Do you really believe all that?"

"Isn't it true?"

"Of course not." How can Rosanna think I'm so shallow?

We didn't get off to the best start the day we met. That was my fault. But I thought I fixed things between us. I took her out to dinner, bought her those new clothes and accessories. I've been supportive of the whole Shayla situation. We've been getting along really well. Or so I thought.

Have I been wrong this whole time?

EIGHTEEN
ROSANNA

I'M OVER THE WAY DARCY acts like she can do whatever she wants and the rest of us will take care of everything.

First she just sat on the couch while I started doing the dishes. Would it have killed her to offer to help? I didn't want to be doing the dishes any more than she did. But there I was, doing her dishes while she stretched out like a show cat whose owner caters to its every desire. Then I dropped a glass. It broke into a million pieces on the tile floor. Darcy reluctantly hauled herself off the couch, clueless about where we keep the dustpan. Maybe she'd know if she did any cleaning. But Sadie and I do all the cleaning for her.

So yeah. I'm being a bitch. I do not like myself right now. Where's the map that shows how to get to the shiny new version of myself I'm supposed to be? Darcy wanted to know what's wrong. There was no way I could begin to explain without bursting into tears. I'm irritated that D is spending time with Shayla. I'm irritated that Addison keeps ignoring my calls. I'm irritated that Frank isn't doing anything about Momo. I'm irritated that my friends and family are so far away. And I'm irritated that financial anxiety is my new best friend.

"Here." Darcy nudges herself next to me at the sink. "Let me help you."

"Do you even know how to wash a dish?" Wow. Now I'm just being unnecessarily bitchy. Crossing the line bitchy. But the words are out there before I can stop myself from saying them.

"What's that supposed to mean?"

"You never wash your dishes. You always leave them in the sink."

"That's not true. I washed my glass out the other day."

"Did you? Or did you leave it in the sink filled with water?"

"There was dish detergent in it. It was soaking."

"You don't even rinse your plates and utensils when you leave them in the sink. You leave them there with bits of food stuck all over. Do you know how annoying it is to scrub off dried food?"

"That's not all me. I hardly ever eat here."

"Sadie washes her dishes when she's done. Either that

or she rinses them off and washes them later. And I always wash everything right away."

"Well, not everyone always has time to wash their dishes right away," Darcy protests.

"How much time does it take to put your stuff in your room?"

"What stuff?"

"Seriously? Clothes, shoes, books, bags—your stuff is everywhere."

"All of our stuff is everywhere. It's called three people living in the same apartment."

"Two of those people put their stuff away in their rooms. Look around." I gesture over the breakfast bar to the living room. A jumble of Darcy's shoes are piled by the couch. Mugs and glasses that she used are scattered on every available surface. Part of what might be a top or a skirt is peeking out from behind a couch cushion. All of it is Darcy's.

"Last time I checked, I wasn't living at home with my parents anymore."

"That's not an excuse to trash our apartment." Darcy has no idea how hard it is to keep a three-bedroom apartment clean. How would she know? She grew up with cleaning ladies to pick up after her.

"Okay." Darcy puts a hand up like *stop right there*. "This? Is not trashed. This is the cleanest apartment ever."

Yeah. Because I do almost all the work. I'll bet she

doesn't even know the difference between a sponge and a scouring pad.

"Would it make you feel better if I put my things away?" Darcy pouts at me as if this is all a game. Does nothing faze her?

"That would be a start."

"Seriously?" Darcy goes into the living room and starts gathering up the mugs. "What else is wrong?" She fumbles one of the mugs, almost dropping it.

I need to get a grip. I am out of control. Fortunately Darcy is tolerating my venting. If I'm not careful, I'll end up with an enemy for a roommate. *Simmer down, Rosanna. Remember who you want to be.*

"Nothing," I say. "Sorry I'm being such a bitch."

"No, it's okay. I want to know what's bothering you. Get it all out, girl!"

"You really want to know?"

Darcy drops the mugs into the sink. "Lay it on me."

"Well . . . you know how I divided our medicine cabinet into shelves for each of us?" The divisions were necessary. Darcy's makeup and eyelash curler and moisturizer kept migrating over to my area. I accidentally took some of her Tylenol before I realized it wasn't my bottle. Of course I replaced them. But that's not the point. The point is that everyone should be entitled to a dedicated area of bathroom space in a shared medicine cabinet. So I divided our sections into areas by shelves: Darcy got the bottom shelf, Sadie was the middle, and I took the top shelf. But a mere two days later, Darcy's lip gloss and tweezers were tossed on top of my eye shadow. The chaos erupted from there.

"Yeah?" Darcy prods.

"That lasted two days."

"Did it?"

"The medicine cabinet is completely destroyed."

"Okay, I don't think we can classify a medicine cabinet as 'completely destroyed' just because some things are out of place."

"It's not some things. It's everything."

"Are your things still on your shelf?"

"Buried under your things. And if you keep putting your stuff on my shelf, I won't be able to fit all of my stuff there anymore."

She leans against the counter, pouting at me again.

"You wanted to know," I say defensively. I start washing her mugs. If I don't wash them, they will sit here forever.

"You do realize it's just a medicine cabinet. It's just stuff. What's the big deal if some of that stuff is out of place?"

I shake my head, rinsing the first mug. She just doesn't get it.

"What else?" Darcy asks.

"You never take your shoes off when you come home."

"So?"

"So your shoes track dirt into the apartment."

"That's what the floor is for."

"You're saying you don't care if the floors get dirty because you keep coming in with your shoes on?"

"The floors are going to get dirty anyway. I don't think my shoes are tracking in that much dirt."

"But how hard is it to take your shoes off when you come in?"

"It's not something I think about. When I come home, I'm either racing to get ready to go out again or I want to relax. Taking my shoes off the second I walk in the door wouldn't help me with either of those."

"It takes two seconds."

"So does cleaning the floor."

Darcy's ignorance makes me bristle all over again. Is she really that out of it? Not that she would mop or vacuum or even sweep when she spilled something on the floor. The other day she spilled sugar on the kitchen floor and didn't even bother to attempt cleaning it up. She just left the sugar on the floor like she still had a cleaning lady to take care of it. She's probably never had to clean a floor in her life. But that's no excuse to be ignorant. Darcy is technically an adult. She should act like one.

"Actually," I say, "cleaning the floor takes a while. This is a three-bedroom apartment."

Darcy goes over to the couch. She yanks her skirt out from behind the cushion. I don't even want to know what her skirt is doing in the living room.

"I don't need this place to be spotless," she says. "You're the one who's obsessing."

"So I'm the one who should do all the cleaning since I'm the one who wants our home to be clean?"

"I said we should get a cleaning lady. But you guys didn't go for it."

"But that doesn't mean you shouldn't help us."

"I wanted to help by getting a cleaning lady!"

"Who we would all have to pay for! Some of us can't afford a cleaning lady!"

We stare at each other.

Like I said. She just doesn't get it. And no amount of explaining is going to change that.

NINETEEN
SADIE

QUIRKY NEW YORKERS WORSHIP MANHATTAN-
henge. Two nights a year (one in May and one in July),
the point of sunset is aligned with the Manhattan street
grid such that every street running straight across from
east to west perfectly frames the sunset. This year the
July Manhattanhenge is happening tonight, July 12. I
can't wait to share it with Rosanna and Darcy.

I also can't wait to tell them about Austin. I wanted to
tell them everything he said after he showed up last night,
but Darcy wasn't home and Rosanna was in her room with
the lights out. When I saw her this morning, Rosanna
told me she wanted to give me space last night in case I
brought Austin upstairs to talk. She wanted to know what
happened. But I was running late and said I'd tell her and
Darcy together tonight. Darcy doesn't even know Austin

showed up. Will they think I'm crazy for talking to him? Will they believe the things he said?

Would it ever be possible to trust Austin again?

"Are we there yet?" Darcy whines.

"Almost," I reassure her. "Just two more blocks."

"Two more blocks! We've already walked like sixty."

"Um, I think you mean six." The best Manhattanhenge viewing point is the farthest east you can get at the end of any street with an unobstructed view of the horizon. The three of us are walking to 14th Street and 1st Avenue. I'd be up for walking even farther east. Rosanna was down with that, too. She wanted to see Alphabet City (mainly because it sounded like something from *Sesame Street*, which she has love for). But Darcy has not been charmed by our walk, even though we're walking the pretty way instead of the efficient way. Walking the efficient way is all about getting from Point A to Point B in the shortest amount of time. I only walk the efficient way when I'm running late. The top efficient ways of walking are 14th Street (basically a bunch of fast food places and discount stores) and 6th Avenue (too frantic and grungy). That's why we're walking over on 13th Street instead of 14th. I prefer to walk on quieter streets with more interesting things to look up at, even if it takes me out of my way. Surrounding yourself with beauty is worth an extra five minutes.

"Why did you wear those shoes?" Rosanna asks Darcy.

"I refuse to sacrifice style for comfort." Darcy holds

her head high, expertly maneuvering her skyscraper heels around a subway grate. "The east side can eat me."

We finally get to the southwest corner of 14th and 1st. There are about fifteen minutes to go before sunset. A skinny older guy with gray hair, retro teashade glasses, and a T-shirt that says FIGHT ON is taking pictures with a professional camera. A couple people crossing the street notice him taking pictures and turn to look west. But we're the only ones camped out on this corner so far. We gaze west down 14th Street. The sun looks like an orange blob suspended in a lava lamp. As we watch its apparent motion, the sun perfectly fills the gap between the rows of buildings on either side of the street, centered on the horizon. Its rays glow brilliantly, illuminating all the building glass in radiant shades of red and gold. When the streetlight turns red, I yank my girls into the middle of the street. A few other people gather in the middle of the street with us. This is the best vantage point to take pictures. Darcy snaps a few beautiful ones.

"The light's turning green!" Rosanna yells.

We run back to the sidewalk. A bunch of people are watching the sun now. The sun dips below the horizon. We watch the sun set until its last slick curve disappears.

"And that's why I moved here," Rosanna says.

"That was amazing," Darcy proclaims. She gives me an appreciative smile. "How many Manhattanhenges have you seen?"

"I try to catch one a year," I say. "But the last few have either been too cloudy or I had plans. This is the first one I've seen in a while."

Darcy stares down the long street as if she's still watching the sunset. "If anyone needs to learn how to be present in the Now, they should watch Manhattanhenge. You can't look away. Even after it's over."

We all stand together in silence. In stillness. In respect and awe of our city. Darcy and Rosanna have shared enough about their pasts during our late-night talks for me to feel like I know them well. Their history is palpable at this moment. The years Rosanna worked so hard to create a better life for herself, hoping that she could live here one day, her biggest dream. The years Darcy battled for her dad's attention, only to be bested by his career, now throwing herself into a summer of excessive boy affection. I feel Rosanna's struggle to be the best version of herself in New York. I feel Darcy's need to be loved in New York. In this moment, we are not three girls who just met. We are one, and one with the city.

I'm treating the girls to fresh fruit drinks at Bubby's. Ever since Austin took me to the Bubby's in Tribeca for pie, Austin and Bubby's have become irrevocably intertwined. But I have no problem going back to Bubby's. I've decided I will not avoid places that remind me of Austin. I will not allow the places formerly known as mine that became ours to be off-limits forever. I'm determined to take back the New York City I knew before him. My first city love that will always be here for me, no matter what.

So I'm taking back Bubby's. Maybe I'm not ready for the Tribeca Bubby's. But it's a start. We're going to the Bubby's across from the High Line. It's all the way over on Gansevoort Street near 10th Avenue. There is no way Darcy's walking nine avenues in those heels.

"I'm getting us a cab." Darcy lifts her arm at an approaching cab. It races over, lurching to a halt right in front of us.

"Damn, girl," I say. "Hail that cab."

"Didn't even have to hike up my skirt."

The High Line Bubby's is even more fabulous than the Tribeca one. This location has an old-school soda fountain. They have sodas, sundaes, shakes—anything you want. All of their ingredients are super fresh. They even make their own ice cream in-house.

"Oh my god!" Rosanna exclaims when she sees the menu at the bar. "They have watermelon juice!"

"Dude, they have all the juices," I rave.

"You do not know how hard I've been craving watermelon juice. This is . . . I freaking love it here."

Darcy peruses the scene from her perch on the high bar stool. She's on the prowl for cute guys. Not in the desperate, obvious way I've seen so many girls scan the crowd for cute guys. Or the way I've glanced around anxiously in countless cafés and bookstores over the years, searching for my soul mate. Darcy is the one in control. She's not waiting for a cute guy to happen to her. She's scoping out potential guys who would be lucky enough to have her happen to them.

We decide to get our drinks to go. Being inside on this gorgeous summer night would be a travesty. The girls like my idea of taking our drinks to the High Line. I'm on a roll tonight, also taking back the High Line.

The bartender places Darcy's Meyer lemon soda and my blood orange juice in clear plastic cups in front of us. Darcy flirts with him a little. He flirts back because she's Darcy. Then Rosanna's watermelon juice arrives. A wedge of watermelon is sticking out of it. Rosanna almost falls off her stool in a fit of ecstasy.

"It's been too long, watermelon juice," she coos at her cup. "Way too long."

I smile as I pay. Rosanna is adorable.

"Thanks, Sadie," Rosanna says.

"Yes, thank you!" Darcy chimes in. "Next time we're doing late-night pancakes at Coffee Shop. My treat. Gotta get our summer ritual on."

Rosanna tenses at this. I know she's grateful when Darcy and I treat. But I also know she feels a lot of pressure to treat back equally, something she can't afford. The two of us have a sort of unspoken agreement that she'll do most of the cleaning around the apartment and I'll cook for everyone occasionally, and we'll call it even. Darcy knows Rosanna is scraping by. You'd think she'd be more aware of the pressure Rosanna feels to keep up with us. But Darcy doesn't see it that way. Treating her friends is something she loves doing. It's a way of showing she cares about us. Treating is a gift, like the clothes she bought Rosanna. Darcy doesn't expect anything from Rosanna in return. Darcy wouldn't care if Rosanna didn't clean. Cleaning is Rosanna's choice.

"Let's keep Coffee Shop as is," I say. "Everyone can pay for what they order."

Rosanna smiles at me gratefully. She sips at her watermelon juice with more enthusiasm than a six-year-old on Christmas morning.

The High Line is dazzling at night. We climb the stairs at the Gansevoort Street entrance. The second I get to the top, I fall in love with this place all over again. It doesn't matter how many times I've been here. Every time is like a new beginning, a new opportunity for possibility. The High Line is an instant mood adjuster. Kind of like yoga for the mind. Any anger simmering under my surface is diffused when I slip past the tall grasses and trees and colorful flowers. I am transported to another dimension. I am free from my past, and the future is wide open.

We walk to section two of the High Line, which begins at 20th Street. Illuminated plants rustle in the breeze. The sweet smell of hyacinths is in the air. City lights sparkle in the distance. I don't look across the river to New Jersey. Nothing can be allowed to harsh my High Line mellow.

We perch on the top row of the Seating Steps bleachers. The High Line rules at repurposing materials. These bleachers were made of reclaimed teak from old industrial buildings. We have plenty of room. Even though it's a gorgeous night, the High Line usually isn't crowded this late since it closes at eleven in the summer. That gives us over an hour for boy talk. I can feel the boy talk coming on even before Rosanna says that she wants to come here with Donovan.

"When's the last time you saw him?" Darcy asks.

"Three days ago." Rosanna puts her juice down next to her, then picks it up again. "He's been busy putting in more time at his internship. And he's planning some more apartment renovations. And . . ."

"And what?"

"He's . . . hanging out more with Shayla."

"Seriously with her? He needs to be hanging out more with you. It's summertime. You guys should be seeing each other every night."

Rosanna drinks her watermelon juice. She doesn't look like it's Christmas morning anymore.

"Have you talked to him?" I ask Rosanna.

"Yeah. I told him it bothered me. But I know it shouldn't. I need to stop being the crazy jealous girlfriend who can't handle her boyfriend being friends with a girl."

"What did he say when you told him it bothered you?"

"That they're just friends. That he can have friends who are girls just like I can have friends who are boys."

I don't want Rosanna to worry more than she already is, but I can't help asking this next thing. "Not to be paranoid? But do you think they really are just friends?"

"He says they are."

I hope that's true. Only, I can't help thinking about how Austin lied to me so easily. I mean, he was freaking married and I had no idea. Is it that much of a stretch to wonder if Donovan is being honest with Rosanna?

"We cannot endure another manwhore fiasco," Darcy trumpets. "We're done. D has to be telling the truth. Demand a dating prenup. If he's playing you, we get his apartment. How much fun would we have living there?"

"I like our place," I say. "We don't need anything fancy."

"Speaking of fancy . . . check out this necklace Logan gave me last night." Darcy pulls a Tiffany box out of her bag. She lifts a delicate silver necklace out of the box. A round tag pendant that says TIFFANY & CO. NEW YORK dangles from the chain.

"Wow," I gush. "It's beautiful."

"He enjoys spoiling me. And I enjoy letting him."

Rosanna and I exchange a look as Darcy puts the necklace on. We're not Logan's biggest fans. Yeah, it was incredible of him to come after Darcy to get her back. And yeah, he seems like a nice guy. But how nice can he actually be after the way he broke up with her? Once a boy breaks your heart, can you ever trust him again?

"Logan wasn't the only boy adventure last night,"

Rosanna informs Darcy. "Sadie had one right outside our door."

Darcy gapes at me. "Austin came over?"

"Not up to the apartment. I went down to talk to him on our stoop."

"Because seventy-three messages weren't enough communication," Darcy snorts.

"Twenty-three."

"Oh, sorry. Only twenty-three."

"What did he *saaay*?" Rosanna is dying.

I tell them everything Austin said. How if he could have only one thing in the world, it would be to be with me. How he'll do anything to get me back.

"Sounds familiar," Darcy says. "Isn't it awesome having a boy beg forgiveness after he was a total meathead?"

"Are you thinking of getting back together with him?" Rosanna asks.

I hesitate. "No. Not after what he did."

Rosanna's look lingers on me.

"What?"

"No, it's just . . . I mean, he *did* leave his wife for you. And he told her about you."

"But not how much I mean to him. Not that I'm the love of his life. He told her we're soul mates, but he hasn't broken it down for her."

"What does that even mean?" Darcy says.

"Soul mates? You know when you feel it. It's this

connection that's so intense it feels completely different than anything you've felt before. You feel the way you'd always hoped you would when you found the person you're meant to be with."

"Um-hmm."

"And the chemistry is off the charts."

"Oh, I hear that. I'm just wondering . . . like, would a soul mate lie to you the way Austin did?"

Darcy doesn't get it, so I explain. "I don't think it's black-and-white. You can meet the right person at the wrong time. If I'd met Austin ten years from now, he might have been divorced already and this whole situation would have been completely different. Austin is still my soul mate. Even after what he did. But just because someone's a soul mate doesn't necessarily mean you should be with them."

The girls contemplate this. The soft sounds of a flute float over to us as a roaming musician strolls by. A couple sitting on the grass next to the bleachers are kissing. Another couple walks by, holding hands and smiling at each other like nothing will ever stand in the way of their love. Like nothing will ever change.

"Are you saying you might get back together with him?" Rosanna asks again.

Maybe that wouldn't be the worst thing. Maybe there's even a chance it could work out. Being here in my Zen place, the summer night and big sky all around, the history of my longing to find a soul mate as present as the soft breeze, it feels like anything is possible. Even the possibility of us.

"I don't know," I admit. "Part of me wants to believe him. But I mostly feel like I need to protect myself. I could be setting my life up to be destroyed like his wife's is." I lean forward on the bleacher, hugging my arms around myself. "It makes me sick that I hurt a woman I didn't even know existed. This woman's husband walked out on her and it's all my fault."

"No it isn't," Rosanna says. "You said yourself that Austin wasn't happy with her. He was thinking about leaving her before he even met you. You're not why they broke up, Sadie. You can't break up a happy marriage."

I've heard that before about how no one can break up a happy marriage. But if Austin hadn't met me, they'd probably still be together. And his wife wouldn't be suffering the way she is now. What if Austin was the only one who was unhappy? What if his wife really loved him?

But I'm starting to see the situation in a different way. Maybe what happened will be better for his wife. She feels horrible now, but someday she'll be free to meet the man who will love her in a way Austin never did. Now Austin knows true love is bigger than what he was settling for. And his wife has the chance to find that kind of love, too.

Everyone deserves to find true love. Everyone deserves to love someone the way I loved Austin . . . and the way he keeps saying he still loves me.

TWENTY
DARCY

KITCHENS AND I HAVE NEVER gotten along. The extent of my culinary capability does not stretch beyond making toast. Which I've burned way too many times. I don't even buy groceries. The refrigerator would be empty if I lived here by myself. So the fact that it's stocked right now with groceries that I bought from not one but two different stores is astonishing.

Even more astonishing? I'm attempting to cook dinner for Logan tonight. No, I *will* cook dinner for Logan tonight. How hard could it be? Millions of people cook dinner every night. To be on the safe side, I'm starting two hours early. That way I'll have everything under control if I encounter any recipe mishaps. This is my first time following a recipe. The way you have to time everything down to the minute is kind of freaking me out. And I've never seriously cooked before with special ingredients and flamboyant tools like whisks. So initially I was a little intimidated. Then I was like, Excuse me. You are a badass. You stare down creepers on the subway and hook up with random hotties in dressing rooms and throw drinks in bad boys' faces. You will not be intimidated by some measuring spoons.

There are several key components to this dinner I'm making. I want it to look like dinner at any decent restaurant. We're talking roast pork loin with sides of creamy au gratin potatoes, stuffed mushrooms, green beans with toasted almonds, and warm sourdough bread. Boom.

Preparing the stuffing for the mushrooms comes first. My eyes water when I start chopping the onion and are on fire by the time I chop the last slice. Mental note: Avoid recipes with onions. Washing and drying the mushrooms takes way longer than I thought it would. By the time I've mixed the stuffing, it's half an hour later, I forgot to preheat the oven, and the potatoes won't be done in time if they're not in the oven ten minutes ago. And I don't need a mirror to know that my mascara is smeared.

Now I remember why I hate cooking.

My aversion to all things culinary is a bigger issue. When I was fourteen, I decided to take on the monumental task of making Daddy breakfast for Father's Day. Except I didn't know how monumental making eggs, bacon, and hash browns would be. Multiple pans sizzling concurrently flummoxed me. My mom had asked if I needed help like five times before I started cooking. I had to ban her from the kitchen so I could concentrate. I wanted to do this all on my own, something sweet for my dad that he would notice and remember. But when I put the plate down in front of him at the dining room table, what he noticed were the burned eggs and soggy hash browns. And what he remembered was that I couldn't even cook a simple breakfast.

"Looks great," he said with a forced smile. He didn't want to be sitting at the dining room table, which I had carefully set with one of the fancy placemats we only used for company and the good silverware Mom kept in the sideboard for holidays. Daddy wanted to kick back in the breakfast nook with a strong coffee and an onion bagel, devouring the financial section of the Sunday paper. He was only pretending to be happy about his ruined breakfast.

That night I overheard my parents talking in the living room.

"Who burns eggs?" Daddy said.

Then he laughed.

Whatever. Moving on.

Sadie comes home sometime between a pork loin rebellion and a dustup with potatoes that would rather not be sliced. She does a double take when she sees me in the kitchen actually cooking.

"No. Way." Sadie comes around the breakfast bar. The

kitchen looks like a bomb exploded, followed by a tornado that swirled every pot and pan in all directions. Making a huge mess of the kitchen wasn't my intention. But I can't say I'm surprised. My first attempt to cook a grown-up dinner is not going as smoothly as I'd hoped. "You're cooking?"

"You could call it that. Or racing with the clock to produce something remotely edible before Logan comes over."

"Do you want some help?"

"You are so sweet. But I want to do this myself."

"Okay, well . . . I'll be in my room if you need me."

"Oh wait, there is one thing." I sift through the pile of eggshells and scrunched paper towels and potato peels until I uncover a cookbook. The au gratin recipe snarls at me with a vengeance. "What do they mean by 'combine'? Do they mean mix together? Or just put in the same bowl?"

"I'm not sure."

"Are you supposed to stir?"

"Let's see the recipe." Sadie reads the directions. "I think you can just mix them together lightly."

"How do you know?"

"I don't, but that's my best guess from cooking over the years. You pick up on techniques."

"You're like the recipe whisperer."

Sadie reads some more. "You know this has to cook for an hour and a half, right?"

"And Logan will be here in an hour and this is nowhere near done and I haven't even gotten in the shower yet?

Yeah, I know." I am trying not to freak out. Epic fail. Why is cooking so hard? Did I not start early enough? Two hours should be plenty of time to throw together a main dish and a few sides. This whole cooking thing is supposed to be something anyone can do. I must be doing it wrong. Just like those burned eggs on Father's Day. Daddy was right. Who burns eggs?

"Do you have something in the oven?" Sadie asks.

"A couple things. Why?"

"Is one of them burning?"

"The toasted almonds!" I yank the oven door open, shove my hand in an oven mitt, and pull out the cookie sheet. The almonds are so burned they're smoking. I was only supposed to put them in for ten minutes. And I was supposed to toss them halfway through.

"Do you—"

The smoke detector goes off with the loudest, most annoying beeping I've ever heard. The beeping is so loud I can't hear the rest of what Sadie is saying. She puts her fingers in her ears and looks up at the smoke detector. I look where she's looking. I didn't even know we had a smoke detector.

"How do we turn it off?" I yell.

Sadie pulls a chair up to the stove and stands on it. She tries to reach the smoke detector, but she's at a weird angle that's not letting her reach it. I motion for her to get down. Then I switch places with her. With one foot on the chair,

I wedge my other foot against the edge of the counter. Part of being a badass means showing loud smoke detectors who's boss.

"Get the broom!" I yell at Sadie.

She rushes out and back with the broom. I smack the broom wildly at the smoke detector. Sadie is yelling at me about some button I'm supposed to push to make the beeping stop. But we are way beyond buttons. Plastic pieces go flying. A battery pops out. The beeping finally shuts up.

"That was the loudest. thing. ever," I gasp. Being a gangsta smacking a broom around in the kitchen is already a thing of the past. Now I'm reduced back to being the girl who not only can't cook, but who pretty much sets her kitchen on fire when she tries.

Something else is burning in a pot on the stove. I know I need to take the lid off and look, but I am afraid.

Sadie helps me get dinner together. She calms me down enough to let her take over while I get in the shower. I throw on the outfit I mentally planned in the shower and rush back out to finish up. Dinner is far from perfect, but at least it's edible. Mostly edible. Like 70% edible. Okay fine, 50%, minimum. Logan won't get food poisoning or anything. Fingers crossed.

"I think you're all set," Sadie says right before Logan is supposed to get here. "I'm taking off so you can have the place to yourself."

"Are you sure?"

"Totally. Rosanna's out with Donovan. You guys can have a romantic dinner."

"With the stench of burned almonds in the air."

"Trends have to start somewhere."

"Can you imagine? Welcome to Per Se. Enjoy the freshly crisped almond aroma."

"Crisped would actually smell really good."

I glance at the clock on the kitchen wall. "Logan will be here any second."

"I'm out." Sadie dashes to her room and grabs a smaller bag than usual. "Have fun!" she trills on her way out.

I frantically scoop food onto plates. This is not the chic scene I was envisioning. The mushrooms are inexplicably falling apart, the au gratin is still in the oven, and the second batch of almonds wasn't toasted enough. Oh, and I totally forgot about the bread. It's not warm. I could stick it in the oven, but I'm afraid I'll forget about it and burn down the entire apartment.

The doorbell buzzes. I run to the intercom and buzz Logan in. Lighting! We need romantic mood lighting up in here. I get a few candles from my room and put them on the table and bar. Where are the matches? Why are there never any matches when you need them? Rosanna might be right about organizing. At least then you know where everything is.

I open the door for Logan right before he knocks.

"Hey, babe," he says, all lanky sexy sloucher.

Maybe I'll eat him for dinner.

I let him in. Then I kiss him like I haven't seen him in weeks.

Logan breaks away. "What's that smell?"

"You mean the freshly crisped almond aroma? It's a new trend. Per Se started it."

"Is something burning?"

I grab the front of Logan's shirt, yanking him toward me. He came straight from work. He took that job at the bike shop and apparently didn't change his shirt before coming over. But the grease stain on the front of his shirt isn't even bothering me. I press up against him, avoiding contact with the grease. "Oh yeah. Something's definitely burning."

"No, I mean . . . for real."

How is Logan not all over me right now? Since when can he resist a sexy innuendo?

"There was a culinary mishap," I disclose.

"Was Sadie cooking?"

"Guess again."

Logan smirks. "We know you weren't cooking."

"Then how did I make you this?" I sweep my hand at the table, hastily set with incomplete dinner plates, an absence of silverware, and unlit candles.

"You cooked?"

"Only for you."

"Why?"

"Um, because I wanted to make you dinner?"

"Oh," Logan says. He looks mildly disgusted. Maybe the burned almond stench is making him nauseous.

"What's wrong?"

"I thought you were ordering in."

"That was what I told you to cover up the surprise. See? I cooked dinner for you. You're the only one I've ever cooked dinner for. *Ever.* And it turned out to be a complete disaster. Surprise!"

Logan attempts a smile. "That was sweet of you, babe. I appreciate it."

"But . . . ?"

"No, it's just I thought you were ordering from Strip House. I was psyched for steak."

"Seriously?"

"You made it sound so good."

"Yeah, no, I planned a whole thing. I went to Whole Foods *and* Trader Joe's for ingredients. I started cooking two hours ago and it didn't even turn out right. After I followed recipes and everything." Why is he being such an asshole? Has he always been an asshole and I just never realized it before?

Logan stretches his arms out to me. "Come here."

"You are the only one I've ever cooked dinner for," I repeat.

He puts his arms around me, hugging me softly. "I'm sorry. This is coming out all wrong. I'm flattered you cooked for me."

"Attempted to cook. Everything is ruined."

"Let's see." We go over to the table. Logan examines the plates.

"The au gratin is almost done."

"It looks good," he says.

"Really?"

"Yeah."

"Because it's not."

"I'm cool with eating everything you made." He pauses. "But we can go out if you want. Your call."

Not cool, Logan. Not cool. You should be sitting down and digging into this meal the girl you adore put her heart and soul into. Even if it's only 30% edible. You should not be shifting awkwardly by the table, hoping to go out and eat somewhere better.

Would he even treat for dinner? Or is he expecting me to treat again? I pay almost every time we go out. Which, whatever, I love treating my friends. But Logan is more than my friend. He was my boyfriend before and apparently wants to be my boyfriend again. He paid almost every time we went out in Santa Monica. Shouldn't he be trying harder to win me back?

"Would you treat if we went out?" I ask.

"I can treat. Do you want to go out to dinner?"

"Of course I don't want to go out to dinner!" I snap. "I just spent two hours cooking for you!"

"But if you don't like how it turned out . . ."

"You should be more supportive. You should be eating this gourmet fail no matter how bad it tastes."

He looks at me blankly. "You'd really want me to eat something that tasted bad?"

"Hello, I'm exaggerating. It's not that bad."

"Then why did you say it was?"

"Because I was embarrassed! Cooking is supposed to be this easy thing anyone can do. Except me, apparently."

"So it's not for everyone. So what? You're talented in lots of other ways."

Now he's saying I suck at cooking. He took one look at the dinner I made him and can't wait to get out of here.

I give up.

"Hey." Logan slides his hand through my hair. His dark eyes smolder. I try not to lose myself in them. "It's okay. We'll do whatever you want."

"What if I don't want to do anything?"

He tries to touch me again. I shrug away from him.

"Do you want me to leave?" Logan asks.

"That's the best idea you've had all night."

So he leaves. No kiss. No see you tomorrow. He just walks right out.

I may be talented at lots of other things, but Logan is a master at leaving me behind. Good to see that making a huge effort for someone who is supposed to love me has such awesome results. But didn't I already know relationships come with way too much disappointment?

TWENTY-ONE
ROSANNA

WHEN D TOOK ME TO Central Park movie night, it was like a big, friendly outdoor party. People were respectful of our space. I had the best time leaning back against D, watching the movie and getting swept away by what was probably the best summer night of my life.

Bryant Park movie night is different.

They haven't even let people in yet, and I can already tell things are about to get real. D can't come until later, so he told me to save us a spot. But he also warned me that Bryant Park movie night was cutthroat. Sadie advised me to get in line before five. She explained how everyone lines up on the gravelly path around the rectangular grassy area where you sit to watch the movie. At 5:00 on the dot, a whistle blows. That's when you are allowed on the grass. I heard it gets insane when the whistle blows. People run to stake out spots so fast Sadie nearly got knocked over one year. All the good spots are pretty much taken by 5:15. Five seemed way too early to show up for a movie that doesn't start until after eight. But I got here early anyway just to be on the safe side. I'm glad I did.

We have a few minutes to go until the whistle blows. Like Sadie said, we're all lined up on the path surrounding the lawn. I can't believe how many people are here already. We're lined up two deep on the path. Some people behind the front row are even trying to push their way up to the front. A low rope extends around the perimeter of the grass. I wonder what would happen if someone stepped over the rope. Not even if they went all the way onto the grass. Just put one foot over. Would an emergency siren go off? Would that person be restricted from movie night? I wouldn't be surprised if there was a no-watch list.

A college girl carrying a heap of blankets drops her big Ikea bag. She slowly lowers herself to retrieve the bag, the blankets blocking her vision as they mash up against her face, and feels around for the bag's handle. I want to go over and help her. But I'm worried that if I step away from the rope, I will be trampled when the whistle blows. Then I'll never get a spot and D and I will have to stand in the back or something. I'm about to go over to help her anyway when a guy standing next to her picks up her bag. He does the right thing. I need to get better about jumping into action when someone needs help. There's no excuse for my behavior.

New Yorkers waiting for the Bryant Park movie night whistle are wound up so tightly you can almost hear them twanging. Being a part of real New York life is thrilling. I am blending in with New Yorkers as if I'm officially one of them. Feeling included in a way I never have before makes me so happy that sometimes I bust out smiling just walking down the street, or on a crowded subway where you're not supposed to bust out smiling for no apparent reason. But this experience might be a bit too scary for me. I might not be ready for cutthroat movie night.

The whistle blows. The crowd engulfs the lawn in a human tsunami. This surge of people running onto the lawn is so powerful that someone could seriously get trampled. Like, to death.

I snap into action. People are throwing sheets and blankets down on the first available spots. I run farther onto the center of the lawn and frantically fling out the old sheet I brought with me. It unfurls enough to spread over a small patch of grass. By the time I bend down to try spreading it out more, people have taken up all of the spaces around my sheet. My sheet is already completely bordered by hardcore New Yorkers with sharpened blanket maneuvering skills. I can't spread my sheet out now. I look around for a larger free spot, but there are none. You can't even see the grass anymore. In the space of one minute, the entire lawn was covered.

What just happened?

I collapse on my sheet. A huge group to my left managed to put a bunch of blankets down so they can all sit together. How did they pull that off? They must have done this before. Bryant Park movie night might be an annual thing for them. Or even a weekly thing.

People are taking off their shoes to use as anchors along the edges of their blankets. The shoes are also boundary markers. One guy arranges his flip-flops in a line along the edge of his blanket. The girl on the blanket next to his places her bag right up against his flip-flop divider. Everywhere I look, people are exhibiting major territorial behavior. A tiny blond girl behind me whips off her sandals. Then she proceeds to shove a sandal against my butt.

"You're on my blanket," she informs me.

"Oh." The edge of her blanket is overlapping my sheet. By about three millimeters. "I think your blanket is on top of my sheet."

The tiny blond girl chomps her gum. "That's how far it spreads out."

"You're lucky. I didn't even get to spread my sheet out all the way."

"But you have enough room."

"My boyfriend's coming later. There's barely enough room for the two of us."

"That sucks." For a second I think she's going to offer to pull her enormous blanket back a little to make enough room for D. Instead she says, "You're still on my blanket." Her beady eyes are defiant.

Seriously with this?

I scooch up two millimeters. Then I take my book out and start reading so she'll stop hounding me. I am the only one reading. Everyone else is laughing with friends and spreading out picnics and reclining on their fully unfurled blankets. I either need to come to movie night every week until I master the mad dash or never come again. Can't decide yet.

The buildings surrounding the park are beautiful. They remind me of when I was younger, watching movies that took place in New York. I would watch movies like *The Family Man* and *In Good Company*, longing for the time when I could live here. Even when I read books that took place in New York, I knew this was my true home. Sitting here alone surrounded by clusters of friends talking and laughing and eating their picnic dinners, I try to feel like I belong. That feeling I had before about blending in with real New Yorkers is gone. Now I feel out of place by myself, adrift in a sea of groups.

The sky melts periwinkle into azure. I sit up, craning my neck above the crowd to see if D is looking for me. He was supposed to meet me here at six. But it's almost seven and I still don't see him. He can't call me on my nonexistent cell phone. I would borrow someone's phone to call him, but I don't want to seem even more pathetic than I undeniably am. All I can do is wait and hope we see each other in this insane crowd.

I wait. And wait. And wait.

Reading is impossible. I'm afraid that I'll miss D while I'm staring down at my page. I keep reading a sentence, scanning the crowd for D, then glancing down to read the same sentence all over again. Some girls on a sheet next to me are giving me weird looks. They're sharing food containers from a big Zabar's bag, passing around roasted chicken and macaroni salad and sautéed red potatoes. You are not supposed to read here. You are not supposed to come alone. You are supposed to be eating your gourmet picnic dinner with your friends and laughing hysterically like you're having the time of your life. If I were those girls, I'd be giving me weird looks, too.

I scan the crowd again. Not only am I trying to find D, I want to make it obvious that I'm not here alone. Or that I won't be alone for much longer. I have a boyfriend. He's meeting me here. He wants to be with me. I exaggerate the motion of looking around, turning my head more than I need to so anyone looking at me knows that I'm waiting for someone.

My thumb is snapping against my middle finger again. I really need to get this nervous tic under control. How long have I been snapping? Have I been sitting here snapping like a spaz the whole time? I put my other hand over my snapping fingers to calm myself. Just like D put his hand over mine when he caught me snapping at Press Lounge.

The Zabar's food containers smell amazing. My stomach growls. I grabbed a bagel on the way over here, thinking that would be enough for dinner. But these elaborate picnic spreads are making me hungry.

The azure sky blends into the darkest shade of blue. The guy who set up the flip-flops barrier is telling a loud story involving a blue French horn on the wall of a restaurant. The Zabar's girls are eating cheesecake drizzled with caramel and chocolate, gushing over how good it is. The tiny blond girl behind me is popping her gum as her boyfriend rubs her back. I am alone and miserable. Should I get up and look for D? Not if I want to get back to my spot. Once I leave my sheet, it will either get covered with overspill from the surrounding groups or I won't be able to find my way back. Either way I have to stay put.

The movie starts. I point my eyes at the screen. I try not to cry.

My boyfriend stood me up. I've never been stood up before. Probably because I've never had a boyfriend before. Although you'd think a boyfriend would be less likely to stand you up than a casual date. There's a chance we missed each other. But the sick twisting in my stomach tells the truth. He was never here.

Of course this is happening on Friday the 13th. Classic.

D will blame this on me not having a cell phone. That tends to be what people do when they are running late or decide not to show up because a better offer came along. But I don't think a cell phone would change anything. D would call and tell me he's not coming. Or I would call him to find out he's not here. Yeah, already picked up on that.

The tiny blond girl behind me is leaning back against her boyfriend, a wide pool of free blanket space around them. She's leaning the way I leaned back against D at Central Park movie night. I wonder if that night was remotely as intense for him as it was for me. Does he even care about me the way I care about him? Making time for him is my priority. But he's been working late at his internship, putting in extra hours to get a stellar recommendation letter for grad school. Between that and hanging out with Shayla, it feels like he's slipping away.

Maybe I just have to get used to him working late. Everyone seems to work late in New York. Sadie told me that even people like teachers who leave work earlier take home tons of work. She's seen lots of teachers in cafés grading fat stacks of papers. New York runs on the energy of millions of people with the strongest career drives and the highest aspirations. D will be like that when he starts working on Wall Street. He's already like that now.

What if we stay together? What if we're still a couple after he's done with grad school and he's starting out as an investment banker? D told me those new guys put in the longest hours. They can work 110-hour weeks with no days off. That only gives you eight free hours a day. Would D choose to be with me during those few free hours? Even if he did, he would still have to sleep. Is our relationship enough of a priority for him? Will he get sucked into the Wall Street world so hard that his obsession with success will push him to work longer hours than he needs to?

When we first started going out, I was okay with not seeing D every day. I wasn't even sure if I liked him enough to want a relationship with him. But everything's different now. I'm different now.

Now I'm in love.

Sitting alone in the crowd, I wonder if moving here was the right decision. Yes, New York City has been my dream forever. And yes, I love it here. But it might be too hard to try to survive in an outrageously expensive city when I'm barely scraping by.

I tilt my head back and look up. I can't see the stars. Somehow along the way, the stars got lost. Before I came here, I knew where I was going. I had a clear vision of how I would achieve my goals. There was an inner light guiding me, pushing me forward on the days when I was afraid. But now, under a purple sky without stars, I feel like I've lost my way, lost my sense of direction, lost the light that was guiding me.

Maybe some dreams are not meant to come true.

TWENTY-TWO
SADIE

I HAVE TO GIVE DARCY credit for cooking Logan dinner. If Darcy were a *National Geographic* subject, the kitchen would not be considered part of her natural habitat. I felt bad that her dinner was kind of a bust. She just took on too much. But it freaking rules that she never gave up. Even after smacking the smoke detector to smithereens. I'll have to talk to the landlord about replacing it. Or am I supposed to call UNY student housing? I don't want them to know we smashed the smoke detector. If they think we're rowdy, they might not let us stay here freshman year.

After calming Darcy down enough to get ready for Logan, I left to give them private time. I thought about calling Brooke and some other friends to get together, but I decided to go for one of my night walks. Night walks always give me an epic feeling of anticipation. I get so excited thinking about the possibility of everything. Friday the 13th has always been a lucky day for me. I took ownership of Friday the 13th back in middle school. That's when I decided that just because everyone says a certain day is unlucky doesn't mean it has to be unlucky for me. And it's been a lucky day ever since.

I walk down Perry Street. Tourists are taking pictures in front of Carrie Bradshaw's stoop. Even after all this time, *Sex and the City* fans still migrate here for photos. The brownstone owners must be so over strangers loitering outside their place. They put up a chain at the bottom of the stairs to discourage people from sitting here with their Magnolia cupcakes. I weave my way from Perry to West 11th to Bank, glancing into lit apartment windows. Not in a deranged stalker way. More like in an entranced admiring way. The homes on these streets are gorgeous. They have fireplaces and floor-to-ceiling bookshelves and grand staircases. It's not my fault these apartments are so alluring. Or that their blinds are wide open. The people who live there are practically inviting me to look inside.

I start heading back to the apartment after giving Darcy and Logan enough time to have dinner. They'll probably be out hitting the clubs by the time I get home. Walking past Bus Stop Café, I glance at everyone having dinner outside. A cute boy around my age locks eyes with me and smiles. He's sitting at two tables pushed together with three other guys. But that doesn't mean he doesn't have a girlfriend. I walk on by without smiling back. I'm on Sadie Time. I'm on a boy break and loving the idea of it more every day. The single girl thing is super empowering if you let it be. It's Friday night, I have a new self-empowerment book called *Your Dream Life* waiting for me on my bed, a whole season of *Prison Break* to binge-watch, and a pint of Blue Bunny Bordeaux Cherry Chocolate ice cream in the freezer. Plus a bag of fresh cherries I can't wait to dig into. I'm all set.

No one's at the apartment when I get home. Just as I'm settling into the big puffy armchair with my bowl of cherries and the remote, Rosanna comes home.

"Right on time," I say. "Have you seen the final season of *Prison Break*?"

"Shouldn't I watch season one first?"

"Are you seriously telling me you've never seen *Prison Break*?"

"Is it good?"

My mouth falls open. I pop my eyes at her. The cherries almost go flying out of their bowl. "Is it good? *Good* isn't even—I think the word you're looking for is *spectacular*. Or *phenomenal*. Or *magnificent*."

"So . . . it's adequate?" Rosanna teases.

"Dude. You must watch this with me right now. You need to watch this show so bad that I will start with the pilot. The final season can wait."

Rosanna slumps on the couch like a deflated balloon.

"What's wrong?" I ask.

She shakes her head. Then she presses her lips together. Her face scrunches up and she starts crying.

"Oh no!" I go over and sit next to her on the couch, putting my arm around her. "What happened?"

"I got"—Rosanna's voice hitches—"stood up."

"By Donovan?" That doesn't make any sense.

She nods. She's crying too hard to talk. I get her a glass of water and rub her back until she calms down enough to speak without words catching in her throat.

"He never showed up at Bryant Park," she says. "I got there before five, like you said. I sat there like a moron until the movie started. I wanted to leave, but I was too embarrassed. And there was no way to get out without stepping on a hundred body parts. Could that place be any more crowded?"

"Sorry you had to sit alone. That sucks. Why didn't you . . ." I was going to ask Rosanna why she didn't call me. I keep forgetting she doesn't have a cell phone. "I would have come to meet you if I'd known."

"Why wasn't he there?" she asks. I wish I knew the answer.

I look over at the voice mail screen of the house phone. Rosanna told us she was ordering phone service along with internet before we moved in. Darcy and I were cool with splitting the total bill three ways. I wonder how many other UNY students in our building have a land-line. We might be the only ones.

We have new messages.

"He probably called hours ago," I say. I reach over to play the messages.

Rosanna stops me. "Don't. Nothing he could possibly say would make a difference. He wasn't there. That's all that matters."

"Are you sure he wasn't there? Finding people in that crowd is ridiculous."

"He wasn't. I was looking for him the whole time. The people around me thought I was a freak for going to movie night alone. Who does that?" Her eyes fill up again.

"Not you. You were waiting for your boyfriend."

"Who chose not to be there."

This isn't the first time Rosanna has sat on this couch all miserable over Donovan. Lately it seems like he makes her more sad than happy. But I don't want to judge. How can I after what I went through with Austin? All I can do is be here for Rosanna. Whatever she needs.

When I put myself in her shoes, I can't believe how strong she is. She moved here with nothing. Rosanna's story reminds me of one of my favorite quotes: "Leap and the net will appear." She took a giant leap to turn her biggest dream into reality. The net appeared to catch her. I just hope it's strong enough to keep her from falling.

Rosanna sniffs the air. "Is something burning?"

"You mean when Darcy cooked an elaborate dinner for Logan? Which was the first time she ever tried cooking a real dinner? Um, yeah, there was burning involved."

"What happened?"

I fill Rosanna in on the details, playing up the funny parts to make her laugh. She's smiling by the time I finish.

"Did she really smash the smoke detector that hard?" Rosanna asks.

"Yes! Don't be surprised if you find pieces of it all the way in your room."

"I wish I could have seen that. How did she even know where the broom was?"

"She asked me to get it for her."

Rosanna glances back toward our rooms. "Are they here?"

"No."

"Because it doesn't look like they finished their dinner."

I look at the table. She's right. The plates of food look like they haven't been touched. How did I not notice that when I came home? "That's weird," I say. "It doesn't look like they ate anything."

"Do you think . . ."

"What?"

"Never mind. I don't want to say it out loud."

"Say it. We're probably both thinking the same thing."

"Would Logan, like, reject Darcy's dinner? After she

worked so hard on it?"

"It's possible. He doesn't strike me as the most sensitive guy."

"I know, right? I mean, I'm happy Darcy is happy with him, but . . ."

"We're not founding members of the Logan Fan Club."

"Exactly."

Darcy poured her heart into that dinner. It's sad to see the untouched plates sitting there ignored on the table. "Do you think she can trust him?" I ask. "After what he did?"

"Refusing to eat her dinner?"

"No. Breaking up with her before she moved here."

Rosanna shakes her head. "She must have been in so much pain when we met her. I wish I would have known."

"I wonder why he broke up with her."

"Darcy said he couldn't deal with being in love. He told her he got scared."

"Boys don't get scared of being with a girl. Girls tell themselves the boy got scared to rationalize his behavior after he broke up with them. If a boy wants to be with a girl, he's going to make it happen. A highly reliable source told me that."

Rosanna is skeptical. "Who?"

"My friend John. Dude tells it like it is. He said guys use excuses like that all the time to justify being cowards. Like when a guy says he's going to call and then he doesn't? He just wants to make an easy escape without admitting that he's never going to call. Guys don't want heavy confrontations with girls they're not into. They don't want to deal with the repercussions of admitting the truth." I realize too late that this is probably not what Rosanna wants to hear right now. I should be telling her something more positive about boy behavior. Something that will reassure her that everything will be okay with Donovan. But thinking about Logan and Darcy's abandoned dinner is not inspiring any shiny happy ideas.

"So why do you think Logan really broke up with Darcy?" Rosanna asks.

"I don't know. But he came all the way here to win her back. He gets points for realizing he was wrong." I'm trying not to let Austin influence my opinion of Logan.

Rosanna leans back against the couch cushions. She pulls one of the cute Graphique de France throw pillows Darcy bought into her lap. "There's something about Logan I don't like. I know that's a horrible thing to say, but there's something off about him."

"So it's not just me! I totally feel you. Yeah, there's something about him that's not exactly creepy. More like . . ."

"Not right."

What bothers me about Logan is hard to define. The times I've seen him and Darcy together made me unsettled.

Not because of anything Logan did. He knows how Darcy likes to be treated and he brings it. Rosanna and I were swooning when Darcy told us how he re-created their first three dates in one night. But Darcy isn't completely Darcy when she's with Logan. Darcy doesn't have that sparkle in her eyes that she had when she was with Jude. Even though Rosanna and I have never met Jude, he obviously brought out the best in Darcy. Darcy's energy was shining when she was with Jude. Being around her was like basking in bright sunlight on a clear day. Now her energy is more partly cloudy. Still good. Just not the best it could be.

"Remember the way Darcy lit up when she talked about Jude?" I say. "They seemed perfect for each other."

"I know."

"The way she described him, it was like she met a soul mate. She's never talked about Logan that way."

"Jude was better for her than Logan."

"Jude was magical. He was literally a magician. He totally—" And then it hits me. An epiphany so big I spring up from the couch. I don't even know how to contain the enormousness of this moment. "We have met Jude."

"When?"

"In the park! He was the magician we saw the first night here!"

Rosanna contemplates this. "How do you know?"

"I just do." Darcy never showed us pictures of Jude. She

didn't overshare Jude specifics. But how many magicians perform in Washington Square Park? The way she talked about him, the way she described how he made her feel or his chill surfer-boy Cali vibe or his infectious upbeat attitude . . . the magician we saw had to have been him. I remember telling Rosanna how much I loved him when we were watching his act. I remember how you could feel his radiant positive energy. How could I not have realized this before?

"I had a feeling it was him the first time Darcy was telling me about him," I say as things keep clicking. "We were having lunch at Chat 'n Chew and I almost said something, but the conversation went in a million directions from there. I totally forgot about that until now." I gape at Rosanna. "Jude."

"We love him," she breathes.

"Yeah we do!" We stopped to watch his show our first night at the apartment. Rosanna had seemed nervous all day. Edgy. Displaced. Imbalanced. I wanted to take her out for a while to have dinner and show her around, hoping a mini tour of her new neighborhood would make her feel more settled. We saw Jude performing with a huge crowd around him laughing and applauding and loving every second. He was so sweet to this little boy watching up front. Jude was freaking adorable.

I'm loving how Friday the 13th keeps getting luckier. I can't keep it in. I bust out a dorky happy dance right here next to the coffee table. Rosanna whoops and throws the pillow in the air. She catches it smoothly before it can bounce off onto the floor.

"We love Jude for Darcy!" I yell. "And we're going to get them back together!"

Rosanna's smile vanishes. "Wait. What?"

"The only reason they're not together is that Logan showed up. If he had stayed broken up the way he was supposed to, Jude and Darcy would be together."

"I thought Darcy didn't want a real relationship with Jude."

"That's only what she said. But the sparkle eyes said something else."

"But what about Logan?"

"Fine. Pros and cons." I flop onto the couch and put my feet up on the coffee table. "Logan pros. Go."

"He and Darcy have a ton of history together. You can't underestimate the power of a shared history."

"Noted. What else?"

"He was her first love. And he did come all the way here to get her back."

"I did enjoy that real-life movie twist."

"Isn't that supposed to be the ending?"

"Not when the story isn't over. Can you honestly say that Darcy is meant to end up with Logan?"

"Maybe we're judging him too harshly."

"Or maybe what we were saying before is right. Our

instinct is telling us he's not the one for Darcy. Right?"

Rosanna sighs.

"We love Jude's energy," I forge ahead. "We loved the way Darcy was when they were together. Like you said, something about Logan is off. She's with him because he made this grand gesture coming here, but if she waits too long, she's going to lose Jude. He'll start seeing someone else who would kill to be his girlfriend. Then it'll be too late for Darcy to see he was the right person for her all along."

"Okay. So . . . ?"

"How many pros was that for Logan? Three?"

"Yeah."

"Any more?"

"Not that I can think of."

"Well, there are one, two, three—like twenty-five pros for Jude. Case closed. We are Team Jude."

"Agreed. Team Jude."

"Our first and only mission: Bring Jude back into play."

"How do we do that?"

"If only we knew where to find him. Oh, wait . . ."

TWENTY-THREE
DARCY

WHEN JUDE COMES OVER TO our table with a double espresso for me and a coffee for him, the Dean & DeLuca déjà vu rams into me something fierce. It feels like we were just here yesterday. Me wanting to dive into Jude like a clear blue sea. Him wanting more than I could give.

Both of us wanting what we couldn't have. Isn't that always the way?

Jude is wearing his MULTI-TALENTED tee. He doesn't need to advertise that on a shirt for the world to know it's true.

"How's your project going?" I ask. Jude is working on an invention he thinks will be huge. It's this pump/spray mechanism for bottles that makes the bottle way easier to use. You can spray a cleaner holding the bottle in any direction and it will still come out. Even upside-down.

You can pump the last bit of lotion or shampoo out of a bottle so none is wasted. No more ripping off the top of a big bottle of lotion and banging the bottle to get the rest out. With Jude's invention, it's smooth spraying and pumping all the way, baby.

"Good." Jude blows on his coffee. "You know those potential investors I told you about?"

"Yeah?"

"They invested."

"That's amazing! Congrats!"

"Thanks. Yeah, we're excited. Can you believe I have employees now?"

"How many?"

"Three."

"Already? So this is officially a thing."

"It would appear to be official."

"You have employees."

"Like a *boss*."

I sip my espresso. Hearing about how Jude's business is taking off makes me want to gulp instead of sip. He makes me feel like I'm not doing enough with my life. Like I need to go whip up a ten-year plan. And if I seem like a slacker, what about Logan? For the first time ever, his lack of motivation is agitating me. Jude is this revolutionary genius. What is Logan doing?

I guess I'm still annoyed from last night. After Logan took off, I stood there in shock by the table with our plates of food getting cold. If you looked up *flabbergasted* in the dictionary, you'd see a picture of me gaping at the door. Boys don't walk out on me.

Except Logan.

Again.

Why do I keep doing this to myself? Did I really expect this time to be any different? Just because he's spending the summer here? We don't even see each other every day.

After my flabbergasted fit, I bolted. Didn't even have a particular destination in mind. I just grabbed my bag and flashed into the night. I ended up at some sketchy bar on Orchard Street with desperate chicks posing along the wall and pool in the back. Anger clawed at me while I ordered a foghorn. No one asked for ID. I was so angry at myself for opening up to Logan all over again . . . and standing there like an idiot while he walked out the door. I'll never forget that gross feeling I had when I moved here, lugging so much anger it was heavier than my duffel. Not that I would let the weight of being dumped anchor me in any way. I'm free as a bird. Summer Fun Darcy waits for no boy. Especially not the boy who's making me feel like an idiot all over again.

Which is why I'm here with Jude.

He called a few hours ago. Normally I wouldn't rush to have coffee with a boy who wants to get together the same day. But I was so relieved that Jude wants me back in his life. Or I'm assuming he wants me back in his life. Why else would he have called?

"I was happy you called," I tell him.

"Your roommates make a compelling argument."

"What?" I have no idea what he's talking about. Has he ever even met my roommates?

"They didn't tell you?"

"Tell me what?"

Jude leans back in his wire-framed chair. He runs a hand through his blond hair, a shade lighter from the sun than when I met him.

"Sadie and Rosanna came to see me in the park," Jude says.

"When?"

"This afternoon. Right before I called you."

"How did they know where to find you?"

"They saw me in the park before. The night they moved in? Sadie was showing Rosanna around and they watched my show. They figured out it was me from stuff you've said. And that I'm the only nineteen-year-old magician working Washington Square Park."

Way to knock me off my game, ladies.

"What did they want?" I ask.

"They said I should fight for you." Jude smiles into his mug.

Now if you looked up *flabbergasted* in the dictionary, you'd see a picture of me sitting right here across from Jude. Wondering why in the world my girls would tell a boy who told me it's over to fight for me. And why they didn't give me a heads-up.

"What else did they say?" I ask.

"That information is classified."

"I didn't tell them to find you."

"I know. They had their reasons."

"Which were?"

Jude tips his chair back, balancing it on two legs. He studies me in silence like he's trying to gauge how much to reveal. The suspense is killing me.

He tilts forward to bring his chair back to normal. "They think we belong together."

"But they know Logan's here."

"So your ex showed up. What we become isn't his decision."

"He didn't just show up. He came here to get me back."

"How's that working out for you?"

Did Sadie and Rosanna tell Jude about my epic dinner fail? They were asleep when I got home last night and they were gone when I got up. I haven't even seen them. The dinner leftovers were stored in the refrigerator by the time I got home last night, stacked neatly in Tupperware containers. The table was cleared and the dishes were washed. Zero evidence of my cooking disaster could be detected in the immaculate kitchen. It wouldn't take a mastermind to deduce that no one ate the dinner I cooked. Obviously, the girls felt bad for me.

I stubbornly jut my chin out. "Fine."

The light that used to be in Jude's eyes when he looked at me is back. Like a lost star I found again. His eyes feed on mine intently. Passionately. He sees exactly who I am. He sees everything we could be together. The potential of us. His starlight is flaming.

I look away before I get burned.

Jude leans toward me. His tan arms rest against the round marble table.

"Want to know what I think?" he says. Challenge sparkles in his eyes.

Between the light and the sparkle, it's getting harder to breathe. "You'll tell me anyway."

"I think you want me to fight for you. I think you know how good we are together. You're conflicted. Your ex showed up for the summer and you have to deal with him. I get that. But I can't give up on what we have."

The scary thing about being completely honest with yourself is that it can be super inconvenient. Jude would never walk out on a dinner I made for him. Jude is sweet and caring and compassionate. The connection we have is the strongest connection I've ever felt with anyone. But if I admit that I feel the same way about Jude, that being with him makes me feel alive in a way I've never felt before, then I would have to admit that Jude is better for me than Logan.

Maybe now is the time to admit it.

"You don't have to tell me you agree," Jude says. "But I do need you to be honest about one thing."

"Okay."

"Were you seeing anyone else while we were together? We weren't together that long, so I'm guessing you weren't. But I need to know for sure."

"Why does it matter?"

"It just does."

That night when Logan appeared out of nowhere, I was bursting to tell Jude that I wanted to be exclusive casual. That I only wanted to be with him. The wanting I felt that night builds up inside of me again.

I begin to explain. "You know how I ran down to see you that night Logan showed up? When I thought it was you?"

"Yeah?"

"There's something I wanted to tell you."

"What?"

"I was going to ask if you wanted to try being . . . exclusive."

"But I thought you were all about having fun with no strings attached."

"I was. I just . . . I wanted to be with you. Only you."

Jude rubs his hand against his scruffy cheek. I love when he doesn't shave for a few days. "So if Logan hadn't shown up at your door ten seconds before I did, you and I would be together?"

"Yes. And no."

The light in Jude's eyes dims.

"I was going to ask if you wanted to be exclusive in a casual way. Where we only see each other, but without the demands and expectations of a serious relationship. We would have fun being together, but we'd also have the freedom to do our own thing."

"So . . . you wouldn't have started seeing Logan again? Even though he came all the way here to be with you?"

"That part is unclear."

"But you weren't with anyone else while we were together, right?"

If a genie in a bottle showed up this instant and granted me one wish, forget wishing for more wishes. I would wish that I could tell Jude he's right. Or that Jude would never ask me this again. But I want to be completely honest with him. I don't want to hold anything back. When you care about someone, you put yourself out there. All of you. The true you. And you hope that person still likes what they see.

"Not exactly," I admit. "But it was nothing."

Jude leans forward on the table again, staring at me. "What was nothing?"

"It didn't mean anything."

"What didn't mean anything?"

"There was . . . I hooked up with someone. While you and I were together."

"Who?"

"Some boy I met at the Strand."

"You didn't even know this person?"

No one has ever made me feel ashamed about having fun with boys before. Not because they haven't tried. People have judged me. People have made snide remarks. People have called me everything from a slut to a sinner. But no one has managed to pull off making me feel ashamed of my choices.

Until now.

At the time I told myself that Jude and I weren't really together. We'd just met. We weren't a thing. But if I were being honest with myself, painfully, completely, inconveniently honest, I would have to admit that we were a thing. We were a thing from the first second I saw him. We were a thing before he even knew my name.

"I'm sorry," I say. "I know that's not what you wanted to hear."

"When you say 'hooked up' . . . what do you mean?"

"We . . . made out."

"Where? At a club?"

This is the part I don't want to talk about the most.

"In a dressing room. At the Gap."

Jude pushes his chair away from me a little. He crosses his arms over his chest.

"To clarify," he says, "you made out with a stranger in a Gap dressing room. While we were together."

"Yeah."

"That's all you did?"

"We didn't have sex. But we did . . . other things."

"Other things you didn't do with me." Jude picks up his mug. He puts it back down again without drinking. "See, that's what I don't understand. You're saying that you only wanted to be with me. But then you go and hook up with some random in a dressing room?"

I try to lighten the mood. "Did you want to hook up in a dressing room? Because I'm free right now."

"Are you? Because I thought you were tied up with your ex-boyfriend." Jude pushes his chair back even more. Then he stands up. "This was a bad idea."

"No it wasn't!"

"I want to fight for you, Darcy. I just don't know what I'm fighting for."

"What are you saying?"

"I'm saying . . . good luck with Logan. I hope everything works out the way you want."

He leaves while I stare at his empty chair. I don't turn around to watch him go. I cannot watch another boy walk out on me.

TWENTY-FOUR
ROSANNA

WHEN WE TALKED THIS MORNING, D explained why he wasn't at Bryant Park last night. He got stuck at his internship. He said he was really sorry for not being there and that he would make it up to me tonight.

Taking the subway to D's place, all I can think about is how I am going to afford August. Covering my expenses for the second half of July will be challenging enough. I'm barely scraping by. But camp ends the third week of August. How am I going to pay for everything that last week?

I'm so out of it I almost miss my stop. The train jerking to a halt shakes me into action when I realize we're at Franklin Street. I leap out of the subway after the doors have already opened, expecting them to close on me with a death grip so tight I will be dragged to the next stop with assorted body parts dangling above the subway tracks. Then I look like a fool who leaps out of subways that aren't going anywhere. An announcement comes on saying the train is being held at the station due to traffic ahead.

A mom pushing a stroller gets on the subway. As I'm walking toward the turnstiles, I see a tattered pink stuffed bunny on the platform. It must have fallen out of the stroller. Her baby starts crying in the subway car. The mom spots the bunny by the turnstiles, her face twisted with indecision. She can't risk running for the bunny. How awful would it be if the subway doors closed right then and the train took off with her baby? She could wheel the stroller back out to pick up the bunny, but then she might miss the train if the doors closed before she got back on. She stares at the bunny as her baby wails louder.

In one swift motion, I dash over to that tattered pink bunny, pick it up, and toss it through the subway doors just as the *bing-bong* tone sounds and the doors slide closed. The mom mouths *thank you* at me. I wave to her as the train leaves the station.

That's two for two.

When Sadie and I were walking to the park to find Jude this afternoon, a middle-aged guy on the sidewalk in front of us dropped a twenty-dollar bill. I ran ahead, picked up the twenty, and said, "Excuse me."

The guy turned around.

"I think you dropped this." I held the bill out to him.

"Thank you," he said, taking it. "Most people would have kept it for themselves."

"That pretty much sums up what's wrong with the world."

He laughed. "Well put."

Sadie said she was impressed with how I ran after that guy. She didn't even have time to react.

So it seems like I'm getting better about reacting quickly when people need help. I just wish I didn't get so nervous. My heart was pounding when I ran after that guy with the twenty. Adrenaline tore me apart as I whipped the tattered pink bunny through those subway doors. But I didn't let being afraid prevent me from taking action.

When I get to D's building, I tell myself to remain calm. It hurt a lot that D didn't show up last night. But he had a valid reason. I do not want to be the crazy girlfriend anymore.

D's doorman recognizes me. All of the doormen for his building wear the same uniform: black suit, white shirt, black tie, and shiny black cap. He smiles as he opens the door.

"Good evening," he says with his fancy doorman inflection. "Is Mr. Clark expecting you?"

"Yes," I say. The yes comes out all garbled. I clear my throat. "Yes, he is." This doorman always makes me nervous. They all do. How can you not be nervous around someone who holds doors open for glamorous, polished people as they sail through them, exchanging pleasantries effortlessly, accustomed to speaking eloquently with doormen on a regular basis? I feel like doormen can tell I grew up in poverty, and having a door held open for me is a much bigger deal than it should be. The ironic thing is, this doorman could be struggling to make ends meet, spending his days opening doors for people with more money than they know what to do with. I need to work on not feeling so intimidated.

The doorman calls D on the phone that sits on the podium by the front doors. The podium phone is the fancy way in which guests are announced. "Rosanna to see you," he reports. Then he hangs up the phone with a clipped nod.

"You can go right up," he tells me.

"Thank you." It's not right that he knows my name but I don't know his. I need to learn all of D's doormen's names.

I have the elevator to myself. When the doors close, I scrutinize my reflection in the glossy silver paneling. Why oh *why* did my hair have to choose tonight to freak out? Yeah, it's hot and humid. My hair always puffs up and frizzes out when it's hot and humid. But can't I ever get a break? I frantically paw at my waves. As if anything I could possibly do in an elevator would improve the situation.

The elevator doors glide open on D's floor. His hall smells like roasted chicken. And something else. Warm biscuits.

He opens the door right away when I ring the bell. Like

he was waiting on the other side.

"Hey," he says.

"Hi."

"Thanks for coming over." He steps aside so I can come in. I can't help smiling when I realize the delicious dinner smells are coming from D's place. Takeout containers are spread out on the coffee table in the living room. Candles are lit on the end tables around the big sectional couch. The blanket D bought for us to use on Central Park movie night is spread out on the floor in front of the TV with some pillows scattered around it. Subtle acoustic guitar plays from the overhead sound system.

"What's all this?" I ask.

"I suck for not showing up last night. It was unacceptable and I'm really, really sorry. So I redid movie night. True, it's inside, but it's gross out anyway. Better to have movie night where we can be cool and comfortable."

D did all of this for me. I can't believe it.

"Sorry I had to work late," he says. "All this stuff went down with a top client account I'm working on. And then one of the guys took us out for drinks after. I didn't want to go. It was a political move; he has a lot of pull with the guy I'm trying to get a recommendation from. I'm sorry I didn't tell you what was going on, but there was no way to get in touch with you. You need to get a cell phone."

D will never know the truth about why I don't have a cell phone. I'd rather die than admit I can't afford something everyone else has. As far as D knows, I'm just making a statement about the importance of being an individual by refusing to succumb to societal pressures.

"Did you stay for the movie?" D asks.

"Yeah. It was so crowded and I was kind of in the middle. Leaving early would have been impossible. And I was afraid that if I left, you would show up and then we'd lose our spot."

"I hope you weren't looking around for me the whole time."

"I wasn't." I totally was. I'm sad all over again when I remember how it felt to be floating solo in a lake of groups. But then I look around at the takeout containers and candles and the blanket with floor pillows. D put a lot of effort into tonight. Everything looks and smells amazing. "Dinner smells really good," I say.

"We're watching *Her*."

"Who?"

"The movie."

"Oh! You remembered." I mentioned to D that I've been wanting to see *Her*.

"I ordered in from Landmarc. Have you been there? Of course you haven't—you just moved here. Sometimes I forget you're still new to New York. It seems like you've been here forever!"

Yay that he thinks I blend in with the real New Yorkers.

"Should we eat?" D says. "I don't want it to get cold."

From the array of food containers spread out on the enormous coffee table, it looks like D ordered about a hundred sides with the roasted chicken.

"Hey." D takes me in his arms. He kisses me gently. "I really am sorry about last night. Let me make it up to you."

I look into his striking hazel eyes. He clearly feels bad about what happened. He's making it very easy not to be mad anymore.

"Okay?" he asks.

"Okay."

D puts his arm around me, guiding me into the living room. "Take your pick. Couch or blanket."

"The blanket would be more authentic, but I'm going with the couch. It's too comfortable to reject."

"Excellent choice."

I sit on the plush couch, suddenly shy. D shakes out a cream-colored cloth napkin and drapes it over my lap. He makes a plate for me, filling it with so many delicious things my eyes water up in gratitude. We've come a long way from D catching me sneaking packs of chips into my bag. I blink my tears away quickly before he can see, embarrassed that I'm emotional.

We talk about work while we eat. D complains about the douche he shares a desk clump with. I complain about Frank, who still hasn't done anything about Momo. D tells me about the trainer he started working with at Equinox. I tell him about the volunteer jobs I'm considering.

"Did you have movie nights like this back in Chicago?" D asks.

"You mean . . . at home?"

"Yeah. I can totally see you and your brothers and sisters having movie nights when you were little. All piled on the couch in the living room in front of a huge TV."

I take another bite of my extravagant dinner.

"Why do you always do that?" D says.

"What?"

"Avoid answering when I ask you questions about your past."

"No I don't."

"Yes you do. Every time I ask about your home life, you deflect."

"I told you about my family! And my friends." He's right. There are certain questions I refuse to answer. I told D all about my brothers and sisters, about their personalities and idiosyncrasies and the funniest stories that have accumulated over the years. But when the conversation leads to more specific details like our house (that wasn't big enough) or family vacations (that we never took) or the size of our TV (way too small and falling apart), I either change the subject or let the question hang awkwardly in the air. Not just because I can't admit how poor my family is. I'm paranoid that D's questions will expose the most damaged parts of me. He's so easy to talk to. I'm scared the truth will come out. Would D still want to be with me if he knew I came from nothing? If he knew I was molested? Could he ever love me, knowing I am broken?

My anxiety must be showing on my face because D says, "No pressure. I just want to know you better."

"I know."

"I care about you." D says this so tenderly that all I can do is nod to keep from bursting into tears.

We finish dinner while D tells a hilarious story about this obnoxious guy at his gym. Then he makes cappuccinos with his swanky Lavazza coffeemaker. Like a grownup. I sit at the long, sleek kitchen island to watch him. He grinds fresh coffee beans and measures the coffee out with a little triangular scoop. The open bag of coffee beans sits on the counter in front of me. I can't stop sniffing it. I put the bag right up to my nose, inhaling slowly and deeply. If there were a way to capture the aroma of finer things in a bag, this would be it.

It is routine for D to make cappuccinos on his upscale machine. I wonder again what it's like to be him. Growing up in that gorgeous Upper West Side brownstone, watching the seasons change right outside his window in Central Park as if it was his backyard, having everything he needed and most of what he wanted provided for him. Going to an exclusive private school that cost as much as tuition at an Ivy League university. Donovan Clark is stable, well-adjusted, and confident. He's not struggling to be normal like I am. He's not running from anything. He's not fighting to forget dark secrets. His future is bright.

Is it wrong that I'm jealous of my boyfriend? Of course I'm happy for him. Every kid deserves to grow up the way he did. No one should grow up scared or mistreated or hungry. D doesn't have any idea what my daily struggle is like. He doesn't have to worry about paying for college. Or paying rent. Or buying groceries. He can just live. He will always be taken care of, no matter what. I'm horrible for being jealous of him. But sometimes I just can't help myself.

Materialistic is one of the last words anyone would use to describe me. If anything, I am anti-materialistic. But I can't deny that I'm admiring the view from the high life. Being in D's gorgeous home, imagining how good it must feel to come home every night and wake up every morning to this simple elegance, surrounded by beautiful objects that make every part of the day run smoothly . . . it all adds up to a life I wouldn't mind living. Can there be a way to have some of this but still stay true to who I am?

D pours foam over each of our cups, then sprinkles cinnamon on top. He puts a little stick with crystallized sugar into each cup. They had these sticks at Butter. As you stir your cappuccino, the sugar melts. I never knew coffee drinks had accessories. There's so much I never knew before D.

"To new beginnings," he says, poising his cup to toast mine.

"To new beginnings," I say.

TWENTY-FIVE
SADIE

SOMETIMES YOU THINK YOU'RE JUST buying Ruffles at the deli. You have no idea what's about to go down.

There's something about Ruffles that makes them taste better than any other potato chip. I don't know what it is. Maybe the ridges trap in extra flavor or make the chips the exact right amount of greasy. Unlike baked chips. What's the point of a potato chip if it doesn't taste like it's not good for you? That's why I'm burrowing behind packs of potato chips on a shelf at my old deli like a squirrel gathering a nut stash, digging for plain Ruffles. Not sour cream and onion. Not that weird cheddar flavor. Plain.

It's strange being back at my old deli. Even though I only moved last month, the last time I came in here seems like much longer ago. New Yorkers tend to frequent the same deli on a regular basis, and it's usually the deli closest to their apartment. That's why I haven't been back here since I moved out. But I just went home to pick up a few things from my old room that I forgot to pack in my frenzy of moving out. My parents were there doing their usual Sunday thing of reading the *New York Times* with NPR on in the background, drinking coffee from their matching mugs (Mom's has two smiling peas holding hands; Dad's has a pea pod), and reading interesting parts of the paper out loud to each other. I let them attack me with their rapid-fire questions for a while before I made my escape.

My persistence at digging around on the deli shelf pays off when I find a single pack of plain Ruffles all the way in the back.

I get in line to pay. The guy in front of me has a peach Snapple. Who drinks peach iced tea? Why do they even make that?

Peach Snapple Guy holds his disgusting beverage up to the cashier. A Korean family owns this deli. They're all super nice. I've been coming here for years. The daughter always apologizes to me when they are out of plain Ruffles, even if I'm not buying potato chips. She's working the register now.

"Two-fifty," she tells the guy.

"For a Snapple?" he booms. "That's highway robbery."

The cashier glances down at the counter. She's a sweet person. Not someone who enjoys confrontation.

The guy huffs in frustration. "Fine." He holds out a credit card.

"Cash only." There's a sign that says CASH ONLY on the side of the cash register. The sign this guy apparently didn't notice while he was waiting in line.

"I don't have any cash on me," he says.

She points at the ATM by the front door.

"Oh, so not only are you underreporting your income, you're raking in exorbitant ATM fees?"

She doesn't respond.

He shoves his credit card at her. She shakes her head.

"You're making me pay for this with cash?" he yells. "I never carry cash anymore. What if I refuse?"

"Cash only," she repeats.

"Is that the only English you know?" The guy turns to me with an incredulous expression. "Can you believe this?"

I throw the cashier a sympathetic look. She doesn't deserve to be harassed like this. No one does. But she won't let herself get upset in front of this lunatic. Her face remains stoic.

This enrages him even more.

"You're un-American, you know that?" The guy looks so disgusted for a second I think he might punch her. Then he does something even worse.

He spits at her.

I gasp. She wipes spit off her neck with a napkin. He

knocks over a Tastykake display as he storms out, still gripping the peach Snapple.

"Are you okay?" I ask.

She nods. She can't even look at me.

"That was crazy," I say. "He was crazy. He had no right to say those things to you." And he totally stole that Snapple.

"I've heard worse." She rings up my Ruffles, composing herself.

"That's horrible." I'm so angry at Enraged Guy I have to restrain myself from running after him and schooling him on the way the world works. How can anyone treat another human being like that? What happened to him to make him so hideous? Doesn't he realize how he's hurting people?

Just like those enraged guys on the subway when I was seven.

The anger that's always under my surface like a live wire is humming. The humming gets louder and louder until I can't even hear what the cashier is saying as she hands me my change. I smile and tell her to have a good rest of the day.

I never know what's going to trigger it. The anger. Most of the time I can play it off like it's not even there. Like I completely believe the positive outlook I project. People tell me all the time that I'm the most positive person they know. They love my warm fuzzies. They love that I appear to be an eternal optimist, despite the dark secret I keep hidden from them.

No one knows my secret. Except Austin.

He was so supportive when I told him about those two guys on the subway. How they scuffled for whatever stupid reason. How one of them shoved my mom. Who was pregnant with my little sister. A little sister I never got to have.

I do everything I can to combat random rage with random acts of kindness. But it doesn't matter how much I do. I will never be enough. I will never be able to protect everyone.

Out on the street, I forget where I was going. I'm carrying a bag of potato chips I don't want anymore. My mind instinctively directs my body around corners and down side streets until I'm walking toward the river. My self knows what it needs to feel better.

After my mom lost the baby, I couldn't stop picturing what my little sister would have been like. Her personality. How much we would look alike. Whether her mannerisms would be the same as mine. Or if she'd be different enough that you couldn't tell we were sisters. In my heart, I know it wouldn't be like that. We would have so much in common there would be no question that we're sisters. Like me, she'd be all about the little things. She would be a dreamer. She'd know that soul mates are real, regardless of how many times her heart got broken. She'd love kids, surprises, badminton, and rooftop gardens. She would even love New York City as much as I do. We'd live here forever, bonded not only by family but geography. We would have each other, no matter what.

What would it have been like to be an older sister? All I know is being the younger sister. But with Marnix away at college in Arizona, everything feels different. He doesn't even come home in the summer. The only time I really see him is at Christmas. Even before he left for college, we were never close. He shut me out a lot. Hid in his room too much. He wasn't the kind of big brother I wanted, but he was all I had.

Being an older sister to a girl would have been a whole other thing. I would have been the one to teach her about kindness and karma. I would have been the one she would have come to with questions she'd be too embarrassed to ask anyone else. And when she had her first breakup with a boy she thought might be the one, I would have helped her put the pieces of her broken heart back together.

I will never get over the loss of the sister I never knew. The missing piece of her has been carved out of me permanently, leaving a gaping void. The loss is profound. Bottomless. I try to channel my sadness into a positive lifestyle. I make choices that improve my life and help others. But no amount of happiness will make up for what I've never had.

All because of some asshole on the subway.

That night I have another nightmare. I'm walking with a little girl down a dark alley, holding her hand. I can sense that I need to protect her from something scary. Dark figures appear at the end of the alley. They have fiery red eyes, glowing in the blackness. I know that the creatures will get us before we can run away. I turn away from them and immediately feel clammy claws scraping down my back. The scraping is so real that I bolt awake. I can't go back to sleep. The sensation still lingers hours later.

I've had some scary nightmares about my sister. But this was by far the scariest.

Sometimes you think people are just arguing on the subway. You have no idea what's about to go down.

TWENTY-SIX
DARCY

"YEAH, SO. I WAS KIND of a dick."

"Kind of?"

"I was a dick."

"Now we're getting somewhere."

"Sorry for walking out like that."

I switch the phone to my other ear. If this two-mornings-after call is Logan's lame attempt at making up with me, he's going to have to bring it harder. Way harder.

"Why did you?" I ask. "Walk out."

"I don't know. There was just, like, all this pressure."

"What do you mean?"

"To like . . . act a certain way you wanted me to be."

"I just wanted you to be supportive. I cooked for you."

"Yeah, I know. That's why I should have been support-ive. I was stupid."

Seems like there's a lot of that going around. But Logan regrets his bad boy behavior. I remember what he said that night he showed up at my door.

I was wrong. I should have never let you go.

"I'm sorry I walked out," Logan says.

Which time? I almost ask.

"Don't sweat it," I say, rummaging through a pile of new clothes on my bed. When I saw some fresh merch in the window of Free People, I had to go in. You can never go into Free People without leaving with at least a few cute pieces. Or, um, two large bags.

"What are you doing today?" Logan asks.

"I have a paper due for Social Foundations."

"When's it due?"

"Tuesday."

"So you don't have to finish it until tomorrow night."

"If by 'finish,' you mean 'start,' then yeah. Although I think starting it today would be smarter."

"Since when do you choose smarter over more fun?"

"Did you have something in mind?"

"Actually, I did." I hear Logan take a sip of something. Ice cubes clink against the glass. "You know that hotel over the High Line? The Standard?"

"Their rooftop bar is overrated. We should go to that one next to the—"

"I'm not talking about the bar. I'm talking about the hotel."

"Oh."

"We should get a room."

"When? Today?"

"Why not?"

"Wait, so . . . you want to have Sunday Funday in a sexy hotel?"

"With sexy you."

"That's the best idea you've ever had."

He's waiting for me in the lobby. Leaning against the wall. Hair falling over one eye, giving me that half-smirk smile. Like we're about to do something naughty.

I slink over to him in my four-inch metallic Gucci stilettos. I take my time, letting him drink me in. My Dior newspaper print dress flutters as I pass an air-conditioning vent. Logan's half smirk busts out into a full smile.

"Happy to see me?" I ask, gliding two fingers down the front of his worn Nirvana tee.

"You look . . . incredible."

"Well, it *is* the Standard. A girl best come correct. There are certain . . . standards."

"Sorry I'm underdressed."

"No worries. You're not going to be dressed much longer." I grab the front of his shirt and pull him toward me. He kisses me so passionately that people are staring when we break apart.

"We should get a room," he jokes.

We hold hands on our way to the check-in desks along the back wall of the lobby. There's a line at the desks. Logan puts his hands around my waist, kissing my neck. His shampoo smells like lemons. He must be using a new shampoo. His hair never smelled like lemons before.

"The things I'm going to do to you," he whispers in my ear.

A shiver runs down my spine.

People are looking. People are always looking.

By the time it's our turn, I want him so badly I'm delirious with lust. It's so obvious what we're here for. We have no luggage. We can't take our hands off each other. The lady behind the desk gives us a tight smile when Logan asks for the room choices. He reserves a standard king room with High Line views for one night.

"Which credit card will you be using?" she inquires.

Logan pulls his wallet out of his back pocket. He takes out a card. The lady gives him another tight smile as she takes the card from him.

"I'm sorry, sir," she says after tapping on her keyboard. "This card was declined. Would you like to try another?"

"Are you sure?"

"I can run it again if you'd like."

"Please."

She runs it again. She shakes her head, handing the card back to Logan.

"Okay, uh . . ." He takes out another credit card.

Same problem.

"Here." I fork over my own credit card. Daddy isn't going to be rejoicing that I paid for a night at a boutique hotel. Or any hotel. Like I said, it's no secret why we're here. But I don't think Daddy even looks at my statements. He has assistants to take care of all that.

I don't know what's going on with Logan's credit cards. And right now I don't even care. We need to get up to a room. Any room. ASAP.

We make out in the elevator up to the thirteenth floor. We go the wrong way down the hall before finding our room. The green light blinks on when it recognizes our key, Logan pushing the door open as he rushes us inside.

We don't look around the room at all. We just fall onto the bed and into each other.

"We forgot to check out the view," Logan says, lying next to me on the bed.

"We should probably do that," I say. "To make sure the world's still there and all."

"I wouldn't care if it wasn't." Logan slides his hand over my stomach. His fingers trace the curve of my hipbone. "All I want to do is be here with you."

"We could stay another night."

"We could stay for a week."

"We could move in. Like those people who live in hotels instead of apartments? My parents know a couple who lives in a Trump Tower penthouse. Their place must be sick."

"Are we really talking about your parents?"

"No. Although . . . Daddy's going to see this charge on my card."

"You'll think of a way to explain it."

"How would you explain it?"

"I don't know. Research?"

"For what, Human Anatomy? I'm not even taking that class."

Logan laughs. "Too bad. This would be my kind of field trip." He traces the curve of my hipbone again, up and down in lazy loops.

"That was weird with your credit cards," I say.

"Stupid magnetic strips. They can get deactivated if they're too close together."

We both know that is not what happened.

I get up and put my bra and panties back on. Then I go over to the windows, pull back the curtains, and look down at the High Line. A tourist in an orange shirt notices me. He waves.

"That guy's waving at me!" I yell.

Logan comes over in his underwear. He looks down below us. "Where?"

"Orange shirt!" I wave back. He takes a picture of me in the hotel window high above him. I try to imagine how we look to everyone down there. Leaning against the glass of our floor-to-ceiling windows. With the curtains pulled all the way open. Wearing nothing except underwear. When I was on the High Line a few nights ago with Sadie and Rosanna, I looked up at the tall lit windows of the Standard as we walked under it. Sadie was talking about the unique building design of how the Standard straddles the High Line. I was only half listening. I was too busy looking up at the windows and noticing a couple kissing in one of them.

When I told Logan about that couple, he said the Standard is famous for people having sex in the windows. It was like a thing when the hotel first opened. Now the hotel staff apparently knocks on your door if you're being too frisky with the PDA.

We'll take our chances.

Logan moves behind me so we're both facing the window. He lifts my arms up, then presses his hands behind mine against the glass. I don't care if anyone comes knocking on our door. I almost hope they do. That would be badass.

Summer Fun Darcy is loving this. She doesn't care who sees. But when a little kid holding hands with a lady who's probably his mom points up at us, I step back from the window. Damaging little kids for life is not my idea of fun times.

"What, are you suddenly shy?" Logan says.

"Not shy. Just over the voyeurs."

"But we still have some clothes on."

I close the curtains so only a thin strip of bright light shows between them. A sliver of light washes over Logan, gilding him like something supernatural. Something from another world where good girls break bad and bad boys get away with whatever they want.

"That's about to change," I say.

TWENTY-SEVEN

ROSANNA

I COULD SERIOUSLY LIVE ON Donovan Clark's roofdeck. Colorful flowers are growing in big stone planters placed all over the roof. The whole roof is landscaped into different sections. There's a section with tables and grills where you can have dinner parties. The northern wall is designed for you to enjoy the view, which is ridiculous. You can see all of Manhattan. I've taken over the lounge chair area. It's perfect for laying out on a sunny Sunday morning like this.

This morning didn't start out as relaxing. D took me running along his route in Hudson River Park. He likes to start his day by running. We're both morning people, so I like the idea of that. I respect how he starts his day in such a healthy way. In South Beach, I told him I want to get more into fitness. I did not say that I can't afford to eat as many fresh vegetables as I want. Or that running is a good option for me since it's free and easy. I mean . . . I thought it would be easy.

D said I should run with him a couple mornings a week. We started today. All it took was three minutes of running for my chest to feel like it was about to explode. I was bent over trying to catch my breath on the sidelines, begging D to slow down. We'll have to work up to getting me in good enough shape to run with him like a normal person. I really want to get good enough to run with him.

Having a fitness partner increases your chances of sticking to a new routine. D is the only person I know here who's into working out. I know I would be way more motivated to get into a workout routine with him. Sadie doesn't like the gym. She thinks the classes are too crowded and the machines are too boring. Sometimes she does outdoor activities like badminton and swimming, but I'm not into either of those. Darcy was a hardcore backpacker last year, but that was just so she could explore Europe within the budget her parents agreed to. She's not the workout type, either. She's so lucky to have a naturally athletic physique. Darcy has that tight, toned look I would give anything for. Anything except being spoiled on D's gorgeous roofdeck.

The bottom half of my beach towel slides off the lounge chair as I flip onto my stomach. I reach down to pull it back up. But D is already leaning over from his lounge chair next to mine to fix my towel. Well, his towel. Because of course D has a huge basket of rolled beach towels on the floor of his guest bathroom. There are also classy bath amenities in silver trays on a glass shelf above the sink. He brings those samples back from hotels he stays at on family vacations. I recognized the Bliss body butter samples from whichever W Hotel he stayed at. Sadie's mom is a concierge at the Times Square W. She's always giving Sadie Bliss body butter samples. You can find like five of them at any given time in Sadie's ginormous bag.

Speaking of bliss. This is it. Our secluded summertime spot high above the greatest city in the world. We're having the best time, relaxing and remembering highlights of our South Beach vacay and geeking out over obscurity that isn't on most people's radars.

"Did you see the one with the clock?" D asks.

"And they think it's a person?"

"Yeah, because it has—"

"—a face and hands!"

"Classic."

"Or the one with the phone."

"Earth book!" D does another imitation of the Yip-Yip Martians from *Sesame Street*. He sticks out his lower lip and pushes it up. He makes his eyes pop. He goes, "Yip yip yip yip! Nooope nope nope nope nope! Earth booook! Book book book!"

I laugh so hard I have to flip back over so I can breathe. A guy listening to music with earbuds a few chairs away is the only other person laying out. He gives us an odd look. Maybe he's jealous that he's not up here having fun with someone. Or maybe he can tell we are total dorks. I didn't even know D had a dorky side until recently. D said he only lets it show with his closest friends. I guess he feels safe enough with me now that he knows I'm going to geek out along with him instead of running in the other direction.

This sundeck area is never crowded. How are more people not taking advantage of it? If I lived in this building, I would be up here all the time. D says a lot of people go away for the summer. Or they go down the shore or out to the Hamptons on weekends. He says August is a ghost town in Tribeca. That's so weird. I mean, I get that this is one of the most expensive neighborhoods to live in. People who live in Tribeca generally can afford to go away for the summer. But if I lived in this beautiful building in this beautiful neighborhood, why would I want to go anywhere else?

"That's what we should be for Halloween," D says.

"What?"

"The Yip-Yips."

"*Yes.*"

"Except no one would be able to tell it was us."

"We would know it's us. That's all that matters." I refrain from freaking out that he is planning ahead to October. Meaning he thinks we will still be together three months from now. Meaning I'm not the only one who sees the potential of our relationship.

D takes off his sunglasses. He polishes them on the edge of his beach towel. "Have you heard of the Halloween Parade?"

"No."

"It's fantastic. You see the most creative costumes. Huge crowds come out to watch. It's on the news and everything." D puts his sunglasses back on. He looks at me. "We should walk in it this year. You want to?"

"Anyone can walk?"

"Anyone in a costume."

"That would be fabulous."

"Okay then. We're walking." D leans back on his chair so our faces are inches apart. He rests his hand on my chair to hold my hand. "I like making plans with you."

When D says things like that, things about our future together, it makes me happier than I've ever been in my life. He doesn't just hint or imply that he wants to stay with me. He comes right out and says it like the confident, secure man he is.

"I'm proud of you," he says.

"For what?"

"For being exactly who you are. For following your dreams. For moving here even though it was scary. You're like, 'This is what I want to do and I'm doing it. End of story.'"

As if that's anywhere near the end of the story. If only he knew the whole truth. I can't just decide to do something and then do it. Everything I want to do, every choice I make, is determined by my limited resources. The harsh reality of my life is something D would never understand. Conquering the world is a lot easier when you can afford to make it happen.

A puffy white cloud drifts over the sun. The bright glare on my skin fades. It feels good to get some relief from the intense rays.

"Trust me," I say. "If I can do this, anyone can."

"You're wrong. Most people aren't as determined as you. Or passionate about what they're doing. They don't base their career choices on helping other people or spend time volunteering. They just go along with whatever's easiest. Or whatever will make them the most money."

"Cynical much?"

"Realistic. I see it every day. Been seeing it for years with my dad's crowd."

"But isn't that . . ."

"What?"

I shake my head. "Nothing."

"No. What were you going to say?"

"Isn't that kind of what you're doing? Choosing a career that will make you rich?" I don't add that he's already rich. He could choose a career in community service and not have to worry about scraping by. He could have the best of both worlds.

D sits up, swinging his legs into the space between our lounge chairs. My stomach lurches in alarm when I think he's going to get up and stomp away. Why did I have to go and say that? Why am I constantly saying stupid things I know I'll never be able to take back? Someone should really install a filter in my mouth. But D isn't mad.

"Yeah," he says. "I guess I am. But investment banking is something I want to do. Not just something I'll make a lot of money doing. It's not social work, but it's a way of making other people's lives better. There is value in protecting wealth for families and their future generations. And it's something I know I'll be good at." He scoots across the gap between us to sit on the side of my chair. He turns to face me, reaching out to gently tuck a wisp of hair behind my ear. "You make me feel lacking."

"I'm sorry. I know we keep talking about this—"

"Not lacking in a bad way. Lacking like . . . like I have to work harder to measure up to you. You're such an amazing person, Rosanna. I want to be you when I grow up."

I scoff, brushing off his compliment. Donovan Clark is already a grownup and he's still in college. Even though I'm scoffing on the outside, I'm all warm and tingly on the inside. I love when we have conversations like these. I love it when D opens up to me. He's not afraid to tell me how he's feeling or to talk about what really matters. I twine my fingers through his, smiling up at him, feeling closer to him than ever.

Then his phone rings.

He picks up his shorts from under the lounge chair. He takes his phone out of the pocket. I'm thinking that he wouldn't dare break our magic spell by letting someone crash this moment. He has to feel it, too.

But he answers the call.

"Hey."

Pause.

"Whoa, slow down. What happened?"

Pause.

"When?"

Pause.

"Are you okay?"

Pause.

"How bad is it?"

Pause.

"Did you call your mom?"

Pause.

"Don't move. I'm coming to get you." D hangs up. "I have to go," he tells me. He starts gathering his things.

And just like that, our magic spell is broken.

"Who was it?" I ask.

"Shayla."

I wait for D to explain. He doesn't. He just pulls on his shirt.

"What did she want?" I ask.

"It's an emergency. She hurt herself and needs to get to the clinic."

"Which clinic?"

"There's a twenty-four-hour health clinic near her place. But it's too far for her to walk. She's messed up."

"What happened?"

D puts on his flip-flops. Ever since he answered Shayla's call, he's been doing this thing where he won't look at me. His open door closed when he answered her call. I was feeling more connected to him than ever. Now he's acting like a stranger.

"She fell," he said. "She got wasted last night. She was walking home in heels and she fell right on the sidewalk. Scraped up her face pretty bad. There was blood all over her pillow when she woke up. She might need stitches."

"Why didn't she go to the clinic last night?"

"I guess she didn't know how bad it was. She passed out as soon as she got home."

"So is it . . . I mean, you're going over there?"

"Yeah, I'll get her to the clinic."

"Walking?"

"No, I'll take her in a cab."

"She can't put herself in a cab?"

D sighs. "She left her wallet at a friend's last night. She has no way to pay for a cab."

"Why is she calling you? There's no one else who can take her?"

"She called her mom and a few friends. No one's around."

That sounds highly suspect. Out of everyone she knows, there's no one besides D who can ride with her in a cab? The whole thing sounds like an excuse to make D come running to her rescue. Why doesn't he see that?

He is the one who broke our magic spell. He is the one who's about to leave me. Yet he is the one who's mad.

"Shayla is a person in need," D says. "I'm going to help her. You'd be first in line to help someone in need. How can you be mad at me for doing the exact same thing you would do?"

"It's not the same thing."

"Why not?"

He knows why not. There is something between him and Shayla that's more than friendship. More than history. He knows and he knows I know he knows.

D gets up and snatches his towel off the lounge chair. "I'm sorry for whatever I did to upset you. But I don't think I'm doing anything wrong."

Shayla is clearly manipulating D. But he's too caught up in her to see clearly. The jealous, insecure part of me wouldn't be surprised if Shayla hurt herself on purpose just to get D to spend the day with her instead of me. It wouldn't be the first time a girl whipped up major drama to get a boy's attention.

"I'll be back soon," D says. He leaves without kissing me.

The roofdeck has lost its luster. Instead of feeling like I'm on top of the world, I feel so low I can't even enjoy being up here. I'm torn between staying and going. Would D even care if I were gone when he got back? What if Shayla makes him stay with her at the clinic and take her home after? And stay with her some more? He might not be back until tonight.

Is this who D is? Someone who would leave me for another girl and feel completely justified doing it? Or is this more about me?

My stomach churns as jealousy eats away at me. It hits me yet again that I am not the best version of myself I was supposed to be when I moved here. I am not Shiny New Rosanna.

I desperately want to be her. I just don't know how.

Did I really think I could move to New York and my past would disappear? That I could run away from what happened and never look back? How could I have been so stupid? Trust issues don't go away on their own. Feeling unworthy, like I don't deserve D, like I don't deserve to be *loved* . . . I could end up sabotaging our relationship before it even has a chance to get serious. There will be no Halloween costumes or holiday dinners or New Year's celebrations if I don't stop acting like a freak. There won't be anything unless I stop.

It might be time to get help.

The guy who was giving us an odd look cuts his eyes away when I catch him watching me. If he was jealous of us before, he definitely isn't anymore.

TWENTY-EIGHT
SADIE

HERE'S ANOTHER REASON WHY I'M not Team Logan: He's not taking Darcy out for her birthday. Darcy says it's because he took her to the Standard to celebrate. But that was two days ago. What I don't get is how the Standard prevents him from seeing her tonight. On her actual birthday.

And what's up with Darcy not even telling me or Rosanna that it's her birthday? We would have totally planned something. Rosanna wasn't home to back me up when I found out. I had to advocate for both of us.

"No worries," Darcy said. "I'm not a big birthday person."

Somehow I found that hard to believe. "But it's your birthday. You're supposed to get all the attention on your birthday."

"I wasn't even going to tell you it's my birthday. You only know because you heard my mom singing over the phone."

I was sitting next to her on the couch when she picked up the call from her mom. The falsetto was so piercing I'm surprised the windows didn't crack. Whether I found out about her birthday from Darcy telling me or overhearing her mom is irrelevant. Today was Darcy's birthday and there was no way we weren't celebrating.

Darcy kept insisting she wasn't a big birthday person.

I kept insisting we needed to celebrate.

Of course she caved. The real Darcy is all about spontaneous fun.

"Fine," she relented. "You win. But nothing big. No birthday cake or anything. Let's just explore and see where the night takes us. Low-key activities only."

"Yay! Let's get ready and I'll meet you back out here. And I'll call—oh, wait. We can't call her." I left a note on Rosanna's pillow telling her to call me if she wanted to come out with us.

I'm not sure why Darcy wants to keep her birthday low-key, but I could tell she was serious about that. So my birthday present to her will be showing her my New York. The real New York I've been in love with my whole life that she's just starting to know.

First I take Darcy to Eisenberg's Sandwich Shop on 5th Avenue. This place has been here since 1929. It's an old-school lunch counter with lightning fast service. The cooks behind the counter shout orders at each other while the bustling energy of New York City undulates all around you. I love places like this. Places with character and history that make you feel like you're part of something monumental. That you were there.

After dinner we swing over to Perry Street. I want to show Darcy all the beautiful behind-the-scenes parts of New York I cherish the most. The parts of New York only a native bursting with city love would know. We will walk down Perry Street and she will soak up the amazing energy and forget about Logan not planning anything for her birthday (which must sting despite all the insisting that it doesn't). I convinced Darcy to wear sneakers for a lot of walking around since it's such a gorgeous night. She was down with that. More because she has these limited edition Kate Spade for Keds sneakers than she wanted to be comfortable.

"Brooke lives here," I point out when we pass her brownstone between Bleecker and West 4th. I don't mention that I canceled plans with Brooke and some of my other friends from high school to take Darcy out tonight. They're my girls, but now so is Darcy. There is something surreal about getting together with your high school friends after you graduate. Like we're still the same people, only everything has changed. There's this bittersweet sense that everything we do together might be for the last time. Simple things like getting gelato at Cones or acting all rowdy over pizza around a big table at John's take on this significance that wasn't there before. I wonder what it's going to be like when we get together during breaks. Or even if all of us will ever be together again.

"Wow," Darcy marvels. "Her building is beautiful."

"You should see her room. Her dad had a designer redo everything before she moved in."

"Where did she live before?"

"With her mom in New Jersey. She moved here senior year."

"Why'd she move?"

"She'd always dreamed of living in New York. A lot like Rosanna did. But at the time she thought she came here to be with a boy."

"Go Brooke!"

"I know. She's my role model."

"So what happened? With the boy?"

"There was a better boy here for her all along."

We head east down Bleecker Street. I tell Darcy about Brooke and Scott Abrams, the boy she came here to be with only to realize that moving here was about finding herself, not finding him. And then Brooke and John Dalton, my friend who gives me the best boy behavior insight.

And then I see something that makes me stop in my tracks.

I've seen this store before. Back when it used to be a different store. Then when it closed and was under construction. And even when it opened as the new place it is now. Darcy and Rosanna and I were walking down Bleecker Street the night Darcy moved in, and I ranted about how this street has changed in a suburban strip mall way that makes me want to throw up. But for some reason, seeing it all lit up tonight is making me more enraged than ever.

"That is not right," I announce from across the street. Java Stop is everywhere, muscling in to take over indie stores that can't defend themselves against the giant coffee corporation. Java Stop is overpriced, underwhelming, and relentless in its pursuit to achieve worldwide domination. Java Stop is a bully no one is standing up to.

Darcy is trying to figure out what I'm talking about.

"There should not be a Java Stop on Bleecker Street," I explain. "A Java Stop should not be allowed to exist on the most historic part of Bleecker Street in the West Village. Where Bleecker Street Records used to be. Hello, that store was only here for my entire life!"

I dash across the street and peer into the window of Java Stop. Darcy runs after me.

"This is wrong," I tell the window. The people gurgling in their Java Stop stupor inside don't even see me. They are too busy tuning out with their music or screens or pretentious posing. I turn away from the window to face the stream of people walking by. "There cannot be a Java Stop on the most historic part of Bleecker Street!" I yell for anyone who will listen. A tourist couple clutching an unfolded map of Manhattan shrink away from me as if I might attack them. Yeah, I'm that girl having a meltdown/ enraged fit/full-on rant outside of an insatiable conglomerate where a mom-and-pop store should still be. And don't even get me started on the 16 Handles two doors down. This is not a suburban strip mall. This is the West Village of New York City. Have some *respect*.

"Sing it, sister friend," Darcy cheers me on. She is thrilled by my impromptu protest.

I spin back around, glaring at the traitors sipping their grande skinny mocha half-caf lattes like it's nothing. Like they are anywhere. Like what they are doing isn't a stab at the heart of the greatest city in the world. A heart dies if you stab it. Don't they understand that?

"Are you going in to complain?" Darcy asks. "You know I would fully support that."

"No. I'm going to complain right from here."

"Let's round up some more tourists you can yell at. The last ones weren't scared enough."

"Would you film me if I picket?"

"Of course."

"Thanks." There's a pile of collapsed and sliced cardboard boxes at the curb ready for recycling tomorrow. I go over to the pile and rummage around.

"Oh," Darcy says. "You meant now."

The perfect piece of cardboard presents itself. Big,

uncrushed, and smooth. I yank it from the pile.

"Hells yeah now," I say. "We're going beast mode up in here."

Darcy whoops. "All we need is a marker."

"Try borrowing one from Rocco's."

She goes into Rocco's while I wait outside Java Stop with my cardboard. At least Rocco's is still here after like forty years. It's not that I think ranting in front of Java Stop will make the rents in this neighborhood decrease. I'm sure that's why Bleecker Street Records and some other stores that had been here for decades were forced to move or fold. Rents in the West Village are outrageous. The little stores that were doing fine before can't afford to survive anymore. What's the heart of the Village going to be like twenty years from now? Or even ten? It would be a crying shame if New York ends up looking like any other American city.

Darcy skips over to me with a big red marker. "The cashier totally hooked us up."

"Awesome." I write SAVE THE WEST VILLAGE in tall red letters on my big cardboard sign. Then I stand right in front of the Java Stop window, holding the sign up in front of me. Darcy whips out her phone and starts filming. I don't yell. I don't scare any more tourists. I let my sign speak for itself.

An amazing thing happens as I'm taking a stand. This rush of elation overcomes me. I am confident. Empowered.

Happy. The rush is so strong I can feel it zipping through every part of me. I feel alive in a way I never quite have by myself before. Like I should be wearing a button that says GIRL POWER. Sadie Time is my time to focus on self-improvement. And being happy on my own. And accepting myself as a complete person. That's the power of a boy break. Right now isn't about finding love. It's about loving myself.

"What happened to the rant?" Darcy asks.

Only a few people have bothered to glance at my sign. Most people walking by have ignored me completely. The ones that noticed Darcy filming me probably think we're just some bored teens. Not activists making a statement.

Time to bring back the rant.

"There should not be a Java Stop where history was!" I yell. "Is this what the West Village is becoming? A strip mall you could find in any other city?!"

"Word," Darcy chimes in.

I rant on. Everyone passing by looks at me. More people are reading my sign. A few people hold up power fists. One girl cheers. A European tourist guy in tight red pants snaps a pic.

Then the Java Stop manager comes out.

"May I help you," he states.

"This is beyond your grasp," I say. "But thanks for checking."

"You're not allowed to film inside the store."

"Which . . . is . . . why . . . we're . . . outside?" Darcy snarks.

"You're filming into the store. That's not allowed."

Darcy films the manager telling her she's not allowed to film.

"I'm going to have to ask you to leave," he tells me.

I lower my sign. "The sign makes the most sense here, but I understand you're just doing your job."

"Thanks for not making a scene," he says.

"Oh, did you not see her a minute ago?" Darcy asks innocently. "She was making a really disturbing scene. Have the whole thing right here." She points to her phone, still filming.

A few minutes later, we move on. Physically. Emotionally I am still protesting the demise of my beloved neighborhood. I can't bring myself to put my sign down until a few blocks later. Then I wedge it between two paper recycling bags outside the Washington Mews, this quaint cobblestone path with cute little buildings. Maybe someone who lives there will find my sign and smile. My sign is the crudest warm fuzzy I've ever made, but considering how many people smiled when they walked past me holding it, I think that it qualifies.

I want to tell Darcy how I felt so confident and happy in my girl power moment of taking a stand. Only I can't think of the right words to explain it. Darcy is in girl power mode all the time. Darcy is the most badass person

I've ever met. She might think I'm ridiculous for feeling empowered just from a few minutes of ranting. And it's not like I can explain how my mini protest diluted the horror of Enraged Guy at the deli or the scary dream sensation that lingered from my nightmare. Better to keep moving on.

Live music is spilling out from a bar. The bar is luminous with red light. The front door is propped open with a stool that an enormous, disgruntled bouncer is sitting on.

"Wait," Darcy says. "I know that band."

Darcy goes right up to the bouncer, confident as ever. The bouncer shifts his harsh expression into one of admiration as Darcy charms him. It's so funny how Rosanna thinks I'm confident. She actually said her goal is to be as confident as me. Darcy is way more confident. My goal is to be as confident as *her*.

Darcy waves me over to the door. The bouncer lets us in. He doesn't even ask for my ID.

"I was right!" Darcy yells over the music when we're inside. "I totally know this band!"

"Who are they?"

"Residue!"

We grab seats in the back and watch the band. I love the lead singer's voice. He seems almost shy about singing, mostly looking down and doing this hunching/shrugging thing. But they're really good. As he sings moody lyrics to a slow song filled with longing and regret, I can feel the power of being in the Now that Darcy always talks about. Tonight was supposed to be all about me showing her the real New York. But she is showing me a side of New York I've never really noticed before. I would have never come into this bar with my other friends. Even if I wanted to, there's no way I would know how to get us in. Darcy's New York is like this secret wonderland I'm only starting to discover. She can unlock doors to this city that have never been opened for me before.

The moody song ends. The drummer clicks his sticks to a fast beat. A supernova of sound explodes, all heavy bass and frantic keys and much louder lyrics than I expected the lead singer to bust out. This guy and girl get up to dance, followed by a few more couples.

"Let's dance!" Darcy yells.

"With who?" I yell back.

"Each other!" She grabs my hand and pulls me right up in front of the stage. We dance like maniacs in the red light and the supernova sound in a place that is opening my eyes to the New York that's been here all along, waiting for me to find it.

Residue keeps the beat up for three more songs, stoked that people are so into them. Then they announce they're taking a break. Darcy and I spill back out into the night, laughing and breathless.

"You know what I'm in the mood for?" Darcy asks.

"What?"

"Sugar. Residue has that effect on me."

"Birthday cake time!"

"The deal was no birthday cake. But something else."

"How about warm cookies fresh out of the oven?"

"Girl, you are on fire today."

"This place has seriously delicious cookies. And it's a short walk from here."

"Yes, please."

We walk along East 11th Street toward Insomnia Cookies. I tilt my head back and look up. You could miss out on something magnificent if you don't look up.

"What are you looking at?" Darcy asks.

"See those trees on that rooftop terrace up there?"

Darcy tilts her head back and follows my gaze. "Yeah?"

"That freaking rules. I'm going to have a rooftop garden with trees."

"Are you having parties?"

"No doubt."

"Am I invited?"

"Only if I want my parties to be legendary."

"You know me so well already."

Looking up makes living here even more spectacular. Looking up anywhere does. When you look up, you notice all these beautiful details you would never notice otherwise. You become more in tune with the infinite possibilities this life brings. You open yourself to positive energy. You wake up.

Darcy freaks out at Insomnia Cookies. She gets a peanut butter and I get a triple chocolate chunk. They're warm and gooey. Darcy makes me promise to bring her back here again. We leave with our cookies and eat them as we walk farther east.

"I need to find a birthday candle for your cookie," I say. "So you can make a wish."

"You're forgetting that I'm not a birthday person."

"Not forgetting. Just . . . trying to change your mind."

Darcy looks up. "Check out that octopus mural!" she screams. There's a purple octopus painted high on the side of an apartment building. Tentacles are wrapping around some of the windows. The purple octopus seems right at home here in the East Village with the gritty building exteriors and rusted-out fire escapes and iron bars clamped over the ground-floor windows. It's fun being this far east for a change. Being a west side girl means rarely venturing east of 5th Avenue.

We're almost at Avenue B when I notice a majestic, expansive building across the street with a wide staircase and huge stone columns. You can tell it has remained unchanged since way back in the day. This building is probably one of the historically preserved structures that are protected from being knocked down or altered. Unlike Bleecker Street Records.

"What do you think used to be here?" I ask Darcy. We survey the building. I look up and see that it says FREE

PUBLIC BATHS OF THE CITY OF NEW YORK etched across the top.

"Let's find out." She whips out her phone. One thing Darcy is good at is whipping out her phone. She quickly finds a bunch of info. There was a public bath movement that began here in New York in the 1840s. A lot of apartments didn't have showers or even bathtubs back then. Free public baths in crowded tenement districts like the Lower East Side provided places where people could bathe. This building had seven bathtubs and ninety-four showers. The public baths closed in 1958, and then the building was used as a garage and warehouse. Now it's a posh photography studio. But the heart and soul of this building will always represent what it originally was.

There's a whole new part of New York I'm beginning to discover even though I've lived here my whole life. It's amazing how when you think you know someone or something so well, you can suddenly find out that there is so much more to see. At the same time, the New York City history I love so much is still here. I can find it anytime I want. All I have to do is look up.

TWENTY-NINE
DARCY

WAS IT WRONG OF ME to lie to Sadie when I told her I'm not a birthday person? Possibly. But the truth was too depressing to reveal.

I thought Logan was going to be the first person to call me today. He would call me before my first class and jack up my mood for the day. He would wish me a happy birthday. He would tell me where he was taking me for dinner. We would have this fun night we'd always remember. He didn't say anything about my birthday at the Standard. I thought that was strategic on his part. You know, not mentioning my birthday so I'd be more surprised when I found out what he had planned?

Yeah. Turns out there were no plans.

Logan didn't call me until this afternoon. He left a message while I was in Social Foundations. When I called him back after class, he sounded like he'd just woken up.

"Hey, babe," he slurred.

"Are you drunk?"

"No. Juss hungover. Stayed out too late with the boys last night."

Um, was I suddenly supposed to know who the boys were? Logan never tells me about his New York friends. Or where they hang out. Or what they do together when they stay out late and get wasted.

I waited for him to say happy birthday.

He didn't say anything. A muffled car alarm went off on his end.

"Are you at work?" I asked.

"Nah. Blew it off."

My stomach twisted in a slow, murky roll.

"So . . . ," I probed. "Do you have anything you want to tell me about tonight?"

"Like what?"

The way Logan said it wasn't like he was playing dumb. He wasn't trying to throw me off. He wasn't covering up a surprise party. Or planning any kind of surprise.

The surprise was that he forgot my birthday.

Oh, and then he said he was busy tonight. Something about the boys wanting a reprise.

When Sadie asked me why Logan wasn't taking me out tonight, I brushed it off with some nonsense about how I'm not a birthday person. That was such a lie. I freaking love birthdays. Mine, other people's, celebs', it doesn't matter. Any excuse to throw a party is a *mitzvah* in my book. My friends went all out on my seventeenth birthday. They did this whole "17 on the 17th" thing at the Penthouse. Everyone was there. We had a cupcake bar, three photo booths, and enough barbecue to feed a small country. They even got Ethan Cross's mixer to DJ. It was one of the best nights of my life.

Unlike tonight.

Don't get me wrong. Sadie is a doll for showing me a good time. The poor girl had like no advance notice. I told her I was in the mood for cookies because I couldn't stand the thought of her buying me a piece of cake somewhere and sticking a candle in it despite our deal that there would be no birthday fuss, which would be a total Sadie thing to do. Being reminded that it's my birthday all over again wasn't an appealing option. What would I even wish for? A boyfriend who remembered my birthday?

The delicious smell of Insomnia Cookies hits me half a block away. Warm cookies and melted chocolate and brown sugar. I could get high on this smell.

"Oh my god, that is the best smell ever," I say.

"Wait 'til you see the cookies." Sadie pulls open the door of Insomnia Cookies. She holds it open for me.

I take one step in. One step is pretty much all you can take in here. This is the smallest shop I've ever seen. Sadie told me how there are all these pop-ups in New York, tiny spaces that rent to stores on a temporary basis. Pop-ups can be even smaller than a food truck. They're sometimes just counters you go up to on the sidewalk. Insomnia Cookies is microscopic. There's a tiny counter along the window where you can eat your cookies. But that's it for staying. Unless you're scrunched up against the counter, you have to grab your cookies and go.

"How cute is this place?" I rave, whirring from a sugar contact high. "They need to bottle that warm cookie smell. I could seriously come here every day. This is—are those the cookies?!" My eyes pop at the cookie display. So many flavors. So little time.

Who knew that a low-key birthday could be so fun?

"I knew you'd love it," Sadie says. She's smiling all big. The girl loves making people happy.

We try to figure out which cookies we want while we're waiting. Way more people than should conceivably fit in here are crammed in line. Two boys around our age are wolfing cookies at the tiny counter. Guys are working back behind the register at the ovens. A fresh batch of peanut butter cookies comes out. So now I have to get a peanut butter cookie.

"What are you getting?" I ask Sadie.

"Triple chocolate chunk. My search for New York's best chocolate chip cookie is what brought me here in the first place. This one is definitely in the top five."

"Has this place been here a long time?"

"Oh yeah. Some Penn student started Insomnia Cookies in his dorm room back in 2003. Now they have tons of locations. I love inspirational stories like that. Can you imagine being him? You're at college in your dorm room, gaming with your roommates or whatever, wasting time. Then you have an idea for a business. But you're not thinking large-scale. Not yet. You're just like, 'Hey, wouldn't it be cool if there was a way to get warm cookies in the middle of the night? Delivered right to your door?' So he started this business at Penn and it exploded. Dude gets the Dream Big Award."

Sadie's excitement is infectious. I can almost hear another piece of my public relations career plan click into place. What if I represented kids like Insomnia Cookies Boy? High school and college students with big dreams, who deserve to be heard. The kind of kids who are making moves to bring their goals to life. Grownups underestimate the power of our energy. Teens are the most enthusiastic, passionate entrepreneurs. They are not afraid to take a chance on something that could fail. They take more risks. They are hungrier for meaning. More desperate to make something big happen in their immediate future. What if I were a publicist for the kids who are going to change the world?

Sadie can't contain herself when it's our turn to order.

"This is my friend Darcy," she tells the cashier. He's a

tall guy with hipster glasses and what might be ironic facial hair. His T-shirt shows a cookie with a bite out of it and a glass of milk holding hands. "It's her birthday."

"Happy birthday! This your first time here, Darcy?"

"Yes, and you will be seeing me again."

The cashier glances around behind him. He leans over to us.

"Don't tell anyone I did this? But your birthday cookie is on the house."

I gape at him. "You. Freaking. Rule." My peripheral vision catches one of the boys at the counter turning to look at me. His look lingers. But I don't look back. This is girls' night. Not about Sadie trying to make my birthday suck less and then me glomming on to some cute boy just because he's looking at me. Boys look in New York. They are not afraid.

I thank the cashier profusely for my warm peanut butter cookie. Then I pay for Sadie's. She deserves a hundred warm cookies. Warm cookies for life.

Some rowdy boys shoving their way in the door crash into the people behind us in line. As I turn around to leave, I get pushed into the cute boy at the counter.

"Sorry!" I apologize.

"That's okay. Anyone staying here to eat is asking for it." He has a nice smile. I can't help noticing how straight and white his teeth are. He must have had braces. His teeth are so white he probably whitens. Should I be whitening? My image has to be polished to a high shine if I'm going to be a publicist. Teeth included.

Back out on the street, we bite into our cookies. Talk about melt in your mouth. That Penn kid had the right idea. I can see myself discovering other young talent like him. Blowing them up even bigger than their wildest dreams. I could be known for finding the next big thing. My reputation would grow quickly. What would I call my agency? Darcy Stewart Public Relations? Publicity by Darcy? Branding is important. What you choose to call your agency speaks volumes. Maybe I'd go minimalist with a one-word agency name. That might add a touch of glamour and intrigue. My list would be highly exclusive.

A motorcycle rumbles by. The rider reminds me of Logan, the way he expertly maneuvers his bike like he owns the streets. So now I'm thinking of Logan all over again. What is he doing tonight? Getting drunk with the boys? Whoever they are? He didn't even tell me where he was going.

I want to get wasted. Why should Logan be the only one who gets to be wild? I'm in a questionable relationship with a boy who can't even be bothered to remember my birthday. And I can't be with the boy who would. If Jude knew when my birthday was, there's no way he'd forget. Jude is the kind of boy who would plan a super special day months in advance.

Boy drama shouldn't be invading my birthday chi. I could make it stop. I could numb the pain. But tonight is about chilling with Sadie. She didn't know me back in my wild days. She probably thinks I'm a wild child now.

If she only knew.

THIRTY

ROSANNA

MY GROUP VOTED ON HIDE-AND-SEEK for free play. Being a camp counselor means getting to play games I haven't played in years. It also means I get to make up rules on the spot while trying to sound like I know what I'm talking about.

"No going out of bounds," I instruct the group. "You have to stay on this floor." Good thing our camp is in a school on the Lower East Side instead of out in the wilderness. I could just see myself losing one of these girls in the woods.

"Can I be It first?" Jenny asks.

"Okay," I tell her.

"What should I count to?"

"Thirty. Count loudly so we can hear you. Everyone ready?"

The girls jump up and bunch by the classroom door. Jenny turns toward a window and puts her hands over her eyes. "One!" she starts counting.

We scatter. I haven't decided if I'm going to hide or supervise yet. When I see one of the girls cram herself into an empty bin in a dark classroom, I decide I better supervise.

"Twenty!" Jenny yells from her spot halfway down the hall. All of my other girls have hidden except for Momo.

"Where are you going to hide?" I whisper.

"I don't know!" she panic-whispers back. "Help me!"

We go into the nearest classroom. There's a tall free-standing closet in one corner. I swing the door open. Empty.

"How about in here?" I suggest.

"No," Momo says.

"There's plenty of room. It's empty."

"I don't want to."

"Twenty-five!" Jenny yells.

"Why not?" I ask.

"No!" Momo yells louder than Jenny. "I'm not going! Don't make me get in there!"

"Okay, okay. You don't have to. Sorry, it just looked like a good place to hide. We'll find somewhere else."

"Thirty!" Jenny yells. "Ready or not, here I come!"

"Um . . ." I look around the classroom. The closet is the only place to hide. Except behind the door. Under the desk is a possibility, but Momo would only be partially hidden. "How about behind the door?"

"Will you hide with me?"

My plan to supervise vanishes with one look at Momo's face. She seems way more terrified about hiding behind a door than anyone playing hide-and-seek should.

"Sure," I say.

We get behind the door. Momo's breathing is heavy. I can feel her shaking next to me. She shouldn't be acting like this. It's just hide-and-seek. But Momo is panting and sweating as if she's being hunted down by a serial killer.

That's it. Frank obviously intends to do nothing to help Momo. Which means I have to be the one to help her.

After camp I don't head to the subway to go home. I go to the main office. Cecelia works in the office for about an hour after camp gets out.

"Hi, Rosanna," Cecelia says from behind her desk. "How'd it go today?"

"Good. How was your day?"

"Oh, you know. Riveting as always." She gestures to a stack of file folders on the counter. "Applications for next year."

"Already?"

"We select our campers for next year by the end of the summer."

"I didn't realize you worked so far in advance."

"That's city-funded day camps for you. The competition is fierce."

"How do you decide who gets in?"

"We take everything into account: school transcripts, behavioral reports, financial need. The kids all write essays on why they want to be here. They're pretty cute. Especially the younger kids' essays."

I wonder what Momo wrote. Whatever it was, she must have appealed to the board of directors.

"So what's up?" Cecelia asks.

"Could I see a camper's file?"

"Frank doesn't like us sharing them, but I can tell you whatever you want to know."

I ask for Momo's address. Cecelia checks her computer and tells it to me. I write the address down in my small notebook.

"She lives in the Mott Haven projects," Cecelia says. "Have you been to the South Bronx before?"

"No."

"It's a pretty rough area."

Cecelia might know why I wanted Momo's address. But if she's guessing why, she doesn't say. And I don't explain. The less she knows, the better. I wouldn't want her to get in trouble with Frank if he found out she knew my plan but didn't tell him.

At the subway station, I ask the lady working in a booth

how to get to Momo's neighborhood. She barks at me through the intercom. Her voice crackles, obscuring her words to the point where I don't even know if she's speaking English. I bend down to the little circle covered with mesh below the window that I am assuming is a microphone and ask her to please repeat that. She barks louder that I have to take the 6 train. It's like she's angry at me for daring to ask a question. People who hate their job shouldn't take it out on the rest of us. Especially when their job involves helping other people.

The barking subway station lady has left me frazzled. I find a map on the wall to get a better idea of where I'm going. Between what Cecelia said about Momo's neighborhood and having absolutely no clue of what I'm going to find once I get there, I'm kind of a mess. But there's no way I'm backing down.

The subway ride up to the South Bronx is long. I take out my book and lose myself in a love story. I can always count on Jennifer E. Smith to soothe me. But I'm nervous about missing my stop. As the street numbers get higher, I peer out the window at each stop to see where I am. Finally the train slows down as it approaches my stop. I bolt up from my seat too early and have to catch myself from toppling over when the train jerks to a stop. Graceful as always. One day I will master the art of subway riding. When I get on the subway, I won't sit down just as the train bolts forward to leave the station, flinging me into whoever is sitting or standing nearby. My timing will be perfect when I get up from my seat to leave. I will be intuitive and effortless, fluidly navigating each subway car I ride like a real New Yorker. No one will be able to tell I moved here from somewhere else.

My heart pounds as I climb the stairs out of the station. Whenever I emerge from a subway station, I have no idea which way to go. It took me like ten different times before I learned which way to go when leaving the regular stops I use to get to camp and back home. So here I am spinning around outside the subway station like a dingbat target in a foreign neighborhood, clearly lost and searching for landmarks that don't exist.

I pick a direction and start walking. I can always turn around if I'm going the wrong way. The last thing I'd do is ask for directions. Advertising that I don't know where I'm going would make me an even bigger target. No one knows I'm here. Cecelia might have her suspicions, but she wouldn't have a chance to save me if I were attacked on the street. Or chopped up in some rapey dude's freezer.

People are giving me strange looks. I'm wearing the T-shirt all the counselors have to wear. It says LOWER EAST DAY CAMP on the front and COUNSELOR on the back. Not exactly blending in with the girls in this neighborhood. Their goal is apparently to show as much skin as possible. Guys are loitering on street corners and stoops. A rowdy pack of boys hanging out in front of a mini-mart catcall as I zoom by. I focus on hurrying and keeping my eyes on the ground.

I hate myself for acting this way. One goal of being a social worker is to help people in low-income areas like this one. Yet I'm acting like I'm scared to be here. Actually . . . I am scared. The South Bronx is a lot grittier than I expected. I don't know what I thought I'd find. Not the burned-out husks of abandoned buildings, vacant lots piled with random debris, and graffiti sprayed everywhere. The energy here is totally different than the West Village. How can two parts of the same city be so different?

I stop for a second outside a Laundromat to surreptitiously check the folded Google Map I printed in the main office before I left camp. The map confirms that I'm going the wrong way. Passing that rowdy pack of boys again is not going to be fun. I take a deep breath, turn around, and tell myself to ignore the catcalls as I zoom by again.

"Coming back for seconds, *mami*?"

"You like a supermodel workin' that runway."

"Lemme get a piece of that white-girl ass!"

My face burns until I can turn a corner a few blocks away. I take more deep breaths until I stop shaking. I'm too afraid to peek around the corner to see if they are coming after me. They might see me peeking and take it as an invitation to harass me some more. But I don't hear their voices getting louder or anything. They're not coming after me.

Momo's building is part of a complex of buildings that all look the same: tall and brown with lots of small windows close together. I find the right one. Her apartment is on the third floor. At first I'm worried that her mom won't buzz me up. Luckily a group of people are going in as I get to the front doors. I follow them inside. They crowd into the elevator with a baby carriage. Instead of crowding into the elevator with them, I step back and take the next one.

The elevator opens on the third floor to a long hallway that wraps all the way around the building. A sign on the wall across from the elevators shows which way to go for Momo's apartment. The hallway smells like someone is smoking in one of the apartments and cooking onions in another. A woman is yelling behind one of the doors. I can hear a baby crying somewhere in the distance. Music blares behind the door next to Momo's.

This is it. This is where she lives.

My heart leaps into my throat as I ring the doorbell. I still don't know what I'm going to say. I've imagined this scenario a thousand times, but all the words I've said in my head seem wrong now. How can I find out if Momo's mom is abusing her without coming right out and asking? And what do I expect her to say? Yeah, I am, thanks for stopping by?

The door opens a few inches. A pretty girl who looks just like Momo peers out at me. She must be Momo's older sister. I wonder why Momo never mentioned she had a sister. She told me she just lives with her mom.

"Can I help you?" she asks.

"Hello," I attempt to say in a professional manner. But it comes out all stuttery. I try again. "Hi. I'm Rosanna Tranelli. A counselor at Momo's camp?"

She opens the door a few more inches. "Is everything okay?"

"Everything's fine. I just . . . wanted to come by. The camp director has been trying to get in touch with your mom. Is she home?"

"My mother doesn't live here."

"Oh."

"Why would he be calling my mother?"

My heart races. How am I supposed to answer that? If I went with the truth, I would have to admit that I reported suspected abuse and he's following up. Then her mom would avoid talking to me like she's avoiding Frank. Of course her mom lives here. Maybe she tells her daughters to lie to any strangers who come by unannounced.

"Sorry to show up like this," I say. "I was just hoping to talk with your mom for a few minutes."

"My mother has no business here. I'm raising my own child."

Wait. What?

"If there's a problem with Momo, you can talk directly to me," she continues.

"So you're . . . are you . . . Momo's mom?"

She looks at me like I'm an idiot. "Who did you think you were talking to?"

Okay. My mind is officially blown. How can this girl have an eight-year-old daughter? She doesn't look much older than me.

The baby crying in the distance is screaming now.

"My work schedule is crazy," she says, unfazed by the screaming baby. "That's why I haven't had a chance to call Frank back. Didn't think he'd send someone in person."

"He didn't send me." Great. Compromise myself more, why don't I. Now I'm some stalker freak. So much for playing this off as official camp business.

"Then why are you here?"

"Um, well—"

"Is she acting up again?"

"What do you mean?"

"She likes to talk back. Has she been giving you sass?"

"Oh, no! Momo is wonderful. She's very sweet."

"Then what's the problem?"

"She seems . . . kind of nervous. Jumpy. Loud noises scare her. And today she was afraid to play hide-and-seek. I was wondering if you knew what might be causing her behavior."

"She's always been a jittery little girl. Nothing to worry about."

Momo's mom hasn't invited me in. We're still standing in her doorway with the door halfway open. I was hoping to see Momo's room. Maybe get a chance to look around a little. That's what a good social worker would do while making a house call. Inspect the premises.

Momo's mom gives me a brief, tight smile. "It was nice of you to come all this way. Tell Frank I'll call him soon?"

"Okay. Thanks for speaking with me."

She closes the door softly.

I linger at the door. The conversation feels unfinished. There is so much more I want to say.

I'm in a foul mood on the way home. Momo's mom was nice enough, but I still feel like something is off. My gut says there is more to the story than what she told me. Which was essentially nothing.

Something is wrong, but I don't know the right questions to ask. How can I uncover the truth when Momo's mom is hiding it? I have no clue where to go from here.

There's a note on my pillow from Sadie when I get home. She said to call her when I get in to meet up with her and Darcy. But I feel gross. I don't want to infect Sadie and Darcy with my foul mood. All I want to do is crawl into bed. After I call D.

I stayed out on the roofdeck Sunday after D left to take Shayla to the clinic. By the time he came back two hours later, my jealousy had already taken control of my emotions again. It wasn't enough to tell myself to stop being so insane. Trusting that D and Shayla were just friends was going to take a lot more than simply wanting to trust him.

D was all smiling and kissing me and pretending like he didn't just leave me for her. Was he trying to be extra nice because he knew he messed up? Or was he just being a clueless boy?

I can't wait to tell D about going to Momo's apartment. He thinks I am someone who takes action, who isn't afraid to make a difference in the world as much as I want to in my heart. D will let me see the experience of talking to Momo's mom through his eyes. He will snap me out of my foul mood. And he will know what I should do next.

Except D doesn't pick up when I call.

I don't leave a message.

We didn't make plans to see each other again when I left his place on Sunday. D said he would call me. That was two days ago. I haven't heard from him since. And now he's not picking up.

My gut is clamoring for attention. It's telling me something is off with us, too. D and I should be getting closer. This weird radio silence where I don't even know if it's okay to call him should not be happening.

I know my gut is not wrong. Not about D. And not about Momo.

THIRTY-ONE
SADIE

WHEN I UNDERSTOOD THE RELEVANCE of that big yellow umbrella on *How I Met Your Mother*, I had to get a big yellow umbrella just like it. I always take my *How I Met Your Mother* umbrella out with me when it's supposed to storm. Searching for an umbrella exactly like the one on the show wasn't easy. But I finally found one. My philosophy was that if I carried the same umbrella around in the same city where the show took place, the same soul mate magic that found Ted Mosby would find me.

I grabbed that umbrella on the way out the door tonight.

That guy Danny who plays guitar at Strawberry Fields said he's there on Wednesday nights. The way he said it, it was like he wanted me to come by. Going to see Danny play was not something I had planned. But I felt like going out after I got home from my internship, and Rosanna and

Darcy were both out and it happened to be a Wednesday. Swinging by to see Danny does not count as a disruption of my boy break. It's just something fun to do on a summer night.

Strawberry Fields is a part of Central Park that's near Hernshead, the hilly section where my annual Remembrance Walk meets. I walk through Strawberry Fields on my way to Hernshead for that event every year, since it's a day of remembrance. Strawberry Fields was created as a memorial to John Lennon. It's across from the Dakota, where John lived before he got shot. Beatles fans, musicians, and tourists flock to Strawberry Fields as a way to be close to him. People sit around the Imagine mosaic on the ground or play Beatles songs on their guitars like Danny. So I'm not going to Strawberry Fields specifically to see Danny. I'm going for the whole experience.

Music drifts over to me as I cross Central Park West toward the park. I twist around to look up at the Dakota. John Lennon would probably still be living there today if he hadn't been shot right outside his front door. He was coming home on December 8, 1980. He got out of a limo by the entrance of the Dakota. He was walking toward the front door when he was shot by a lunatic who was waiting for him to come home. He was rushed to the hospital, but was dead on arrival. John Lennon was murdered by a random act of anger that could not be prevented by his thousands of acts of kindness.

This is not the world I want to live in. People shooting people on the street. People killing people on the subway. Including people who aren't even born yet. The limitations of positive energy are infuriating. Lunatics are everywhere. Enraged Guy at the deli, the dimwits who pushed my mom on the subway, the deranged guy who shot John Lennon . . . Nothing could stop them from unleashing their rage. I want to believe that positive energy makes people more aware of how their negative choices impact the world. I know it does. But damn . . . John Lennon died because some lowlife shot him right outside his home. What's the point of anything when tragedy can happen anywhere, anytime, to anyone?

Danny is perched on top of a backrest of one of the benches that circle the Imagine mosaic. He's jamming on his guitar with three other guys playing "Things We Said Today." The other guys are old, like in their thirties and forties. One of them is sitting on the ground playing an acoustic guitar that looks so beat up it might crumble to bits any second. The other two guys are sitting on the bench Danny is perched on. One of them is playing a flute. The other is singing.

The bench on the opposite side of the mosaic is empty. I sit down and watch Danny play. He has this intensity you don't usually see in guys. You can tell he loves being here. The way he closes his eyes while he plays his guitar, slowly shaking his head. How he watches the mosaic reflectively.

He even turns to look up at the Dakota at one point. I feel this sense of connection to him even though I don't really know him. The vibe he gives off as he strums his guitar to "The Night Before" is familiar. I recognize emotional turmoil. Danny is another broken soul who comes here trying to heal, just like so many others do. Just like I do.

Eventually Danny sees me. At first I can't tell if he recognizes me. He gazes over the mosaic and catches my eye. His gaze is dreamy at first, then sharpens into focus. He smiles and kind of bows his head at me. I smile back.

The jam session ends after a few more songs. Tourists take pictures around the Imagine mosaic. The musicians stick around to talk to people. Danny packs up his guitar and crosses over to me.

"Hey," he says. "Thanks for coming."

"You were awesome."

Danny sits down next to me. He leans back on the bench, stretching his legs out in front of him. "Trying to be awesome, anyway."

"No, you're officially awesome."

"Possibly remotely awesome."

"How did you meet those other guys?"

"They've been coming here for years. They were down with letting me join in when I started playing guitar about a year ago. I'm hoping they'll still let me jam with them after my grown-up job starts. Don't want them thinking I sold out."

"You're like the opposite of selling out."

"Aw." Danny nudges his shoulder against mine. "Go on."

"You're a genuine person. I hardly know you and I can tell you're the real deal."

"How much am I paying you for the compliments again?"

I laugh. Danny is helping me remember how mellow summer nights like this can get heavy and introspective, but can also make me so happy. Instead of worrying about one of the many Austin mines buried around this city, ready to explode, I finally feel like I'm reclaiming my city. Like I'm remembering who I really am. Reconnecting with the heart of me.

Tree leaves rustle. The comforting smell of warm pretzels from the cart outside Strawberry Fields wafts over. With the cool summer breeze, I remember the essence of those epic feelings I had before I met Austin. I knew my soul mate was here somewhere. I knew we would meet someday soon. Despite the devastation with Austin, deep down I can never give up hope of finding the person I'm meant to be with. I can't let negative experiences prevent me from living the life I want to live.

"So what's your story, Sadie?" Danny asks. "You into the Beatles?"

"Who isn't?"

"You'd be surprised. This world is filled with an abundance of ignorance."

"Tell me about it. I was thinking about John Lennon before. How he was killed right outside his building."

"Unreal, right?"

"I hate that something so tragic can happen anytime. It shouldn't be allowed."

"By who?"

"By anyone. The world just shouldn't work like that. We should be better than this." Rosanna is always saying how people could be better versions of themselves by caring more about the world around them. And I know how powerful kindness can be. Why don't people care more about how they're affecting others?

"That was John's message," Danny said. "'Give peace a chance.'"

A wave of sorrow hits me. Danny feels it, too. I don't have to tell him about my personal grief for him to get me. We can just sit here like this, on a contemplative summer night, sharing the loss.

One second we are staring in silence at the Imagine mosaic.

The next we are nearly drenched in a sudden downpour.

Girls shriek. Guys yell. Everyone makes a run for it.

Danny springs up from the bench, grabbing his guitar

case. "Come on!" he yells. He wants to make a run for it, too. But I pop open my big yellow umbrella and shelter him. It's a big enough umbrella for both of us.

We walk calmly out of Strawberry Fields as people race past us. Car tires make slick fizzing sounds on the wet street as they roll by. I can't wait until after the rain. I love it when the air is fresh and everything shines in the city lights. That's when New York feels the most glamorous to me. The classic city of Tiffany's and FAO Schwarz, high tea at the Plaza and drinks at the Rainbow Room, the Empire State Building and Rockefeller Center. The contemporary city of Soho galleries, green architecture, and infinite possibility around every corner. My beloved New York City, then and now.

"Which way are you going?" I ask as we cross Central Park West.

"One train."

"Same here."

"*Yes*. I don't care if I get soaked, but my baby is another story." Danny pats his guitar case.

"Don't worry. I would walk you wherever you had to go. I wouldn't let either of you get soaked."

Danny gets a twinkle in his eye. I get a twinge of wanting to break my boy break. But tonight isn't about Danny. Danny is a symbol. He's a sign from the Universe, telling me that more soul mates are here. The key is to never give up. If you never stop believing the love of your life is out there, if you know in your heart that true love is your destiny, you will find the love you want.

People aren't perfect. Neither is love. Soul mates aren't always people you can, or even should, be with. But now that I know how it feels to be with a soul mate, I refuse to settle for anything less.

THIRTY-TWO
DARCY

WHY HELLO, DOLCE FAUX-ALLIGATOR STRUC-TURED tote winking at me in the boutique window. I think I'll come on in and snatch you up.

I stride into the boutique, making a beeline for the Dolce totes display. This was not a chance occurrence. The instant I flipped through the pages of *Vogue* and saw this exquisite bag, I knew I must possess it. The way the bag is flirting is further proof that it was made for me. Darcy Stewart knows what she likes and she knows how to get it.

The cashier takes my credit card. And the world as I know it starts to crumble.

"I'm sorry," he says. "Your card has been declined."

"What?"

"Yeah, it's . . ." He tries running it again. "The same alert keeps coming up."

This is exactly what happened to Logan's cards at the Standard. Did my card get switched with one of his? I was crushing so hard on this tote I didn't even look at my card when I took it out of my wallet.

"Can I see it?" I put my hand out for him to give me the card back. But he doesn't hand it over. He holds the card up in front of me so I can see it. My name, my card. "Oh. That's my card."

"I'm sorry about this." The cashier presses his lips together, giving me a sympathetic look. "The bank is saying I have to confiscate your card."

My heart hammers. This is the only credit card I have. I use it every day.

"There must be a mistake," I say. "It was working fine yesterday."

He shakes his head, looking at the screen again. The screen that's telling him to confiscate my credit card like I'm some kind of criminal.

"Is there someone I can call?" I try. "This is the only credit card I have. It's basically what I use for everything."

"The only thing you can do is call the credit card company and have them send you a new one. If there really was a mistake, they should be able to get a new card out to you tomorrow."

How weird is this? First Logan's cards are all denied. And now mine? What the hell?

"Would it be okay to take my card back? Just until I find

out what's going on?"

He throws me another pity look. "I'm supposed to cut it up."

Slow your roll, Cashier Boy. No one's destroying my credit card.

"Wait, let me just . . ." I take my phone out and call Daddy. It goes to voice mail. "My dad's not answering. He would know if there was a problem."

"There *is* a problem. I'm sorry, but—"

"It's okay. I know you're just doing your job. I'll call him later and have a new card sent out. This one probably died from overuse."

The cashier smiles, relieved I'm not diving over the counter and tackling him for the card. "That has been known to happen." He takes a thick pair of scissors out of a drawer. I watch him cut my credit card in half. Then in quarters. And then he throws the pieces away.

I try calling Daddy again as I leave the shop. My mom isn't going to know anything about this. Still no answer. He's probably in a meeting. I'll keep trying him until he picks up. I start walking home, telling myself to keep calm and rock on. There's always the ATM if I'm desperate for cash.

When my phone rings a few minutes later, I'm expecting it to be Daddy. It's Logan. My first instinct is to tell him about my card being confiscated. But then I remember that none of the cards he tried at the Standard were confiscated.

They were denied, but he got them all back. The thing with my card was probably a glitch on Daddy's end. Maybe the card reached its limit or something. Unless . . . Daddy didn't cut me off, did he? The deal was that I get good grades and he covers the credit card bills. My art history grade is questionable, but grades aren't out yet. What if he saw the Standard charge, flipped out, and canceled my card? How am I going to explain why I stayed at a swanky hotel?

"Hey, Gorgeous," Logan drawls when I pick up.

A tight *hi* is all I give him back. I'm super tense about the credit card annihilation. And I'm still pissed that he forgot my birthday. Three days later and he still hasn't mentioned it. There's been no "I am so sorry I forgot your birthday! I'm such an idiot. But you already knew that," or "Will you ever forgive me for forgetting your birthday? Let me spend every single day making it up to you," or "I'm taking you out for the birthday dinner that should have happened on your birthday. Prepare to be spoiled like you've never been spoiled before." Logan has said none of those things. He hasn't even cared that I've been blowing him off. For a boy who supposedly came here to win me back, his attempts aren't exactly dazzling.

"What are you up to tonight?" Logan drawls some more.

"I don't know yet. Maybe going out and getting wasted."

"Want to get wasted with me?"

It's Friday night. I tackled three major exams this week. There's a massive paper due on Monday that I do not even want to think about. Daddy's threat to cut me off if my grades suck looms over the rest of the summer like a dark storm cloud. And that was before the possibility that he went ballistic over the Standard charge. Oh yeah, and Logan's hot for me one minute, cold the next. All I want to do tonight is go out, find where the party's at, and forget about everything else.

A ridiculously gorgeous guy coming my way locks eyes with me. He doesn't drop the eye lock as we pass each other. I could have talked to him if I wanted. I could have hooked up with him. The control I potentially have over him brings a whoosh of endorphins, making me feel insanely powerful. Boys are like the only thing I consistently have control over.

"You still there?" Logan asks.

"Tonight's not going to work," I tell him.

"How about—"

"I gotta go." I hang up before I let Logan talk me into anything. He's not the one I want to see.

Before I realize what's happening, I'm at the park. Jude's park. Somehow I walked here without planning to. But I don't go up to Jude. I keep my distance, hiding behind a tree and convincing myself that I am exhibiting completely normal behavior. Spying on the boy I like from afar does not make me a creeper. I'm simply being respectful of Jude's need for space.

Jude is performing a trick with a glittery gold Hula-Hoop. He holds the Hula-Hoop up and throws a gold foam ball through it. The ball doesn't come out the other side. It vanishes into thin air. He repeats the trick a few times, smiling like he's having the best time ever. I'm not close enough to hear what people are saying, but I know they are in awe of Jude. We all are.

Watching Jude in action, I can't help wondering what my summer would have been like if we were together. What if Logan never showed up? What if Jude and I had the whole summer to be in lust? Or maybe even to fall in love? I wasn't expecting to find love when this summer started. But watching Jude now and remembering how amazing it felt to be with him, the possibility of loving him feels right.

Watching from a distance is too painful. It's time to go home.

When I open the front door of my building, the momentary high I got from watching Jude vanishes into thin air like that gold ball. Actually, not thin air. More like heavy, humid, oppressively hot air. The dark storm cloud is back. It follows me up the three flights of stairs to the apartment. The only thing I can think about is getting in a cool shower with lots of soapsuds.

When I open the door, I'm engulfed by even more hot air. The apartment is stifling. The air in here feels like it's been baking all day and then got hotter when the heat was accidentally turned on. I didn't even know an apartment could get this hot.

Rosanna comes out of her room. I can't believe she's home.

"Why didn't you turn on the air conditioner?" I say. "It's broiling in here." I go over to the living room air conditioner and snap it on.

"Do you know how much our electricity bill is?"

"Of course I know. We each pay one-third of it."

"More like your daddy pays one-third," she mumbles.

I whip around. "Excuse me?"

"We each pay one-third. Meaning I pay one-third. So I have a say in whether I want the air conditioner on."

"Well, I'm getting ready to go out and I'm not leaving here looking like a hot mess. The air conditioner stays on."

"Fine. Then you should pay more than one-third of the electricity bill this month."

"Fine, I will."

Rosanna stares at me. It's a hard stare I've never seen on her before.

"Are you okay?" I ask.

"No. No, I'm not okay. Not at all."

She looks like she's about to have a breakdown. Or maybe she already has. I could be walking into some sort of freaky aftermath. How much do I really know about this girl? Only what she's told me and what I can deduce from her behavior. I'm beginning to think she has mood swings on the reg. Could she be bipolar? There aren't any prescription meds in our medicine cabinet, but she could be hiding them in her room. She could be covering up a whole other side of her she doesn't want me or Sadie to know.

I follow Rosanna into her room. The contents of her closet are strewn everywhere: all over the floor, on her bed, hanging from the door. Her closet door is flung open. All that's left hanging are the hangers.

"What's going on?" I say.

Rosanna scoops up a bunch of clothes from her bed. They are all clothes I gave her.

"Take these back," she says.

"They're yours," I say slowly, surveying her room. "I want you to have them."

"I didn't earn them. I didn't buy them. They don't belong to me."

"They were a gift."

"It doesn't matter how hard I work, does it?" Rosanna stands there holding the pile of clothes, that hard stare freaking me out all over again. "I must have been delusional to think I could reinvent myself."

"Look, I don't know what's going on—"

"You'd never understand. You people think you can

buy anything. But some things aren't for sale."

Seriously with this girl? I tried to be patient. I tried to be understanding. When she ripped me a new one that night she made me clean the living room, I restrained myself from blowing up at her. But she can't keep attacking me and expect me to just take it. Whatever's wrong with Rosanna, I've had enough. She needs to know that I will not be pushed around. Especially after executing a major fashion hack with her new wardrobe, thank you very much.

"What is your problem?" I ask.

"My problem. Is spoiled rich kids who don't know how lucky they are. You have everything you want and you don't even appreciate it."

I sweep my hands toward the heap of clothes she's holding. "Did I not buy you all of those clothes?"

Rosanna throws the clothes she's holding at me. Some flop against my stomach. The rest fall to the floor. "Take them! Take them all back! I told you I didn't want them! I asked you to return them and you wouldn't!"

"I was trying to help you!"

"I don't need your charity!"

"And I don't need you blasting the same song on repeat a thousand times or skulking around in your ratty robe like some crazy bag lady, but here we are!"

We stand there glaring at each other. Clothes scattered around me. The suffocating heat making my head throb.

"At least I don't snore!" Rosanna jabs.

Oh no she *didn't*. "If you want to be ungrateful, that's your problem. But I'm not taking these clothes back." I stomp toward the door, whipping back around to have the final word. "Any time you want to apologize, you know where I live."

Rosanna doesn't come to my room to say she's sorry while I'm getting ready. I look in her room on my way out. She's bent over her bed, picking up the last of the wardrobe explosion. The clothes I gave her are packed away neatly in a big, clear bin.

She snaps the lid shut.

THIRTY-THREE
ROSANNA

SOMEONE WATCHING ME RIGHT NOW wouldn't notice anything unusual. A camp counselor putting her group of girls on the bus that takes them home every day. Hugging a girl who gave her a necklace she made with pink and purple beads. Laughing at something another girl with rainbow tie-dyed shoelaces said. Telling the girls to have a fun weekend. The same routine someone would see if they were watching me out in front of the school any Friday after camp.

There is someone watching me right now. She's standing across the street, leaning against the chain-link fence, one leg bent up behind her. She is too far away for me to tell if I know her. But I get the feeling I've seen her before. Normally I wouldn't even notice someone standing across the street. Only . . . this girl is fixated. Her concentration is so blistering it's radioactive.

The bus pulls away. I shade my eyes under the blinding sun, trying to figure out who that girl is. She pushes off from the chain-link fence. She starts walking toward me.

When she crosses the street, I realize who she is.

Nasty Girl. Addison.

The girl who spilled punch on me at the camp party. Who lied about working at the other camp.

The girl who told those horrible lies about me to Mica. Mica, who was going to be my good friend. Mica, who won't talk to me anymore.

The girl who hates me even though I'd never seen her before in my life.

I wipe nervous sweat from above my mouth. I cannot believe Addison is so twisted she's stalking me at my job. My heart is racing like it's going for a state record, doing wind sprints and jumping hurdles. Am I finally going to get answers to the questions that have been hammering away at me every single day?

Addison comes right up to me like she belongs here. All the other counselors are gone. The campers have all been picked up by guardians or taken away in buses. No one else is around. A shot of panic makes my heart race even faster. Addison could do anything she wants to me. Right out here in the open. There would be no witnesses. A few people are walking by across the street, but I seriously doubt any of them would notice us. Unless I screamed.

"Hello, Rosanna." Addison doesn't bother fake smiling. This time she's practically seething.

"What are you doing here? I know you aren't a counselor at the sister camp." I hope my pounding heart isn't showing. I would glance down at my shirt to check, but I don't want to break my gaze. A steady gaze implies confidence. She cannot know how afraid I am right now.

Addison is unfazed by getting called out. "Thanks for the discovery, Nancy Drew. Do you also know I don't really live in Mica's building?"

"What?"

"Yeah . . . I lied to Mica about us having the same housing. I actually lied about a lot of things. Sound familiar?"

"Why did you tell her those lies about me?"

"But I do live here," Addison continues, ignoring my question. "In New York, I mean. Born and raised. So when I heard you were going to UNY and working here this summer, it was perfect."

My heart stops racing. No more sprints. No more hurdles. My blood is cold as ice.

"How do you know about me?" I ask. "All that stuff you told Mica. How do you know all of that?"

"Oh, did I forget to introduce myself? My bad." Addison sticks her hand out for me to shake, then drops it. "You know my uncle. Or, you knew my uncle. Back in Chicago? There was this rumor going around that he molested you. Do you know who started it?"

Oh.

My.

God.

The man who molested me when I was eleven was someone's uncle.

He was Addison's uncle.

Addison takes a step closer to me. Mascara is smudged under the outer corner of her left eye. There's something tangy on her breath. Sugary orange. No, grapefruit. Her gold metal bracelets clink together when she reaches up to tighten her ponytail.

"Because I heard it was you," she says.

My mind begins to wrap around the horrifying reality that Addison is the niece of the man who molested me. But she's not on my side. She isn't about to apologize for what her uncle did.

She doesn't believe he did anything wrong.

"If you can spread lies about my uncle? One of the kindest, most generous people I've ever known? Then I have no problem spreading lies about you."

"I didn't lie."

"Did you really think you could get away with it? He's a good person. A real person. With a real family. A family who cares about him. A family who would do anything for him." Addison shoves me. Not hard. Just hard enough to jostle me. "Including revenge."

"Why would I lie about that?"

"Duh, for attention. Stupid girls do stupid things."

"Addison. Think about it. Your uncle threatened to hurt my little sister if I told anyone what he was doing to me. The only reason it got out there is because I told my best friend and she told her mom. It's not like I was broadcasting what he was doing."

"But your lies about him got out there." Addison traces a manicured finger over the loop of her gold hoop earring. She squints at me like I am a lab specimen she's been assigned to observe. "You pushed him out of his town. He was forced to move away, which he couldn't afford. He's still in debt because of you. You destroyed his entire life."

What about how he destroyed my life? What about how it's such a challenge for me to trust D, or how I'm scared to move forward with him physically? Why is Addison so determined to believe nothing happened to me?

"I didn't lie," I repeat. But I can tell no matter how many times I repeat the truth, Addison will never believe me. She made up her mind about me a long time ago. Nothing I can do will change her beliefs.

"Did that punch stain ever come out?" Addison asks innocently.

"Why were you at that party if you don't work at the other camp?"

"Because I knew you'd be there, silly! Donovan's sister is super friendly. She didn't even question me when we met and I said I was a counselor. She told me about the party and everything. So I wasn't technically crashing. I haven't seen her since the party. How *is* she?" Addison blinks at me with icy eyes. "Oh, that's right. You and Donovan don't hang out with his sister, do you? Why do you think that is?"

My face burns with shame. I've been wondering the same thing. He hasn't introduced me to his parents yet, either.

"Yeah." Addison sneers. "That's what I thought. You know what else I think? I think things are about to get ugly for you. Real ugly." She pokes me hard in the center of my chest. "I know where you work." *Poke.* "I know where you live." *Poke.* "I know more about you than you want me to know. And I'm not shy about using any of it. Oh, and I know all about Donovan, too. Which reminds me . . . how gorgeous is Shayla? We hung out last night. Shayla was at this club I just happened to be at."

Fear tightens my throat.

"We didn't talk for that long, though," Addison continues. "Just long enough for me to tell Shayla that you're going to break up with Donovan. You know, just so she would know he's available. As if she's not already acting like he is. But don't worry—I swore her to secrecy."

I can't breathe. There's so much I want to say to Addison. But I can't breathe. I want to tell her off. I want to tell her to go to hell. I want to be fierce and confident and say that if she ever comes near me or anyone else in my life again,

I will take her down. But none of these things come out. The sad truth is that I'm afraid of her. I'm afraid that if I say any of these things I want to, she will come at me even harder. She's already angry enough. One wrong move and I could tip her over the edge.

"Anyway." Addison gives me a bright smile. "Be seeing you around." She turns on her heel and leaves me speechless and shaken under the blazing sun.

I mentally beat myself up on the subway ride home. Why didn't I say more? Why didn't I stick up for myself? That was my chance to speak up. I had a chance to defend myself and I blew it. I hate myself for letting her intimidate me. I feel so repulsive I can't even stand to be in my own skin. I am completely violated. Addison ripped me apart until I was naked. She scraped out my insides, ground them into the hot gravel, and smeared them down my chest. And I just stood there and let her do it.

By the time I climb out of the searing subway station, my fear and pain have expanded to fill every crevice in my body. I catch my reflection in some storefront glass. Frazzled. Sweaty. Gross. On the verge of tears. Is this how I look? I'm disgusting. My hair is spazzing out. The heinous combination of unbearable heat and humidity has whipped my hair into a curly, frizzy mess. This is my hair for the rest of my life. I'll never be able to afford to straighten it. Or even to afford better products to tame it. I am, and will always be, at the mercy of external variables.

The more I think about Addison and how her uncle took advantage of me, the more depressed I become. I try to be a good person. I'm struggling to scrape by even though I work hard. That's okay with me. But when it's still not enough to prevent abuse, torment, and deceit, that's not okay. I'm working harder than ever and for what? To be taken advantage of all over again? I thought I could start a shiny new life here. Reinvent myself in a city where no one knew me. But I was wrong. My past will always follow me. People like me will always get shafted while people like Darcy will keep getting more privileges. Darcy will never have to worry about the things I do, from big picture to trivial details. Right down to her hair. She has the kind of straight hair that does exactly what she wants it to do. Everything has been served to Darcy on a silver platter, superior genetics included.

By the time I get home, the subject of my miserable mental ruminating has shifted from Addison to Darcy. What kind of fantasy world was I living in, accepting those clothes from her? Darcy bought those clothes for me out of pity. She obviously sees me as a charity case. I thought we were actually becoming friends. What a joke.

The apartment is sweltering. But I don't care. Turning on the air conditioner would be like throwing money out the window. I'd rather sweat and save. I strip off my camp clothes and put on the skimpiest shorts and tank I have. Then I yank every piece of clothing Darcy gave me out of my closet and throw everything in a heap on my bed. I rip all of my other clothes off their hangers mercilessly, the way Addison ripped into me.

My face burns with shame as I think about how I've been prancing around in these fabulous clothes Darcy gave me. Like I belonged in them. Darcy doesn't know what it's like to be so poor you can't afford to buy the yearbook, pretending like you're bringing back autograph books that year. Or what it's like to rummage through used clothes at thrift stores that kids from your school donated during charity drives, only to be exposed by one of the most popular girls in front of the whole class when she was like, "Isn't that my shirt? I thought my mom threw it out. Ew, did you dig through my garbage?" Darcy never had to pretend to be sick and stay home because she couldn't afford the extra fee for a field trip. She was encoded for success before she was even born.

Darcy comes home while I'm flinging my clothes everywhere.

"Why didn't you turn on the air conditioner?" she demands.

THIRTY-FOUR
SADIE

AUSTIN ASKED ME TO GET together with him tonight.

I was looking forward to another boy break weekend while I was walking home from my internship yesterday. I'm working on elaborate warm fuzzies for all of my friends from high school. We're planning a party in August before college starts and most of them move away. Warm fuzzies will look cute on their bulletin boards. My boy break weekend also featured a whole season of *Gilmore Girls* to binge-watch and a whole watermelon to eat while I was watching.

I was thinking about whether I wanted to slice the watermelon or bust out the melon baller when Austin fell into step beside me.

"Hey," he said. "Can we talk?"

"Depends on what you want to talk about."

"Us, Sadie. What else is there?"

The way he said it, the mix of desperation and passion in his voice, made me stop walking. He looked like he was willing to do anything to get me back. He was the Austin I remembered.

"Can you meet up with me tomorrow night?" he asked. "There are some things I have to tell you. Things I think you'll want to hear."

Butterflies flapped wildly in my stomach. That same rush I felt the first time I saw him came flooding back. There was no way I could deny that I wanted to hear those things.

So I said yes. He told me to meet him on the southwest corner of 55th and 5th. The butterflies are back as I stand on the corner waiting for him. I'm trying to figure out why we are meeting on this random corner in Midtown. Tiffany's is two blocks away. For a second I think Austin might be taking me to Tiffany's to pick out an engagement ring. Then I get a grip.

I look up and notice exquisite etching on the building across the street. There's an elaborate ivy pattern etched below each row of windows. A light suddenly blinks on in one of the windows. I love this time of day when city lights start to blink on. When the city wakes up for the night and every wish you ever had about summer city nights could come true.

Austin strides up to me. He must have seen me spacing

out from across the street. I was so deep in city love I didn't even notice him.

"Hey," he says. "Thanks for coming."

"Where are we going?"

"This way."

We start walking toward 6th Avenue. Nobody says anything. Our silence is making everything else sound louder: the snap of my flip-flops, a police siren in the distance, and the tourist couple in front of us speaking a language that might be Hungarian. Walking with Austin used to be one of the most romantic experiences of my life. We would hold hands the whole time, talking nonstop. We couldn't take our eyes off each other. Every few blocks we would stop and kiss up against a building or even right in the middle of the sidewalk. But walking with Austin now is painfully different. It's weird not to be holding hands. It's weird that nobody has said anything for ten seconds. Or that he's not pulling me over to the side because he has to kiss me.

Is it weird that part of me wants all of that back? After everything that's happened?

There's a replica of the *LOVE* sculpture at 55th and 6th. I totally forgot that's where it was. The second I see it when we turn the corner, I know this is where we are going. We walk right up to it like Austin knows I know.

"You once told me you're in love with love," Austin says. "You are the most romantic person I've ever met. So

I wanted to bring you here to tell you what I want to say. I wanted it to mean more than just words."

My heart pounds. I'm having an epic feeling that what he is about to say will be monumental.

"I told her all about you," he says. "My wife. Shirley. I told her that you're my soul mate. I told her that I've never felt the way I feel about you for anyone else. Including her."

"That must have been really hard to hear."

"It was. She said she wants a divorce."

"What do you want?"

"The same thing. She was served with divorce papers yesterday. That's why I waited until yesterday to talk to you again. I wanted to wait until the papers were served."

He actually did it. He actually left his wife for real. They are not only separated. They are getting divorced.

"So this is happening," I say.

"This is happening."

"You're getting divorced."

"Correct."

"How do you feel about that?"

"Relieved. Like a weight has been lifted off my shoulders. Like I can breathe again." Austin tentatively reaches out to hold my hand. His touch feels too good to break. His eyes lock into mine. He says, "Like I can be with the person I'm meant to be with."

Why does this have to be so freaking complicated? We

were meant to be together. Anyone who saw us together before could tell that from a mile away. But people can be soul mates and still screw it up. People can be oblivious to their issues or have no interest in working them out. People can lie and cheat and deceive. When you find true love, it doesn't always look the way you thought it would. Should the forces keeping us apart be forgiven just because the forces that brought us together were stronger? Forces that had been bringing us together for much longer than we were aware, in ways we will never know?

"There's something else I didn't tell you," Austin says.

My stomach clenches. I take my hand back. Then I mentally prepare myself to make a run for it after hearing whatever other horrendous thing he kept from me.

Austin takes a deep breath.

"Shirley cheated on me," he says. "We had only been married for five months when it happened. She reconnected with some old boyfriend from high school. They got together a few times. They didn't sleep together—or so she said, but I'm not sure I believe her. I had no idea what was going on until he called one night."

The irony is not lost on me. Austin found out his wife was cheating the same way I found out he was married. I'll never forget how devastating it was when his wife told me who she was over the phone.

"Why didn't you tell me before?" I ask.

"I was embarrassed. I thought it was my fault somehow,

like I was lacking in a way she needed. No guy wants to admit his wife cheated on him. It sounds lame, but I thought you would think less of me if you knew."

"It wasn't your fault. That was all her. Not you."

"What she did doesn't excuse my behavior in any way. I just wanted you to know there was more to why I was planning on separating from Shirley before I even met you. Looking back on everything . . . I should have gotten the marriage annulled. But I felt obligated to make it work."

"You should have told me you were married. You lied to me. Being honest now doesn't excuse lying to me then."

"I know."

An older couple approaches us. They have that comfortable vibe of people who have been married forever. At first it seems like they are going to ask us something, like to take a picture of them in front of the sculpture. But when the woman takes a closer look at us, she gives me a kind smile and gently pulls her husband away. She obviously could tell Austin and I are in the middle of something.

"I can't tell you how sorry I am," Austin says. "All I can tell you is the truth. From now on, that's all you will get from me. The truth is, every other time I thought I was in love before seems ridiculous now. I love you more than the person I was married to. I love you for all the right reasons. Not just because I'm attracted to you or you live nearby or we have the same internship. The love I feel for you is the ultimate kind of love. The kind of love that makes you want to be a better person. The kind of love that fills up every empty space in your soul. There's no doubt how I feel about you. I don't have to wonder if you're the one. I know you are."

When you meet the right person, there's no doubt in your heart that the search is over. That's how I felt about Austin. How could I have a Knowing about something so right that turned out to be so wrong?

I couldn't. I was right all along. We both know what this is.

Austin messed up. He majorly, historically, catastrophically messed up. The thing is, he knows it. He feels horrible about it. And he's doing everything he can to make up for it. So it comes down to trust. Can I ever trust Austin again?

I know no relationship is perfect. Everyone has challenges to overcome. Maybe our biggest challenge came right away. If that's true, won't everything work out in the end? We have the kind of love people search for their whole lives and sometimes never find. What if I decide we're over and I end up walking away from the love of my life?

"Remember that sunset on Trey's roof?" Austin asks. "I already felt so close to you. We'd only known each other for what, one day? How can you explain a feeling that strong unless we're meant to be?"

His eyes look into me. Searching. Hoping.

"Will you give me a second chance?" he asks.

"I have to think about it."

"Take your time. Whatever you need."

Austin reaches under the middle line of the *E* in the *LOVE* sculpture. He peels off a square envelope that was taped there. He hands the envelope to me. The color of the envelope is almost an exact matching shade of *LOVE* red. There are rainbow heart stickers around my name printed in black on the front.

"I made you a warm fuzzy," he says.

Oh my god. How can I be mad at a boy who made me a warm fuzzy? And came here early to hide it on the *LOVE* sculpture? Austin is too adorable.

I don't trust myself to stick around and get swept up in Austin's magnetic aura. I'm not totally sure I can let him in again, even with his warm fuzzy. So I tell him I have to go. We're both going downtown, but taking the subway together would be awkward.

"I'm going to walk for a while," I say.

"Okay. Well . . . talk to you later?"

I nod, restraining myself from throwing my arms around him and kissing him like crazy. Being impulsive won't help either one of us. I have to think about this.

Austin crosses the street to walk west. I walk east back to 5th Avenue, then start walking downtown. The lions can help me decide what to do. They are outside the New York Public Library on 42nd Street. When I was little, my mom would bring me to that NYPL branch for story hour. One of the books was about the lion statues outside the library on the grand staircase. The story said that the lions' names were Patience and Fortitude. The lions and I became friends that day. I said goodbye to each of them on our way out, petting their stone paws. These days they remind me that most problems can be solved with patience and fortitude. Both of which I could really use right now.

The traffic light across from the library turns green as I reach the curb. It's a good sign. The lions draw me into their protective fold as I approach the staircase. I pick a spot in the middle to let their collective energy envelop me. I focus on being in the Now like Darcy says, not thinking about Austin, not thinking about anything. Clearing my mind to make room for patience and fortitude.

Austin's warm fuzzy pokes out of my bag. I lift the bright red envelope out and open it. Inside is a card with a glossy photo of the *LOVE* sculpture on the front. The card is blank on the inside with this note from Austin:

Dear Sadie,
You are the love of my life.
You are the woman of my dreams.
You are my soul mate.
I will never stop loving you.
Love,
Austin

I'm not sure how long I have been sitting here when my phone rings. It's my mom. She's probably going to give me a hard time for not staying longer when I stopped by last week. But my mom doesn't understand that I needed to move on. Part of moving forward means not looking back.

"Guess where I am?" I say when I answer.

"Where?"

"Sitting between Patience and Fortitude."

"You and those lions always were inseparable."

"Sorry I didn't stay longer last weekend, but—"

"I'm not calling about that."

"You're not?"

"Sadie." Mom clears her throat. "I have something to tell you. About your brother."

"What is it?"

"He's coming home for the rest of the summer."

"No way." Marnix never comes home except for Christmas. He always complains about the humid summers here. Arizona's dry heat works for him. "He loves Arizona in the summer."

"He's not in Arizona. He's upstate."

"What?"

"Marnix . . . was in a rehab facility for a while. Getting better." Mom's voice breaks. "He . . . tried to commit suicide."

I am completely shocked. I didn't know anything about this.

"When?" I ask.

"Near the end of last semester. Your father and I found a good facility for him upstate so we could visit him once a week."

"Why didn't you tell me?"

"Marnix made us promise not to tell you until he was better. Now he's ready to come home."

How could something this drastic have happened to my brother without me knowing anything about it? How could I have been figuring out what to knit him for Christmas instead of how to help him when he needed help the most? True, we don't talk that much. We just don't have that much to say. But I should have been better about reaching out to him. Did he really try to kill himself? That doesn't sound like the Marnix I know.

It's more obvious than ever that I don't know my brother.

Marnix isn't someone I ever really knew. He couldn't wait to leave for college, either. I guess he had his own reasons to move on and not look back. Except now he has to look back. He has to stay at home for the rest of the summer so my parents can monitor him. He might even have to miss next semester.

My brother is coming home. That shouldn't make me

so nervous. Brothers and sisters seeing each other should be a normal thing. But with us, nothing was ever normal.

I guess I'll have to try getting to know him all over again. But this time, I want to know the real him.

Even if he scares me.

THIRTY-FIVE
DARCY

I FOUND SOMETHING AT LOGAN'S last night.

A necklace. That wasn't mine.

Logan was not supposed to be a part of last night. Not at all. When he called me before the Jude stalking and asked about getting together, I knew I needed to go out by myself. I went to a few clubs, met some new people, danced harder than I ever have. I might have gotten drunk. And I might have shown up at Logan's place. Then I sort of ended up spending the night. Which is how I found the necklace.

The necklace was under his bed. The only reason I noticed it was that light was glinting off a couple strands of crystals sticking out from under the bed where I dropped my shoes. I snatched the necklace up and stashed it in my bag before Logan came into the bedroom with beers.

Was it possible that the necklace had been under the bed since before Logan came to New York?

Yes.

Was it possible that the necklace belonged to a girl Logan did not know?

Yes.

Did I think either of those scenarios was true?

No.

Call it women's intuition. Call it a sixth sense. Hey, it could have been that Knowing thing Sadie is always yammering about. Whatever it was, my stomach clenched at the sight of that necklace. My heart stopped beating. I knew why I had been feeling like something was off between Logan and me. Logan knew exactly who that necklace belonged to. And she had been there with him, right in that same bed, not too long before I was.

We drank our beers. We watched TV. I pretended to fall asleep so Logan wouldn't touch me. If he had tried to touch me, I would have screamed.

While Logan was in the shower this morning, I yelled into the bathroom that I was going out for bagels. I picked up his apartment keys on the way out. Then I made copies of his keys at the hardware store across the street like a ninja. We ate bagels when I came back, like nothing was wrong. We left the apartment together. Logan said he was doing something with the boys for a few hours. I pretended I was going home. I told him to text me when he was ready to bounce and I would come meet him.

I waited around the corner for ten minutes. Then I used my new keys to get back into Logan's place.

A girl going through her boyfriend's things is so cliché. And so wrong. But I don't care. I'm on a mission to find that one incriminating piece of evidence that will validate this disgusting feeling I've had ever since the necklace glinted at me. I start with Logan's bag. He tossed his duffel in the corner of the bedroom. I dig through clothes and various boy gear. Nothing. I inspect every drawer, every scrap of paper on the dresser, every shelf. I check under the bed for more girl accessories. Still nothing.

I go out to the desk in the living room. Logan's laptop is sitting there. He assumes I would never touch it. Plus he's too lazy to password protect it. Even his email is open.

It doesn't take me long to find out who she is. The slut is your typical SoCal beach bimbo. Bleached blond hair. Impossibly blue eyes. Completely unrealistic body measurements.

There are naked pictures of her.

Logan sent some naked pictures of himself back.

They wrote long emails to each other. Emails like people used to write love letters back in the day. One of Logan's messages says how much he misses her. That he can't stop thinking about her. That he will be home soon.

One of them from her says some frantic guy came looking for him.

But an email chain with Randall wins the prize for Most Magnificent Display of Asshat Ineptitude. Randall is Logan's friend back home. They work in the same electrical repair shop. These are the top five highlights I discover from their communication:

1. Logan has a buttload of gambling debt.
2. Logan skipped town on a loan shark.
3. Logan is maxing out his credit cards to be here this summer.
4. Logan intends to scam me out of enough money to pay his debt back.
5. Logan is planning to break up with me—again—after he's back in California.

From what I can tell, SoCal Beach Bimbo doesn't know about Logan's gambling debt. All she knows is that he's running a scam. Against me. A scam that has her full support. In one email, Logan told her this about me:

Lifted $200 in total over a few nights while she was sleeping. She doesn't suspect anything. Plenty more where that came from. She doesn't need the money. Daddy pays her bills. She'll never miss what she can get more of.

So the part where Logan showed up at my door, begging me to come back? That was for show. He has been manipulating me since the first second I saw him.

Logan didn't come to New York to get me back. He doesn't even want me back. He only wants my money.

That must be why my credit card was confiscated yesterday. Logan was probably messing with my account. He might have been trying to take a cash advance or something that triggered an alert. Or running some other scam that wasn't supposed to show up. He shouldn't have bothered trying. He's not smart enough to get away with this. I still haven't told him about my card getting confiscated. He thinks he is still getting away with his scheme.

I cannot believe I fell for his bullshit. How could I not have seen through all that bad acting? Is he even out with "the boys" right now? Or are the boys actually a girl? A girl who lost a necklace. A girl who uses lemon shampoo. I checked the bathroom. Logan doesn't have any shampoo that smells like lemons. So why does his hair smell like lemons all of a sudden?

Logan has been playing me this whole time. He's been treating me like some chickenhead he can manipulate, steal from, and then dump like garbage all over again.

Logan = Fake. Darcy = Stupid.

But here's the thing.

I know what he's trying to do. But he doesn't know I know.

No one plays Darcy Stewart and gets away with it. Especially bad boys who get off on breaking good girls' hearts.

No boy will ever make me feel stupid again. Starting right now. Starting with Logan.

I am a live wire. Thrumming with high voltage. Dangerous.

My revenge will taste sweeter than honey.

Ready or not, Logan. Here I come.

THIRTY-SIX
ROSANNA

BATTERY PARK IS A SWEET place to hang out. A mix of everyone from individual runners to families with little kids is here. A refreshing breeze is drifting in from the river. D is in one of his romantic moods. After the weird distance that has been between us, I'm happy he is coming back to me.

D put together another picnic dinner for us tonight. This time we're eating outside on the grass instead of in his living room. It's the first traditional picnic I have ever had with a boy. D spread out the blanket from Central Park movie night on the grass. He has a fancy picnic basket with real utensils and plates and glasses. He takes out a bottle of Martinelli's sparkling cider, opens it, and pours cider into two wineglasses.

"Cheers," he says, holding up his glass. "To summer."

I clink my glass against his.

"You up for running tomorrow morning?" D asks as he starts opening takeout containers from the Palm. I marvel at how he ordered dinner from one of the most expensive restaurants for a picnic. He could have just made peanut butter and jelly sandwiches or something.

"Now that you have me hooked." I love running. My body is adjusting to the shock of moving its parts in ways it is not at all used to. I don't know if it's that running is something special I share with D or if I just needed some cardio action. Whatever the reason, I'm loving the challenge. I want to get better. I want to be able to run alongside D no matter how fast he goes. I don't want him to have to slow down for me.

"I knew you'd love it," he says.

"This smells amazing, by the way."

"Yeah, you know—" D's phone cuts him off with a ringtone I have never heard before. I assume he is going to turn off his phone. This is the first time we have seen each other all week. But he doesn't turn off his phone. He answers it.

His volume is turned way up. That's how I can hear it's Shayla. How often do they talk? This is the second time she's called D while we were together. Does she call him every day?

"What have you been up to?" she asks.

"Nothing much," he says. "I can't talk now. Call you

tomorrow?" He hangs up after Shayla trills a *byyeeeee!*

Why didn't D tell her about our picnic? Or at least mention that he was with me? It's like he didn't want to give the reason why he couldn't talk.

"Sorry," he tells me. "You know how it is with Shayla."

"Do I?"

"What do you mean?"

"Do I know the whole story of you two?"

"We've been over this." D extracts plates from their notches in the fancy picnic basket. "She's going through—"

"—a hard time, I know. But I still don't think you're telling me everything."

"What else is there to tell?"

"Why did you even answer the phone?"

"I didn't know if it was another emergency."

"What kind of emergency would it be?"

"The kind where she needs me."

I chug the rest of my sparkling cider like it's wine and I really need a drink. When did D start putting Shayla's needs ahead of mine? Can't I have just one night alone with my boyfriend?

"She's a good person," D says, refilling my glass. "She feels bad about interrupting our sundeck time. She wants to take us out for a drink."

"Us or you?"

"She wants to get to know you. She knows how important you are to me."

"How important is she to you?"

"She's my friend. You know that."

"And that's it? You guys have always been just friends?"

D hesitates. "We kind of . . . dated. In high school. It was nothing."

Aha! I knew it. I freaking *knew* there was more going on. So not only do they have this big shared history, they were a couple. Who kissed. Maybe more.

Going out for a drink with my boyfriend and his exgirlfriend would be beyond awkward. I'd be sitting there like a dillweed while they lobbed inside jokes back and forth. She would laugh too hard, gushing over how funny he is. And I'm sure she would be clinging to his arm again. There is no way I'm watching that.

I clear my throat. "How old were you?"

"We were juniors. It was only for a few months. I didn't tell you because I knew you'd get upset over nothing."

"Stop saying it's nothing. You were together. That's something."

"But it's in the past. You're my girlfriend now. It's not like you don't have exes."

"Actually . . . it is. You're my first serious boyfriend."

D looks at me like he's seeing me for the first time. Another breeze drifts over from the river, making his sandy-blond hair flash with gold highlights in the sun. His hazel eyes have flecks of gold in the sun, too. He's my golden boy.

"I didn't know that," he says.

"There's a lot about me you don't know."

"You don't tell me much. Every time I try to ask you about your life back in Chicago, you change the subject."

"All that's important is who I am now. Not who I was then."

"I disagree. You are the person you were. You always will be."

"Trust me. You don't want to know who I was."

"Try me."

How much should I tell him? How much do I want to tell him?

I don't give myself time to decide. I just start talking. "Do you know why I don't have a cell phone?"

"You're not a follower. You're original. It's one of the things I admire about you."

"I don't have a cell phone because I can't afford one. My family . . . we struggle to get by. Money has always been tight. That's why I'm putting myself through college."

D blinks. "I had no idea. You don't seem . . . your clothes look expensive."

"They were from Darcy. She took pity on me and gave me like a whole new wardrobe. I wanted her to take them back, but she wouldn't. She took the tags off everything and threw away the receipts. You take me to such nice places that I wanted to look like I belonged. But I won't be wearing them anymore."

"Why not?"

"I forgot myself for a minute there. I felt like I needed those clothes to go out with you. But I eventually remembered who I am. Wearing clothes I didn't buy for myself just isn't me." I glance down at my worn T-shirt and capris. Getting away with this outfit for a picnic is one thing. Getting dressed for more upscale dinners out with D will be interesting.

"You looked beautiful in them," D says. He gives me the plate he made for me and starts eating. He doesn't reassure me that I could wear anything and still look beautiful. His silence makes me feel worse about my situation. I can't help feeling like he is ashamed of me. I thought I would feel better about having to measure up to his lifestyle if he knew the truth. Instead I'm still feeling like I'm not good enough for him. Like I'm not worthy enough to meet his family. Like there is something missing in me that he needs.

D is eating like we're having a normal conversation. Like what he heard didn't even faze him. I hid a part of my past from him, just like he hid a part of his past from me. Maybe he thinks we're even.

We will never, ever be even.

But if there is a chance for us to make it, I have to tell him the rest. I put my plate down on the blanket.

D looks up from his food. "You okay?" he asks.

"Not really. I need . . . there's more I want to tell you."

"Okay . . ."

"There's a reason why I don't like talking about my past. Other than growing up poor."

D puts his plate down next to mine. His laser focus intensifies.

"It has to do with Addison. She showed up at camp yesterday."

"I thought she didn't work at the other camp."

"She doesn't. She lied about that and she lied to Mica about me because she thinks I lied about something first. Something big." My thumb is snapping against my middle finger. I twist my other hand around my fingers, forcing myself to stop. "I know Addison's uncle. Or I knew him back home when I was younger. He . . . he was a neighbor my family trusted. I'd go over to his house to play games and stuff. He took me and my little sister out for pizza and to the zoo. He was like an uncle to us." My throat gets tight. I take a sip of sparkling cider. "One day I was over at his house playing Scrabble and he put his lips on mine. He just came at me out of nowhere. I don't know if he had been planning to start touching me or if it was a split-second decision, but he didn't quit. Things just got worse from there."

"Did he . . . how far did it go?"

"He didn't rape me or anything. But it was bad."

"Are you okay now?"

"Not really."

D moves over next to me and hugs me tight against him. "I hate him for doing that to you. I want to track him down and beat him to a pulp."

"My dad beat you to it. Then he ran him out of town."

"So that's why Addison's such a psycho? She thinks you lied about her uncle?"

I nod against D's chest, breathing in his familiar scent. Breathing in him.

"Now you know why the whole sex thing is complicated for me," I say.

"I hope you haven't felt like I've been pressuring you."

"No. But I've been worried about how we're going to move forward."

D gently pushes away from me. His intense laser focus is back. "Don't worry about that," he says. "We'll figure it out together. Okay?"

"Are you sure you still want to be with me?" I blurt.

"Why wouldn't I?"

"You don't think I'm, like . . . damaged?"

"Are you kidding? I couldn't be more proud of you. What happened wasn't your fault. If anything, I care about you more because I admire how strong you are. How resilient you are. I would be a mess if I went through what you did. You're amazing."

D is saying all the right things. And I feel better now that he knows the truth about me. So why do I still feel like, no matter what D says, I'm not good enough for him?

Is this because of my own issues or because that's how he makes me feel? All I know is that I shouldn't be feeling this way.

And I don't want to feel this way anymore.

The truth is, I deserve to find a kind of love that won't make me compromise who I am. Before I met D, I wasn't sure if I deserved to be loved the way I wanted to be. But D has taught me that I am worthy.

Sadie says there is an epic kind of love you can find if you believe it exists. Even after Sadie found out Austin was married, she still talked about finding it. Nothing can make her stop believing that true love is real and she can find what she's looking for. I want to have that same certainty.

It's dark enough now to see a few stars. Three points of light are shining in the night sky. But even on those nights when I can't see any stars, I know they are still there. Shining just as brightly as ever.

True love isn't about being swept away to fancy dinners or elaborate vacays. It isn't about hiding who you were to become a person someone else wants. I want to get to the good part of life, where my insecurities and fears are behind me. Will D still be a part of my life when I get there? Maybe not. Maybe to get to the good part, I have to break away from everything holding me back. I can't let the fear of how I will support myself keep making me so worried every day. I can't let the fear of what Addison might do next take over my life. And I can't let the fear of my relationship with D possibly coming to an end stop me from dealing with my past. I don't want to be defined by fear. I want to let fear become an obstacle I proudly overcome, not a barrier preventing me from living my dreams.

Here's what I know about the good part. On days you feel desperate, hopeless, and alone, we all have to remember this: You can't get to the good part unless you keep going. And the good part *will* come.

I can't wait to be the best version of myself.

I can't wait to finally get there.

ACKNOWLEDGMENTS

WHEN I WAS IN HIGH school, every summer break had the potential for magic. Not that anything ever happened in Middle of Nowhere, NJ. But being an eternal optimist (even in my teen years, the worst time of my life), every summer began with a sense of infinite possibility. The possibility that I would have a boy adventure. The possibility that I would figure out who I really was and stop caring about what other people think. And especially the possibility that I would reinvent myself. I looked forward to every summer as the Summer of Reinvention, during which time I would completely transform myself into a girl kids would hardly recognize when school started. Of course that never happened. The important thing was that I believed it could. There was always the anticipation that tremendous things could happen over the summer, and that anticipation sparked my passion for this series.

Writing a series about summer love, self-discovery, and sisterhood has been a magnificent journey. But like the journeys of Sadie, Darcy, and Rosanna, I have not been traveling this road alone. My people pave this road, constantly smooth out new potholes, and plant lots of colorful flowers along the way. These are the friendly neighbors who glow brighter than the sun.

I am profoundly grateful for my editor and publisher, Katherine Tegen, who made it possible for *City Love* to shine. Emily van Beek, to whom this book is dedicated, is everything an outstanding agent should be and so much more. Thanks to Brandy Rivers for believing in the potential of *City Love* and working toward seeing this series sparkle on the screen.

Much love to the rays of sunshine at HarperCollins who make *City Love* glitter, like my publicity/marketing dream team of Rosanne Romanello, Lauren Flower, and Alana Whitman. Thanks to Carmen Alvarez, Margot Wood, and the Epic Reads team for spreading the city love.

Erin Fitzsimmons, Amy Ryan, and Barb Fitzsimmons are the most dazzling creative team who have designed yet another gorgeous cover. Ana Maria Allessi was extremely kind to interview me for a HarperAudio Presents podcast, and totally gets why dreaming big is essential for creating a happy life. Thanks to Kate Egan, Jen Strada, Kathryn Silsand, Kathleen Morandini, and Kelsey Horton for polishing this book to a high gloss.

There are so many authors who have inspired me with their radiant positive energy, support, and guidance over the years. I want to thank Jennifer E. Smith, David Levithan, Sarah Mlynowski, Blake Nelson, Laurie Halse Anderson, Sarah Dessen, Judy Blume, and Jodi Picoult for everything they have done for me . . . and for making this world a better place.

My friends continue to dazzle me with their insight, strength, beauty, humor, and talent every single day. You are like warm summer sunshine even on the coldest winter days. You know who you are and you know you are made of all awesome things. Thanks to my fitness for life support team, Careen Halton and Linden Hass, and to our incredible instructor, Kara Doyle. Infinite thanks to my soul mate, Matt. You are the most colorful sunset I could ever imagine. Here's to the power of megadesk taking things to the next level in 2016. Go, karma.

Eternal thanks to my readers. Thank you for all of your warm fuzzies on social. Thank you for sharing your personal stories of hope and triumph with me, and for never giving up. Thank you for making this life possible. You are why I write. I hope the *City Love* series brings you those magical summer feels . . . and that you live every single day like anything is possible.

THE STORIES OF SADIE, DARCY,
AND ROSANNA WILL CONTINUE
IN THE FINAL BOOK OF

CITY
LOVE

FOREVER IN LOVE

CHAPTER 1
SADIE

I NEVER KNEW SILENCE COULD be so loud.

This is the loudest silence of all. Buzzing with things left unspoken. Humming with the discomfort of a forced reunion. But here we are. My parents, my brother Marnix, and me. Having dinner at our small dining room table like we are any other average family. Kind of how we pretended it was before Marnix and I left for college. The throwback tableau appears perfect as long as you don't squint at it too hard.

I can't believe I'm back here in the West Village apartment I grew up in. The one I fled right after I graduated from high school. Even though I moved to another apartment in the same neighborhood, it still counted as a victorious escape. Living with Darcy and Rosanna this summer in our University of New York student housing apartment has been a sweet taste of freedom. Visiting my parents for a few minutes here and there is one thing. But sitting here with them and Marnix at Sunday dinner like the good little family we never were is a joke.

"Can you pass the corn?" Marnix asks Mom.

Mom scrambles to slam down her glass, swallow the water in her mouth without choking, and grab the platter of roasted corn on the cob. Her bustling to give Marnix exactly what he wants, exactly when he wants it, would lead one to suspect that the corn's true identity is a nuclear bomb. If Marnix can't defuse the ticking corn within the next thirty seconds, the entire population of New York City could die.

"This corn is delicious!" Mom gushes. "Best corn of the summer. Nothing beats that farm stand in New Jersey for freshness. Isn't that right, Ron?"

"Best farm stand in Jersey," Dad confirms.

"And the tomatoes! Oh my gosh, Marnix, you should have been here in July. The Jersey tomatoes were bursting with flavor. You could eat them with nothing on them at all. One night we had tomato salads for dinner—just chopped tomatoes, cucumbers, croutons, salt, pepper, and olive oil—and it was unbelievable. The produce has been excellent this summer. Something about the amount of rain we got . . ."

Mom's manic bubble pops when she looks at Marnix and actually sees him. Slumped down in his chair. Clearly wishing he were anywhere but here. There was no way Marnix could have been home in July. He shouldn't even be in New York right now. He should be in Tucson, Arizona where he goes to college. The next time we should be seeing him is Christmas.

But here he is. Back at the table that's been a part of this apartment since before we existed. Eating Jersey-fresh corn on the cob while Mom's forced conversation glosses over everything that is wrong with this picture. Tonight is Marnix's first night back home. Mom has been acting weird since he got here. She's always been a cheerful person, but anyone could see how fake she's being tonight. She has only touched on upbeat, peppy topics instead of drifting into her usual passionate discussions with my dad about everything from endangered species and the overall destruction of our planet to the increasing prices of health insurance and college tuition. Like she thinks being herself around her own son would send him over the edge. Is she going to walk on eggshells around Marnix until he goes back to Arizona?

"We should do this every Sunday night," Mom says. "Sunday family dinner! Wouldn't that be fun?" She beams at me expectantly. "That way we would be able to see you more when school starts."

"Sunday family dinner." I try to match her enthusiasm. "That would be awesome." There is no way I am playing this twisted game every single week. Marnix won't go for it, either.

"Marnix, what do you think?" Mom asks.

"Might as well." He butters the other half of his corn. Marnix has always eaten corn on the cob this way. He likes to butter one half and eat it before he tackles the other half. "Since this is where I live. Again."

Mom beams some more. "It's only temporary. Just until you get your feet on the ground."

Marnix puts down his butter knife, carefully balancing the blade on his plate with the sharp edge facing away. He looks at Mom.

"Is that what you're calling it?" he says. "Getting my feet on the ground? What does that even mean?"

Mom is startled. "I wasn't . . . I didn't mean anything by it. You can stay here as long as you'd like."

"Okay then," he fires back. "How about not at all?"

"Watch your tone," Dad says. "Your mother is only trying to help you. You should be grateful."

"Grateful?" Marnix snorts. "Helping? How is she helping? By having me committed to a rehab facility? By keeping me prisoner in this apartment for the rest of the summer? By threatening that I might miss next semester if I don't snap out of it? If she wanted to help me, she would leave me alone!"

"That's enough!" Dad yells.

I can hear my heart pounding in my ears. Dad never yells. Except for those scary fights he used to have with Marnix.

"What?" Marnix taunts. "You're going to send me to my room? Don't bother." He pushes his chair away from the table, dropping a summery orange linen napkin from his lap onto the table. "I'm one step ahead of you." Marnix pounds down the hall to his room so heavily that my chair trembles with the vibrating hardwood floors. Then he slams his door.

This whole scene takes me right back to high school. Marnix was always slamming his door back then. It terrified me every time.

When I was a freshman and Marnix was a junior, he started having these enraged fits. One day he was the same quiet boy I'd always known, locking himself away in his room for hours and not speaking to any of us at dinner. Then he changed into a boy who would snap over the most minor thing. He had loud fights with our parents that were so awful I hid in my room. One time I even blockaded my door. Mom said it was hormones. Dad said he'd grow out of it. He never did. His door slamming was usually the beginning of one of his fits. By the time he left for college, I was still scared every time I heard it.

I don't know if he's been different at college. Maybe living away from us in the dorms has mellowed him out. I know I'm a lot more aware of my behavior now that I have two roommates. The last thing I want to do is irritate them in any way. So it's possible Marnix could have calmed down in a new environment with new people.

But even if he did, there was obviously still something wrong.

Marnix tried to kill himself. That's why he was in rehab. That's why he came home.

All I know is that it happened in April near the end of last semester. Mom says she doesn't know why he did it. Apparently Marnix wasn't ready to talk about it during the weekly visits my parents made to his rehab facility upstate, and Marnix's psychiatrist told our parents they shouldn't push him. He said that when Marnix is ready to talk about it, he will come to them.

So this is the first time I've seen Marnix since last Christmas. A sister seeing her brother should be a normal thing. But with us, nothing has ever been normal.

I was so nervous walking over here. I built up an arsenal of things to say, conversation starters to use in case we got lost in awkward silence. We never really talked much before, and we definitely weren't affectionate. But when I put my key in the door and came into the living room tonight, Marnix looked relieved to see me. He jumped off the couch and gave me a big hug.

"Hey, you," he said. "I'm psyched you're here. Mom's acting crazy."

"What else is new?" A smile broke out on my face. I couldn't remember Marnix ever hugging me before. I thought that maybe things would be different now.

But then the fight happened at dinner. And Marnix

stomped away to his room, slamming his door. Same old story.

Marnix's abandoned place at the table is sad. A corner of his napkin fell across the buttered half of his corn when he dropped it. The butter has seeped through his napkin, a dark spot oozing over the bright backdrop.

The dark spot kind of reminds me of my life right now. This summer was supposed to be bright and cheerful. But it is not turning out the way I was expecting. Not at all.

CHAPTER 2
DARCY

THE GUY WHO WAS ALL bossy about ordering his drink gets up in my face.

"This isn't two percent," he accuses.

"Um, excuse me." The lady next in line pierces Bossy Guy with a withering glare far surpassing the intensity of his. He was totally asking for it. When I gave him his drink, he scurried off to his table like a good little customer. But then he hustled back up to the counter like we weren't about to set the world record for Longest Line Ever. The withering glarer was in the middle of ordering when he interrupted her.

"I was here," Bossy Guy tells her. "They messed up my drink." He slams his cup down on the counter. Apparently my identity has been reduced to They, regardless of the name tag on my black tank top that clearly reads DARCY.

"Your drink was made correctly," I say. "With two-percent milk."

"How do you know?"

"I'm the one who made it."

We stare each other down for a few eons. Bossy Guy, infuriated that his pretentious coffee drink was made so skillfully he couldn't tell two-percent milk from whole. Me, aka They, standing strong behind the barista counter, mentally willing him to take his drink back so I don't have to make another one.

Because I'm a barista now. At my job. Where I work.

"Whatever," he growls, snatching the cup back.

"Sorry about that." I apologize to the lady he interrupted. "What would you like?" Her makeup is flawless and she's overdressed for a Sunday. My guess is she won't be staying. She is one of the many New Yorkers zipping through Java Stop on her way to wherever she's already late to, expecting her drink to be ready way faster than it physically takes to make. I never realized how impatient New Yorkers were about their coffee before. And of course I never knew how long it took to make any of these drinks. I've always been on the other side of the counter, ordering my double espresso without thinking about the logistics of not only making it, but making it well.

Until now.

Turns out that when Darcy Stewart is facing a life-or-death situation, she can actually learn how to make something without burning the place down. I was the girl who scorched eggs. I was the girl who set off the smoke detector while I was trying to cook dinner. Never in my wildest dreams did I think I would become the girl behind the counter at Java Stop.

And not just any Java Stop. The same Java Stop on Bleecker Street that Sadie protested in front of.

Sadie was devastated when I told her.

"How can you work there?" she wailed. We were having movie night with Rosanna at our place the night I got the job. I was on the couch, Sadie took the puffy armchair, and Rosanna had the violet pouf. "Java Stop is evil. Do you not remember our cardboard sign? Save the West Village?!"

"I didn't have a choice," I apologized. "Trust me, I don't want to be working there any more than you want me to. But they were the only ones who would hire me without previous job experience."

"So . . . are you a cashier, or . . . ?"

"Both. Cashier and barista. Whoever takes the order makes the drink."

"But . . ." Rosanna exchanged a look with Sadie. "No offense, but do they know you're not experienced with making drinks and stuff?"

"Yes. They are training me. Don't worry, they're not

letting me make anyone's drink until I know what I'm doing. The machines do most of the work anyway. How hard can it be?"

Hard. Much harder than I expected. Which is what I found out when I was allowed to start making drinks last week. Fretting over the perfect degree of foam density while a long line of impatient New Yorkers agitating for their caffeine fix are waiting behind you brings stress to a whole new level.

"Here you go." I place Overdressed Lady's small-batch, cold-brewed coffee on the counter. She doesn't tip when she pays for it. I knew she wouldn't. I was surprised to discover that people who look like they can't afford to tip are the ones who tip most frequently.

This line is outrageously long. It's been like this on and off all afternoon. Sadie said Manhattan was empty in August. Is every person not at the beach today here? The only thing getting me through this shift is my plan to meet up with Sadie and Rosanna after work. We're going to walk around and see where the night takes us. Out on the streets, I will feel like myself again.

And that's not all. I am going to tell them why I'm really working at Java Stop. Sadie and Rosanna probably didn't buy the story that Daddy insisted I needed some work experience. That was the only excuse I could think of when I told them I got a job. I've tried to tell them the real reason so many times before. But this is it. They have to know. I have to stop being humiliated about something I can't even control.

At the end of my shift, I burst through the Java Stop door like a prisoner breaking out of jail. Except I will be returning behind bars tomorrow for another day of lattes and long lines.

Rosanna and Sadie are waiting for me at the corner of Barrow Street. Sadie gives me a sympathetic smile.

"How was it?" she asks. She knows I hate working there even more than she hates that I work there.

"Exactly how you think, only worse."

"It kills me to say this, but I do enjoy how you smell like freshly roasted coffee beans after work."

"I know, right?" Rosanna sniffs my shoulder.

"Enough about me." I tap Sadie's arm. "How was dinner?"

Sadie starts walking toward Grove Street, Rosanna and I falling into step beside her. "Oh, I'd say it went about as well as your day," she says.

We wait for her to tell us more. She doesn't.

"How was seeing Marnix?" Rosanna tries.

"Can we . . . maybe talk about this later?" Sadie says. "It was just . . . bad."

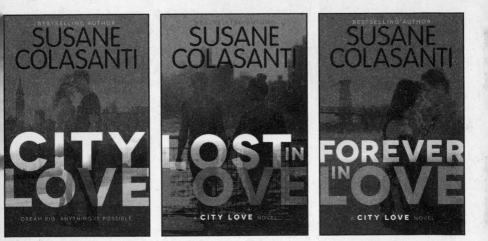

JOIN THE

Epic Reads
COMMUNITY

THE ULTIMATE YA DESTINATION

◀ **DISCOVER** ▶
your next favorite read

◀ **MEET** ▶
new authors to love

◀ **WIN** ▶
free books

◀ **SHARE** ▶
infographics, playlists, quizzes, and more

◀ **WATCH** ▶
the latest videos